Single Action

Jim Williams

RoseDog Books
PITTSBURGH, PENNSYLVANIA 15238

The contents of this work, including, but not limited to, the accuracy of events, people, and places depicted; opinions expressed; permission to use previously published materials included; and any advice given or actions advocated are solely the responsibility of the author, who assumes all liability for said work and indemnifies the publisher against any claims stemming from publication of the work.

All Rights Reserved
Copyright © 2022 by Jim Williams
No part of this book may be reproduced or transmitted, downloaded, distributed, reverse engineered, or stored in or introduced into any information storage and retrieval system, in any form or by any means, including photocopying and recording, whether electronic or mechanical, now known or hereinafter invented without permission in writing from the publisher.

RoseDog Books
585 Alpha Drive, Suite 103
Pittsburgh, PA 15238
Visit our website at www.rosedogbookstore.com

ISBN: 978-1-63937-562-2
eISBN: 978-1-63937-602-5

OTHER JIM WILLIAMS PUBLICATIONS

Beyond Hate
I Never Believed In Ghosts (Contibutor)

Single Action is dedicated to my friends and drinking buddies Jimmy Egan, Sparky Wykoff and the late Tim Ryan, may he rest in peace .... SLAINTE lads.

Single Action is fiction.
Any similarities to any person or place are coincidental.

PREFACE

The 1960's were a defining decade in American history. Vietnam, JFK, RFK and MLK's assassinations, Moon Walk, the Beatles, racial and civil unrest just to name a few significant and world changing events. They were also the high-water time period for organized crime and the long overdue beginnings of the civil rights movement and the passing of significant civil rights legislation.

Single Action is dark, violent but it could have happened. It's certainly not PC by 2021 norms ... but then again, remember it was set in 1966, a very different America.

JSW
September, 2021

Single Action

ONE

Early October 1966

Larry Carson already knew he was smart ... now he knew he was lucky. At 28, he was the youngest department head at the world's premier teaching hospital and research treatment center ... and he did it all without a college degree.

Carson headed up a team of 14 programmers and system analysts. All degreed and one even a PHD. Larry had fallen into computer programming when the occupation was in its infancy, back in 1961. A lucky stroke. He had carried a radio in the army and knew a little about telecommunications ... and he had taken the only course in high school that actually meant anything ... typing ... the combination of these skills landed him into a job as a teletype operator at a New York City brokerage. It was there that he became a computer programmer. He was good, very good and after a bit found a new programming job at the Guardian Memorial Hospital center at a hugh salary increase.

"Got a minute Larry?"

Doug Hayes closed the office door, took a seat across from Larry, handed him a steaming black coffee container and an envelope filled with cash.

"It's 5 big one's buddy and this is just the first month. Oh, and good news, I have one of the girls keypunching another 2,000 numbers for the data base. Didn't I tell you that hooking up with the Preacher was a good idea?"

Larry smiled and put the fat cash filled envelope into his top desk draw without checking its contents.

"I guess you were right about that Doug." But at the same time thinking,

"And we're now hooked up with a criminal organization."

It had all begun a few months earlier. Just one of those routine days at the job. Doug had come in Larry's office to "shoot the shit" and waste time.

"What are you doing after work Larry? Want to hit the Keg for a few beers ... some darts? Oh, and guess what Boss, surprise surprise ... I'm buying tonight."

Larry smiled. Doug was always looking to borrow a few bucks between pay days which he rarely repaid, but he was Larry's best friend on and off the job. They were dart team partners and very good at winning money playing the young drunks who hung out at the Keg. Larry's home life was not great, not bad but not great. He was restless, not looking for an affair, maybe a "quickie" if someone was willing and there were always a lot of girls "willing" at the Keg. It didn't hurt his chances that Doug was a very good-looking black man, ready with a quick joke and an abundance of natural charm. It was the "Swinging '60's and "Black is Beautiful" time in the New York singles bar scene and Doug Hayes was the crown prince of white girl "Pickup Lines". Larry welcomed the chance to be out with Doug after work but wasn't certain that he'd would be covering the night's bar tab.

"So, who died and left you money? Or did your number finally come in?"

Doug laughed and waved a roll of twenties under Larry's nose.

"My number man ... my number ... 518 straight up ... hit 600 to 1. You dig?"

Larry was both surprised and happy for his friend. "Maybe Doug will actually pay me back some of the money he owes me.", he thought.

Almost reading his friend's mind, Doug peeled off three twenties and handed them over. "Here, put that on my tab. Should get it below $1,000."

"Why this is a pleasant surprise. How many times have you actually hit with that number ... 518?"

"This is the first time in over a year. But I knew it was due. The law of averages my man. It was ready to show."

Larry laughed. "Didn't they teach you at St. John's that there's no such thing as the "law of averages" buddy. Any number can play any time. Your 518 could come in again tomorrow or every day for the next month. It's all about probability. Not averages."

Over the next week, their conversation continued along these lines. Doug was always looking for ways to make a quick buck and Larry was intrigued with the concept of forecasting numbers and had the germ of an idea. He would think about it and write a computer program to pick numbers. And he did.

At first, their short list of probable numbers that might come over the next 30 days which his program had forecasted, wasn't even close. But as their data base of previously played numbers grew, it became much more accurate. When they thought that it was reasonably accurate, at least one winner on the list, Doug put an ad in Harlem's Amsterdam News, offering their 30-day numbers pick list for $5. The first month they had three winners, the second, 5 out of 10 … maybe just pure chance or perhaps it was "probability" after all. It was then the money started coming in. Word spread about the computer list that picks winning numbers and hundreds eventually sent in their $5 for the Single Action monthly pick list.

Numbers, or Policy as it was called, was still illegal but it was one of the "crimes" nobody had any problem with. Everybody in New York City played the numbers.

Larry was surprised when Doug came in one morning and told him that the big Policy man uptown, a guy named Preacher who ran everything, wanted to buy their exclusive services and would pay them big bucks each month for the sole privilege of owning the computer's pick list.

"Why would he want to use our list Doug? He doesn't play the numbers, does he?"

"No buddy, but he'd like an idea of what numbers might be hot. He could tell his Street people not to cover them or offer lower odds… it would save him a lot of payouts. You dig?"

It made sense to Larry and he agreed to taking on just a single customer. It made the process much simpler and perhaps more dangerous too. But with three young kids and a dream to buy a house on Staten Island, Larry was willing to take the risk.

TWO

Monday 12:47 AM, October 17, 1966

Sal Caputo nearly shit his pants when the guy in the back seat farted. The loud flat sound and choking stink had caught him by surprise because the guy sitting in the back seat of Sal's Lincoln was dead.

Since he'd never studied biology, Sal wouldn't have known that even after death some biological digestive activities continue and farting was the natural result.

The methane gas that had accumulated in the corpse's bowels was upset from forcing it into a sitting position and then bouncing it from pot hole to pot hole over darkened New York City streets. The agitated gas inevitably erupted into a string of colossal foul-smelling farts that were now choking Sal.

He pulled over, rolled down his window and took quick, deep breaths of crisp early morning New York City air. When his head cleared, he looked over his shoulder at the body rigidly positioned in his back seat – grateful that he couldn't see the stiff's contorted features in the blackness of the car's interior.

"Hey! Are you fuckin' dead or what?", he shouted. "Why the fuck don't you keep quiet like your buddy here?" Sal pointed to the second corpse slumped next to him.

Sal's chuckle turned into a hearty genuine belly laugh that doubled him over. He was not a man normally able to recognize the idiocy of a situation but this time he saw himself sitting in his car, at one o'clock in the morning on a deserted New York City Street yelling at a stiff for farting and then telling him he should be quiet like his dead buddy.

"You guys are gonna make me pee my pants.", was all he was finally able to say while wiping the tears from his fat cheeks. After a while, Sal stopped laughing and closed the open car window. He was ready to go to work.

"Time to get out shit heads.", he announced pleasantly to his two silent passengers.

The car's ceiling light threw a muted glow over the three occupants for only a second before Sal reached up and turned it off. He didn't need or want any light for what he was going to do next.

2:45 AM, MONDAY OCTOBER 17, 1966

The big shouldered freelance TV cameraman hauled himself into his cluttered Ford van and immediately began reloading his sixty-five-pound Portacam X3. It was a simple process, taking only seconds, but one which he religiously followed after every shoot. He went through a dozen video tape cartridges daily since he never, never reused a tape. It was a big operating expense – "But what the hell", he often said, "it all comes off my taxes anyway."

He thought about the shoot he just completed.

"Shoot is right.", he said softly, shaking his head.

He had seen at least ten thousand homicides during his time spent on these mean New York City streets – all kinds – mob whacks, domestic, police and serial killings, hold-ups gone bad and crazy hold-ups that normally included killing the victim. This double homicide looked like a mob hit, but there was something a little off center about it. He'd check the video tape later if he had time.

His mobile radio boomed.

"Hey Mike, what's your 40? Over.", It was his wife, Marge.

Picking up the microphone, Mike pressed the broadcast button.

"I'm just leaving 54th and 9th. Got about twenty-five minutes in the can Marge. Hey babe – good news, the BIX's crew was late – came after the meat wagon left. We have the exclusive on this one kid – get on the horn and call the nets. Who knows, maybe we'll get a grand slam."

Single Action 7

Mike Denton was paid $600 for each shoot used by local TV news - $1,500 if his piece went national. Since his was the only camera rolling at the murder scene, he had a good chance of selling it to all three major New York networks as well as the three locally based TV outlets – a grand slam. It didn't happen often, but it would only happen if, one – he had good clear shots of the stiff; two – no other TV crew got there before the coroner and the homicide guys finished; three, the idiot bystanders who managed to get on camera didn't act like idiot bystanders who managed to get on camera and then behave like it was a New Year's Eve party – and most importantly – there was something unique about the homicide, something that would "sell".

Mike knew this piece met at least the first three requirements – he didn't know about the last, but had a hunch. There was a white stiff and black one – that was different and they obviously hadn't killed each other, not with two or three bullet wounds in each stiff's head. The cops couldn't locate any ID but they were still wearing their watches and rings so it wasn't a stick up. They looked like typical New York middle class civilians – not mob, low lifes, or street punks. "Yeah, there's a story here.", Mike Denton felt it in his bones.

Denton worked the grave yard shift, 9 PM to 5 AM six nights a week since Marge got pregnant again. It was almost 3 AM and he was ready for a break. It had been a very busy Sunday night.

"OK Marge my Queen, I'm out of here, ya got anything for me?", he said with a sigh that didn't transmit over the mobile radio.

"You feel like going to Staten Island?"

"Not really, but talk to me."

"It's the Verrazano Bridge; the first jumper on the "SPIC and SPAN" Mike. They're still talking to him. Should make the networks if he dives. Over."

"Sounds good. OK Margaret, you talked me into it; I'm on my way to Staten Island. Out."

Mike knew his chances for a grand slam on this one was nil since in all likelihood, this would be the lead on every local newscast Monday morning. The Bridge would be crawling with TV crews.

"That's probably why there was no competition at this shoot. But who knows?", he thought. "Maybe the jumper will do a triple gainer or whatever the hell they called those fancy high dives, I'll get the best shot and UBC will use it for the opening of the Big World of Sports!"

He started the van, pulled away from the curb and headed downtown toward the Brooklyn Bridge. He'd take the Gowanus Parkway through Brooklyn and connect with the Verrazano. It was the fastest route. "Hey Marge honey, you still there?"

"I'm here Mike. What's up?"

"I'm rollin to S.I., do me a favor. Check first with Gil Peterson at MBC about the double whack I just got. Tell him I have an exclusive. You copy?"

"I copy. Out."

The streets were still empty this time of morning and he was doing a solid 40 MPH and catching all the lights down Broadway.

"She didn't want to talk.", Mike thought. "Probably had to feed the kid." He could see her shuffling around their kitchen, kid in one arm, microphone in her free hand. He had to get a ten-foot microphone cord for her. Marge always kept busy when she was on the horn with him. Wiping off the counter top, standing by the stove, listening to the Police scanner .... The van's brakes screeched and its tires left rubber on the pavement as it rocked to a sudden halt.

Mike's attention had drifted as he drove the empty streets so he was forced to make an abrupt stop at 33rd Street for the changing traffic light. Sitting there, he stared intently at the bright red stop light and images of the "Shoot" scene flashed in his head.

"Blood!", he yelled, "That's what's fuckin' missing! There should have been more blood. The stiff's clothes were too clean and there was no blood on the fucking street.", a smug grin filled his fat face. "So, they were somewhere else when they were clipped.", he thought. "Big deal; the cops will figure that out pretty quick."

His right foot was almost in the gas tank as he jumped the changing traffic light.

Mike was content – the crime scene loose end was tied up. He turned up the volume on his favorite oldies radio station to full strength and began a loud sing along with Chubby Checker's bouncy "Let's Twist Again".

"Cha Cha Cha.", he sang to the almost empty streets.

4:20 AM, MONDAY OCTOBER 17, 1966

Gil Peterson was pissed. As the night News Producer for MBC, it was his job to put together the local New York stuff used on FIRST LIGHT's frequent morning news breaks.

"Gibbons you tech wienie bastard, you get that AP wire working in five minutes or I'll come down and personally kick your fat Irish ass back to Astoria."

Peterson threw the telephone receiver in the general direction of its cradle and completely missed, knocking over a two-hour old, half-filled coffee cup.

"I'll be a son of a bitch bastard!", he roared – his fat face taking on an even deeper shade of red.

Peterson reacted quickly and began moving news reports and papers on his cluttered desk from the path of the cold, black coffee flood.

"Gil you are a son of a bitch but I didn't know that you were a bastard too.", Johnny Dolan laughingly said replacing Gil's dangling telephone receiver.

Looking up quickly with a bulldog scowl, Peterson's face switched to a grin seeing the arrival of his favorite investigative street reporter. The smile remained while he continued sponging up the coffee mess with his soiled handkerchief.

"Dolan, I'm glad you're back. What happened to the jumper?", Gil asked, throwing his soggy handkerchief into an overflowing waste paper basket.

"A dud – didn't jump, cops talked him down.", Dolan answered.

"Aw shit!", Peterson growled seeing his lead news story lose its "punch".

Dolan read the look and quickly added: "But we got some good film and you know what Gil, the bastards made us pay the Bridge toll both ways."

"Did you get receipts?", Peterson asked shaking his head at the lack of respect NYC officials had for the media.

"Of course, and a few extra just in case."

It was a standing joke around the Newsroom that you could put a chit in for $500 to pay a source without any documentation, but the MBC Accounting Department went "ape shit" if you didn't include a receipt for any expense under $2.

Johnny Dolan appeared small next to Gil Peterson's overweight bulk. Both were in their late 30's but Dolan looked at least ten years younger. He had a "camera ready" face and looked and sounded like any other third string TV street reporter. There was a difference though, John Dolan was a whole lot smarter than most of his peers. He was a West Pointer and Rhodes Scholar with a 140 I.Q.

He had a lot going for him and a lot against him too. He was gay – not swishy gay, but enough people knew about his homosexuality for it to have adversely affected his military career in spite of the Silver Star he was awarded for heroism in Korea. But being a homosexual hadn't been a detriment at MBC because John Dolan was presentable to the viewing public and it didn't hurt that he was networked to other gays behind and in front of MBC's cameras. Dolan wasn't blatant about his homosexuality but he didn't try to hide it either.

"Save those god damn receipts if you want your expense money. By the way – did you see Mike Denton working the Bridge?"

"Yeah, I saw him. Why?"

"Marge Denton just called and told me they had an exclusive shoot on a double homicide on 54th Street. It's already on the wire. It might be a Mob hit Johnny. See what you can find out and take Billy and Ted over to Center Street and find out if the cops are ready to make a statement."

Billy Miceli was the night MBC cameraman teamed with Dolan and Ted Cohen, their regular soundman. Johnny made himself a cup of tea before placing a call to the 24-hour media liaison desk at Police Headquarters on Center Street.

The cops hadn't made a positive on the stiffs and wouldn't release anything anyway until the next of kin were notified. The Information Officer told Johnny that each had been shot multiple times in the head and "for background only", that the black guy had had his penis amputated – probably after death. That's all they were releasing now but there would be a press briefing on Tuesday.

Peterson sent Johnny and his crew over to Police Headquarters anyway to get an outside shot while Dolan described the killings without referencing the details. This clip, together with about ten seconds of Mike Denton's exclusive was only used once by MBC on Monday's FIRST LIGHT show. It had been a busy Sunday news night and there were more interesting stories than two un-named murder victims.

THREE

FRIDAY 8:40 PM, OCTOBER 14, 1966

The three, twenty-two-year-old nurses from Brooklyn simultaneously saw the Ford station wagon begin to pull away from its parking place on 71st Street between First and Second Avenues.

"There's a spot Sharon. There's a spot. Take it!" her girlfriends shouted.

Sharon Boyd, driver of the VW bug, rolled passed the wagon, hit her break, smoothly put the little car into reverse and waited patiently for the big Ford to completely pull away.

"What a break. We'll save ten dollars for parking." She said.

"More drinking money.", Leslie answered from the back seat.

It was almost impossible to find street parking anywhere on Manhattan's East Side. This was especially true on Friday nights when the whole area filled with singles heading for the hundred or more pick up bars lining First and Second Avenues from the 50's on up to the 90's.

"Even you should be able to fit the "BUG" into that hole Sharon.", Kim said sarcastically.

"Yeah, sure", Sharon answered turning to her front seat passenger. "Look who's talking, Miss Parking Champ of 1966."

This little exchange was just enough distraction for Sharon to allow the Cadillac that had pulled in behind her to get its nose into part of the parking space.

"Hey you creep! This is my space!", she screamed at the image in her rear-view mirror.

Her girlfriends were shouting at the other driver as Sharon quickly positioned the VW to gain ownership of the front half of the contested space. The Caddy's horn sounded loud and long; its driver could not be seen clearly by any of the girls.

Sharon banged open her door and indignantly walked toward the gleaming big red car.

"I was here first. This is my spot. Go find your own!"

The Caddy's tinted electric window softly hummed as it partially disappeared in the door frame. The driver, a black man about thirty years old, turned to face her.

"Get your fucking car out of my way bitch. Now!"

He said this so softly and calmly, Sharon wasn't sure she heard him correctly. The window eased back up.

"Fuck YOU and go to hell.", she angrily shouted at the now closed window as a delayed reaction.

Sharon stepped directly in front of the Cadillac; her two friends had left the VW and now stood together on the sidewalk.

The Caddy's engine revved loudly.

"Look out Sharon, he's going to hit you!"

Sharon ignored the roaring engine, Kim's warning and just folded her arms in defiant display. But she screamed when the big car suddenly lurched forward, its bumper banging into her legs hard enough to throw her into the back of the VW but not causing any real injury. The Caddy's engine continued to roar.

"He hit her! He actually hit her! Call the cops!", Leslie screamed.

Sharon was badly shaken but alright.

"This guy is fucking crazy.", she thought. "He's going to kill me if I don't get out of here!"

Leslie was banging on the Caddy's hood and screaming gibberish at its driver when the big car lurched backward almost running over her feet. The engine revved even louder and its horn blasted.

Sharon was certain he intended to crush her between the two cars. "Dumb Brooklyn girl gets killed for parking space" – was the Daily News headline that flashed through her mind.

Somehow, she managed to stumble to the sidewalk just as the Caddy smacked loudly into the rear of her VW. That was all the encouragement they needed, the girls from Brooklyn bolted. Crying and terrorized, they practically threw themselves into the little car and with a grinding of the gears, Sharon lurched the VW back into the Friday night traffic.

Since this was New York, no one had noticed the scene just played out and if they had, probably wouldn't have intervened anyway. Later, when the girls told the story, everyone said they were lucky the asshole didn't kill them. Sharon drove almost two blocks before realizing she had wet herself.

The big red Cadillac backed smoothly into the oversized parking space; it's headlights and engine shut off a full ten seconds before the driver's door opened.

Bunny Ennis walked around his car and quickly examined its front right bumper, the point of impact with the bitch's car.

"No problem. Not even a fucking scratch.", he thought, but he knew that there wouldn't be. The Cadillac was still the best car in America and this was his sixth. It was a 1966 Sedan Deville with a 325 horse V8. He liked the big heavy car. He liked its power, its electric gadgets and the looks it got when he drove it Uptown. Everybody knew the "Bunnyman's" Caddy and nobody messed with it.

Bunny Ennis was a mean mother-fucking, well dressed, good looking dude. He liked to hurt people. He had always liked hurting people, even when he was a kid. Whenever Bunny felt the heat start to cook in his gut, he could only cool it with violence – always quick, unexpected and sometimes fatal. If Sharon and her friends had persisted, Bunny would have hurt them.

Over time, Bunny learned to use violence for profit or pleasure. New Yorkers were used to violence and they tended to avoid any situation where violence might be done to them; except when they were drunk, drugged out, macho or stupid. God help them if their paths happened to cross Bunny Ennis.

He wasn't particularly big, about six feet, or overly muscular but he kept in shape, didn't abuse himself in the usual ways and had boxer's hands; oversized, strong and quick.

Bunny always went armed; a five-inch twisted piece of coat hanger wire that could blind or kill, a small bottle of lye and two

M80 artillery simulators – three-inch quarter sticks of dynamite used by the military in training exercises.

Tonight, he had supplemented his standards with a compact .22 caliber, eight shot automatic pistol; no stopping power but it was quiet and good for close work and Bunny always got close when he worked.

Bunny was looking forward to tonight. He smoothed his jacket and straightened his tie before opening the Keg's front door, a popular hang-out on First Avenue; the loud music and almost choking cloud of cigarette smoke hit him like a vagrant Jones Beach wave as he pushed his way through the giddy crowd toward the mobbed bar.

His eyes and ears quickly adjusted to the Keg's tempo – sexual tension in shrill voices from dozens of singles on the make.

"What'll ya have?", the barmaid shouted over the din.

"Double Jack and Pepsi, sweet thing."

She shrugged and almost said "what a way to fuck up Jack Daniels", but just fixed his drink and placed it before him. He gave her $10 on a $3 drink and told her to keep the change. Bunny always made a point of tipping big on the first drink; he found it was the best way to insure good service.

He began a systematic search of the crowd. The two assholes he was looking for were less than ten feet away playing darts.

"Double top to win Dougy.", someone in the crowd yelled at the shooter.

The tall, good looking coffee skinned black man took careful aim at the circular cork dart board eight feet distant and with a smooth release that bespoke many practice hours, let go his third dart which hit its target – the half-inch space between the double wire band circling the board.

There was a microsecond of silence from the otherwise noisy crowd of on-lookers before they erupted into choruses of "Alright!", "Yes!", "My Man!" and "Shit!", from the losers who had bet against the shooter.

"Way to go Dougy!", his partner exclaimed putting an arm around Doug Hayes' shoulders as he pulled Doug's three dart cluster from the corkboard.

"Rosemary... hey Rosemary, pour me and my partner a beer. Man, you are great in a clutch.", Larry Carson shouted.

"It's in the wrist – the wrist, Larry.", Doug Hayes responded simulating his dart throwing motion.

"Pay up you guys – when you hot, you hot!", Larry moved among the crowd, hand outstretched, collecting his and Doug's winnings.

"And when you not – you not!", the well dressed, dark skinned black man said toasting the winning team of Carson and Hayes with a raised glass of Jack Daniels and Pepsi.

"Let me buy the champs a drink.", he motioned to Rosemary who immediately filled Doug and Larry's beer glasses.

The partners toasted their benefactor and continued to accept the crowd's congratulations. Larry knew he was lucky. He had Doug Hayes as both his dart partner and business partner and lately, both partnerships had become very successful.

The part-time computer programming venture started four months earlier was succeeding beyond their greatest expectations and even Doug, who was always overly optimistic, hadn't forecasted the extent of their success. It was a simple business too – only one customer now – who paid very well for their services. In a few months they would quit their computer programmer jobs at New York's Guardian Memorial Hospital's Data Processing Department and work full time at their new venture.

Larry returned to the dart board to organize the next match and noticed that Doug was talking to the black guy who bought them the drink.

"Come on over here partner! There's someone you need to meet.", Doug was waving his hand and shouting to get Larry's attention over the crowd noise.

Larry angled over to where they were cramped together at the bar.

"Shake hands with another dude who works for the Preacher." Doug threw an arm around each man. "Bunny Ennis meet Larry Carson, my partner and the best white dude I know."

Larry reached out and shook hands with Bunny Ennis whose hand was surprisingly big and very strong and who was now squeezing much too hard. Bunny only released Larry's hand when he saw the white man's eyes squint against the painful pressure.

"Hell of a grip you got.", Larry said shaking his right hand. "Where'd you get a name like Bunny?", Larry shouted over the crowd noise.

Ennis smiled and answered in a normal voice causing Carson to move his ear closer to Bunny's mouth. "Cause' I fuck like one."

"I'll take your word on that.", Larry responded laughingly.

"Hey man.", Doug jumped in. "What do you do for the Preacher?"

"Odd jobs.", he answered with a shrug.

"Such as?", Larry retorted.

Doug had a look on his face like, "Why the hell you asking questions like that?", but he knew his partner had a very direct way in all things. Larry was a very good computer programmer and systems analyst and his success was in getting answers to his questions.

Bunny didn't seem the least bit offended at the question; he even laughed as he answered.

"Preacher told me to check out his new partners – that's why I'm here. He wants you happy and content and old Bunny is the Preacher's happy and content odd job man."

"You happy Doug?", Larry asked turning to his partner.

"Couldn't be happier.", he answered. "You play darts Bunny?"

"I don't play games my man – but you dudes go ahead with your tournament. I'll just sit here; watch you clean up and keep the drinks coming."

And he did. For the next two hours Larry and Doug took on all the comers and held onto their winning streak. After a while the steady flow of cold beer affected their throwing and accuracy and they were ready to call it a night.

"I'm outta here Doug.", Larry said. "Bunny, it was great meeting you and next time we get together, Doug and I are buying."

"Yeah man. Later. We got a long trip to Brooklyn.", Doug added his farewell to Larry's.

"Wait on here. I got my wheels just outside. I'll run you two dudes on out to Brooklyn."

"Naw Bunny, don't hassle yourself man."

"Hey it ain't no hassle. Let's go.", Bunny turned toward the barmaid working the other end. "Rosemary! Buy yourself a new wig baby.", he shouted pointing to the twenty he placed on the bar.

"Thank YOU! Come again!", she shouted to their backs while pocketing the tip.

The three took off for Brooklyn in the big red Cadillac and had only driven five minutes when Bunny told them he had to make a quick stop at one of the Preacher's East-side cribs.

"It's on our way man and I know you dudes gonna enjoy seeing the place.", he told them.

Larry wanted to skip the stop and grab a cab for home but Doug wanted to check the place out. Larry had never been in a whorehouse and was curious and finally agreed to stay for a few minutes. It was on the second floor over a pizzeria on 52nd Street and Lexington. They climbed the narrow staircase and were met by a beefy, middle aged white guy sitting at a small table just inside the door at the top of the stairs.

"Hey Bunnyman, what's shaking?", he asked. Larry sensed that this man was afraid of Ennis.

Bunny laughed and pointed to his two companions. "These are the Preacher's new partners and I want to show them the Man's favorite business. You got something for me Sal?"

"Sure, I got something for you Bunny. You know I always got something for you – I take good care of business, don't I? Go on in and show your friends our prime pussy and then come back out to see me. I'll have your package ready."

Sal then gave Larry and Doug a weak handshake and Larry noticed that he didn't once look them in the eye.

"Go on inside. The Bunnyman will show you around; have a taste, we got the best booze and check the girls out too. Everything is on the house for you guys.", Sal offered with bowed head and hand outstretched toward the room beyond.

Bunny opened the heavy, steel plated door and led Doug and Larry into a large reception area off the entrance foyer. There were three couches and some easy chairs placed throughout and a portable bar padded in imitation leather, occupied the back half of the room. The room's appearance was attractive but its main attraction was not its décor.

Sitting side by side on one of the couches were three stunning young girls who stood as the men entered.

"Bunny baby. Hey Bunny.", they giggled, surrounding Ennis, obviously happy to see him.

Larry knew that he had never seen three more beautiful women. None was more than twenty and each girl's perfect body was completely revealed by the transparent negligee she wore.

Doug seemed less impressed and was amused by his partner's "open mouth" reaction. "Larry, you're drooling man.", he said. "I thought you wanted to get on home."

"Ah, we have time for a drink.", he quickly responded while checking his watch.

Doug just shook his head and smiled at Bunny.

"Hey Bunny, how about introducing us to your good-looking friends.", one of the women asked.

Bunny introduced Monica, Carol and Jackie to Larry and Doug and asked Monica to fix them a drink. She and Larry sat on one of the couches while Doug and the others remained at the bar.

Bunny then excused himself and left to talk with Sal but before leaving instructed the ladies "to take good care of the Preacher's partners".

Monica was a natural blond, about five three, and wore a sheer white penoigh. Larry couldn't keep his eyes from her perfect breasts. He was almost drunk, a little giddy and very aroused. She had a sensual voice, a charming laugh and was stroking his inner thigh with the tips of her fingers.

"I have to come back some other night Monica, when we have more time to talk."

She looked at him with a pretty little grin fixed on her cherry lips. Larry found himself lost in Monica's dark blue eyes which were surrounded by the longest natural lashes he had ever seen. Her perfume was delicious and made his head spin.

"Larry, I'm not here for conversation.", she scolded. "You and Doug have all the time you need, so let's go inside and fuck." She whispered this while gently biting his ear lobe.

FOUR

4:45 PM, TUESDAY, OCTOBER 18, 1966

Detective Al Miller hated TV news press briefings. While he welcomed the opportunity they presented to advance his career, he just didn't like the way he looked on television. Miller was thirty-six years old and had been bald for almost ten years. The baldness made him look fifty and he didn't like that. But he also dressed "older" in dark, conservative suits, thinking this look presented a better image to the Police Department bosses.

Captain Gentner was running this afternoon press conference and it had already gotten off to a rocky start.

"Captain, why hasn't the Department been able to release more information about the murders of Carson and Hayes?"

Miller recognized the questions that came from that queer prick Dolan, a TV reporter from MBC.

"We are conducting a sensitive investigation and it would be inappropriate to release more at this time. Yes, you – next question.", Gentner pointed to the guy from PIX.

The press conference continued another fifteen minutes. Since the Department didn't have much to go on, Captain Gentner's answers were brief, non-committal and non-informative. The Press knew the routine and wrapped up their questioning quickly. This conference might not even air on most of tonight's newscasts.

Dolan approached Gentner and Miller as they started to leave,

"Could I ask a few questions off the record Captain?"

Gentner rolled his eyes in feigned exasperation.

"I got a meeting to go to Dolan. Talk to Miller here. But for Christ's sakes – keep it off the record!"

"OK Captain, no problem – background only. Thanks.", Dolan then turned to Miller. "Come on, let me buy you a cup of coffee Detective Miller."

Twenty minutes later Miller and Dolan sat across from each other in a small crowded diner on First Avenue.

"Let's make this brief Dolan, I have a lot of work to do. What's on your mind?"

Miller didn't like Johnny Dolan and made no effort to hide it.

"OK Detective Miller. I won't take up much of your time. What can you tell me that I don't already know about Hayes and Carson?", Dolan remained pleasant.

"Hayes was killed a good twelve hours before Carson. Both were tortured before they were killed and you already know that Hayes had his prick sliced off, probably after he was dead."

"Was it recovered?"

Miller smiled. "Not by us. You want it for your collection?"

"Do you have any leads?" Dolan answered, ignoring his BS comment.

"No."

"Any theories?"

"Yes."

"Well?"

Miller didn't respond, he just stared out the big plate glass window at the passing traffic. Dolan finally asked, "Look Al, this is off the record. Why do you think they were killed?"

Miller ignored the question for a few seconds and then turned and spoke. "Dolan you know I don't like you.", Miller was staring hard into Dolan's eyes.

"I could already guess, but what has that got to do with it?"

Miller continued. "We think these two were fags and were picked up by some queer bashers and the beating just got out of hand."

Johnny Dolan thought about what he had just heard a few seconds before speaking. He stirred his tea and looked at Al Miller who was still staring intently at him with a smirk on his face.

"You know that I'm gay don't you Al?", he said quietly.

"I heard you were a queer.", Miller answered, lighting a cigarette.

Dolan sighed. "So why do you think Hayes and Carson were gay?"

Miller blew a cloud of smoke toward Dolan's face.

"Hayes was arrested on a vice charge two years ago. He and the Mayor of Nyack were caught wienie wagging in the men's room at Grand Central. It was a political setup to embarrass the mayor and it worked. It made the Nyack papers. The charges were eventually reduced but he never ran for office again."

"What happened to Hayes?", Dolan asked.

"He was let off."

"Have you spoken with their wives?", Dolan then asked.

"Yes, we have. Hayes and his wife have been divorced for three years and didn't have much contact. Carson's wife did have something to tell us. It seems she got a telephone call from Carson about 5 AM Saturday morning – we estimate that was about the time he was killed."

"What did he say?"

"Nothing much. They were cut off almost immediately."

"Did either of them have anal mutilations?"

"You'll have to wait for the coroner's report Dolan."

"OK. Do you have any other theories?"

"Not at this time, but we are still putting Carson and Hayes' last day together. We figure that some black guy they met in a bar they hung out in might have something to do with this."

Dolan thought, "This asshole cop doesn't like anyone does he?"

"Where's the bar Al?"

"Look Dolan, it's too early in this investigation to be giving out that kind of information – off the record or not. Is there anything else you want to know; I have work to do?"

"No thanks Al, that's it. I appreciated your information."

"The only reason you got anything from me was because Gentner told me to talk with you. I told you that I don't like you and I mean it. And stop calling me Al, you're not my friend."

Miller stood, pushing his chair roughly into the table rattling the coffee cups. He gave Johnny Dolan a hard look, turned and walked toward the exit.

"Hey Al. Thanks for your help." Dolan called pleasantly after him.

Miller stopped, hunched his shoulders and it seemed if he was about to turn and face Dolan – he didn't – he just slammed the diner door as he exited.

Dolan finished his tea, paid the check and was back in the MBC Newsroom an hour later.

"Gil, it's important to me. That's why.", Dolan said in answer to Gil Peterson's question.

"Johnny, it's not that big a story. It's yesterday's news. There are a dozen murders every day in New York. These two guys have no special news appeal, you know that. I can't justify putting you on this story full time."

"I have a personal reason for wanting this one Gil."

"Oh damn it, for Christ's sakes Johnny – personal reasons don't cut it. You have a job to do and so do I. Forget about it."

Dolan paused a few seconds and sighed as he started speaking.

"Gil, you know I'm gay. I've never broadcasted it but I've never denied

it either. The cops think Hayes and Carson may have been killed because they were homosexuals. The country is changing Gill. Gay men and women are coming out of the closet and publicly admitting their homosexuality. It takes courage to go against Society. It takes even more guts to come out if there's a chance you might be killed because of it. Someone very close to me was beaten to death last year and I want this shit to stop!", Johnny's voice was beginning to rise. "Exposing the problem might help to find a solution. Besides there's a legitimate story here Gil that needs telling and I'd like to be the one to tell it. Just give me the chance."

As he listened, Peterson saw the possibility of a significant story or even a series. Gays in New York as in other parts of the country were becoming more visible and vocal. A good story here could make the national news desk – that would make him look good. Gil Peterson knew his business sometimes depended on a reporter's commitment to finding the truth. Johnny Dolan was an honest reporter who did his job well and deserved a chance to work on this story, for personal reasons or otherwise.

Peterson sighed. "OK, lad, I'm in. Take a few days and dig. We'll talk again and see where it's going. You'll still have to cover the grave yard shift but I'll get somebody to give you a hand. Deal?"

"Deal and thanks Gil."

FIVE

1:35 AM, SATURDAY, OCTOBER 15, 1966

Larry Carson looked over the room where Monica had left him. It was clean and quite ordinary; a bed and metal folding chair were its only furniture. It was dimly lit by a set of ceiling track lights and he could hear the low sound of some rock and roll radio station playing a Beatles number. There was a small sink with a mirror mounted above it in one corner. The ambiance, if it could be called that, was of a very low budget motel room where people went for afternoon sex.

He stood there wondering what he should do. He had an unreasonable sense that someone was watching and was startled when Monica quietly returned. "What the Hell am I doing here?", he thought as she came toward him.

"Oh, you're not comfortable yet Larry.", she whispered. She was carrying some towels.

"I'm very comfortable, thank you Monica."

"But you're still dressed Larry." She answered with pouting lips.

"I was waiting for you to help me.", He smiled at her and wondered why they were whispering.

Monica placed the towels on the sink and stood in front of him. She was so beautiful and so out of place that he almost asked why she worked here. Fortunately, he was able to stop himself. It wasn't any of his business why, she was a hooker. She wasn't his date; he was here to get layed.

Larry removed his jacket and tie and placed them on the metal folding chair. Monica helped with his shirt buttons and had him sit on the bed while she removed his shoes and socks, then she quickly undid his belt and removed his pants and shorts. He reached down toward the kneeling girl and pulled on the little pink string bows that held up her skimpy costume. The top fell to her waist exposing her well-formed, pink nippled breasts. Larry cupped each in his hands enjoying their feel, shape and weight.

Monica stood and stepped out of her pink peignoir and inched toward him; Larry's face was almost level with her blond pussy. He put his hands on her round solid ass and pulled her forward until his mouth was submersed in her perfume scented pussy hair.

His head was still spinning when she brought him to the small sink and began washing his balls and erect prick.

2:45 AM, SATURDAY, OCTOBER 15, 1966

Larry Carson floated peacefully in a half-awake state; he was vaguely aware that Monica had left him but was so relaxed he never heard Bunny enter the room.

Bunny stood at the foot of the bed watching the steady rise and fall of the sleeping man's chest. After a minute, he took a small glass bottle from his jacket pocket and carefully undid the cap. He tipped it so a single drop of liquid fell, landing on the sole of Larry's left foot. Bunny then stepped back, never taking his eyes off the naked man sleeping on the small bed.

Larry Carson had drifted into a pleasurable dream. He was lying on a beautiful tropical beach. He could hear the rustling of a thousand palms, the distant cries of seabirds and the rhythmic sound of the surf. He was so relaxed and contented he could feel the tepid ocean water reach and touch him where he lay. Then the seawater began to heat.

"It's too hot.", he said aloud.

The ocean had begun to boil and where it touched his left foot, turned it into burning red agony.

Larry was fully awake, his foot on fire, but he couldn't see the flame – all he saw was the smiling face of Bunny Ennis. Carson couldn't speak, couldn't reason, but he could scream and he did at the unbearable, searing pain that now pulsated upward from his foot throughout his entire body.

"Need some help Larry?", the Bunnyman asked softly.

"Ahhh!", Larry Carson screamed.

Sal came in and the two men lifted Larry from the bed and dragged his naked body down the corridor to another room.

Carson's whimpers were punctuated with a high-pitched scream each time his injured foot contacted something solid. He was only vaguely aware that Doug was also in this new location. It never registered in his pain wracked brain that his partner was also naked and bound tightly to a chair.

"Put your foot in the water man.", Sal said as he roughly sat Larry on a hard-wooden chair.

"I said – put your fuckin' foot in the water asshole!"

When he still didn't respond, Sal lifted Larry's left leg and dropped his foot into the basin of water on the floor in front of the chair.

The shock of the ice-cold water on his burning foot was dramatic; the pain immediately subsided and Larry was catapulted back into reality. He and Doug were balls ass naked, in a small windowless room somewhere in a whorehouse over a pizza parlor. Doug was bound hand and foot and Larry could see an orderly pattern of small bloody puncture wounds spread over his chest and arms. Doug's head was tilted forward, chin resting on his chest, eyes closed.

"Doug – Doug. You alright?", Larry croaked.

"He's OK, just a little sleepy. I'll wake him up for you.", Bunny answered Larry as if he was Doug's best friend.

Bunny walked to the slumped figure and smacked him hard with his open hand four times across his face.

"Wake up homo. Time to wake up you fucking fag.", he growled.

Bunny raised his hand to strike Doug again when Larry shouted. "Stop hitting him you bastard!"

Surprisingly, Bunny stopped. He moved to Larry and made quick slashing movements with open hands in front of Larry's face. Larry raised his arms to protect himself, but Bunny was only being playful. He never touched him.

When Bunny finally stopped, Larry managed to ask: "What the hell is going on here Ennis? Why are you doing this shit to us?"

"Think of this as part of your initiation into the Preacher's worker's club. Yeah, we making you and your queer friend over there honorary members of our club. Right Sal?"

"That's right Bunny.", Sal answered.

"But first we got to collect your dues. Hey give me your knife Sal. I got me some cutting to do."

Sal handed Ennis his switch blade.

Bunny ran the deadly sharp knife lightly across Larry's chest, opening a thin red line which formed a drop of blood at one end. It thickened and began running down toward his nipple.

Carson was too shocked to cry out or defend himself. Bunny stepped back admiring his handy work.

"That be pretty – maybe Sal and me play some TIC-TAC-TOE on you."

Carson blanched and Sal laughed.

"Dougy say you the brains of the outfit and I think he be truthful.", Ennis calmly continued.

Bunny then moved behind Doug and pulled his head up and back by his hair. He placed the tip of the knife on his throat and Doug moaned softly but his eyes remained closed. Larry started to rise but fell back from the jolt of pain shooting up from his foot still immersed in the water basin.

"Yeah, old Dougy convinced me and Sal that he was being truthful. Right Sal?", Ennis ignored Carson's feeble attempt to come to Hayes' aid.

Sal smiled and held up a three-foot length of flat board hammered with half a dozen nails, their sharp points exposed and bloody.

"After a few whacks with this everybody tells the truth Bunny-man.", Sal instructed Larry.

"I guess you be wondering why you and your homo partner be

getting the special initiation treatment? Well, it's because you been holding out on the Preacher and we don't allow that.", Bunny said.

Larry's mind screamed for answers. "What could we have that the Preacher wanted?", he thought.

"I don't know what you're talking about Ennis. We gave the Preacher everything we agreed on.", he finally answered.

"Oh, not everything. You and your whiz kid buddy are holding the Preacher's property and he wants it. He asked Dougy for it nice last week, but this fool tell him NO! Now that ain't right is it? All the money the Preacher give you two, you got to be more respectful. You dig what I'm saying man?"

Doug's eyes fluttered open and seeing Larry, gave him a weak smile.

"We'll give the Preacher whatever he wants – just tell me. Let us go and get us to a hospital for god's sake!"

Bunny released Doug's hair and bounded to Larry's side. "Where's the source code to your computer program mother fucker?"

Bunny's face was only inches away from Larry's. His black eyes blazed with hate and Larry felt as if he was being attacked by a wolf ready to rip out his throat if he made the slightest movement. A light flashed in Larry's brain. "All this bullshit was for some lousy computer program code."

"I WANT THAT CODE!", Ennis shouted.

"It's in my office at the Hospital.", Carson whispered.

"Where in your office?"

Carson could smell rot on Ennis' fetid breath.

"There's a file cabinet, the top draw. It's labeled Single Action. That's the program source code. You can have it."

"Great – Now how the fuck do I get in your office shit for brains?"

"Take my wallet. The plastic security card opens the computer room door. Tell the computer operator I sent you. His name is Nick. If you want, let Doug and me go and I'll bring the program to the Preacher on Monday."

Bunny laughed loudly and Sal retained his stupid smirk.

"Too late for that shit for your partner. He had his chance last week, but he fucked up. Ain't that right Dougy? You fucked up, didn't you?" Bunny then placed his oversized hand around Larry's throat. "If you ain't lying to me you might get a break Larry. You might even get out of here. You might even get to keep on working for the Preacher. You know Larry I kind of like you. You ain't gay like this one."

Bunny released Larry's throat and pointed to Doug. "No sir, Monica told me you done her good. She like you. I like you too. Now Doug, he a different case. Get inside with the women and he stay limp dick. You don't like pussy do you Dougy?"

Doug Hayes stared dumbly at Bunny Ennis but made no effort to answer. Instead, he turned to Larry.

"I'm sorry I got you into this shit man.", he said weakly.

"Aw, poor Dougy. I know what you need to make you feel better.", Bunny said soothingly stroking Doug's head.

"Here Sal, cut this piece of shit loose of these ropes."

Bunny handed the switch blade to Sal, removed the pistol from his waistband and held it pointed toward the floor between the two seated men.

Sal cut Doug's bonds and stepping back, pocketed his knife. He then stood with his back leaning against the door, dumbly picking his nose.

"That's right, that's right Dougy. Get the circulation going again. You got plenty of blood left in you. Sal didn't let it all out when he whacked you. Now stand up like a good boy, go on now – stand up."

Doug sat rubbing his wrists and wincing at the obvious pain from the dozens of puncture wounds.

"Sal, get your 'hole-in-one' bat and help old Dougy stand up like he been told."

Sal picked up the obscene club and raised it menacingly. When Doug quickly stood both Sal and Bunny laughed at him. Doug hung his head and began to sob.

"GIVE HIM A WHACK ON THE ASS SAL!", Bunny roared.

Sal swung his club and the penetrating nail spikes made a plopping sound as they entered Doug's buttocks.

"Ahhg!", he shouted in pain, falling to his knees.

"Stop it! Stop it!", Larry screamed.

"Oh, don't worry he OK. Ain't you faggy Doug? You probably like to get whacked. It make you feel good. Now get the fuck on your feet when I'm talking to you."

Doug stood slowly, pulling himself up with the help of the chair; small rivers of blood ran down the back of his legs.

"That's much better Doug. You got to do what I tell you. Now just stand there.", Bunny said, his tone softening.

Doug's eyes began to flutter and his knees buckled.

"Don't you pass out on me now. Don't pass out mother fucker.", Bunny shouted, slapping Doug's face.

Doug's eyes opened and for a second, burned with hate. He gripped the back of the chair to steady himself.

"What does the Preacher plan to do with the source code?", Larry asked, hoping to draw Bunny's attention.

"How the fuck do I know.", Bunny answered, temporarily diverted but his eyes never leaving Doug.

"It won't do him any good if you kill us Ennis.", Larry continued.

Bunny's gaze shifted to Carson. "You think you the only two computer whiz kids in New York? Preacher got his own genius, asshole. He told the Preacher you two fuckin' with him by keeping that source code. So you ain't so fucking smart after all.", Ennis was enjoying himself.

"If you let us go, we'll work for you. You can have the source code. Doug and I will show you how to use it. You'll make a fortune for yourself. Just let us go Ennis."

Bunny took the four feet separating him from Carson in one bound. He was so quick; Larry couldn't even raise his arms to protect himself from the punches that left his face bloody and broke two teeth.

Bunny stepped back from his savaged victim and kicked away the water basin from Larry's still immersed foot, doubling his pain.

Ennis wasn't even breathing hard and his voice sounded almost gentle as he spoke to Larry Carson.

"Listen to what I tell you and don't ever forget it. When you work for the Preacher you in for life. You don't jive with him and you don't fuck with him or what's his. You dig what I'm saying to you?"

Larry nodded. His face had already begun to swell from the deadly punches he had received.

"That's a good boy.", Bunny patted Larry's head and turned toward Sal, "I got to start wearing gloves or something Sal.", he smiled as he shook the pain from the hand that had just delivered the blows to Carson's face.

Sal gave a genuine laugh at Bunny's joke.

"Aw Dougy, we almost forgot about you.", Bunny now moved to the still standing man and put an arm around his naked shoulders.

"How you all doing? Come over here man and say hello to Larry."

Bunny slowly moved Doug across the room to stand before his seated partner. Neither Doug nor Larry had any fight left and escape was out of the question. Bunny had beaten them; he owned them.

"Dougy you gonna help Larry get over his blues? You know what he need? ... No, well let me tell you 'cause I think you gonna like it too. Your man Larry need some head. You think you can give him some? Ain't that right Larry; some head gonna make you feel better."

Bunny pushed Doug to his knees in front of his seated partner. "Go ahead, suck him off."

Doug seemed to revive when he realized what was expected. He shook his head slowly and croaked "No."

"What you say Dougy? You say no? You don't want to make Larry feel better? Hey Larry, what kind of queer ass partner you got here?", he said this as if he was confused and disappointed by Doug's refusal.

"Suck his cock mother-fucker!", Bunny said loudly.

"No you son of a bitch! Go fuck yourself!", Doug answered almost as loudly.

Doug stared defiantly at Bunny as he tried to get to his feet. Larry sat, dumbly afraid, staring straight ahead.

"Dougy, Dougy, why you being so uppity?", Bunny said despairingly while raising his pistol level with Doug's head.

The report of the .22 was no louder than a small firecracker but at this close range its effect on Doug's skull was devastating. The bullet entered his right temple and exited from his left. Doug toppled over and blood pumped in spurts from the exit wound. He began to convulse and his eyes rolled back in his head. His mouth opened in a silent scream and his fists shook rigidly at his sides.

"Aw Dougy, you need another one, don't you? "Bang bang. You dead.", Bunny said firing another round into Doug's head.

One would have been enough to finish him. Larry stared in horror at his dead partner lying at his feet. Sal showed no change in expression and Bunny was smiling.

"We don't need him do we Larry? You the brains anyway, especially now since all Dougy's brains be running out of him. Hey, I got an idea. Let's get you a souvenir of Doug. Something that will help you remember him. What do you think Larry? That a good idea? I don't want you to forget him now."

"Sal, let me see that blade man."

Sal pulled the knife from his pocket and flicked it open and then handed it to Bunny who looked admiringly at it. "I like this blade Sal, where'd you get it man?"

Sal shrugged that he didn't remember.

Bunny just shook his head and putting his arm around Larry's naked shoulders whispered, "Cut his cock off Larry."

He placed the opened knife into Larry's shaking hand and then forced him to kneel before Doug's body. Bunny rolled Doug onto his back with the toe of his shoe, being careful not to get any blood on himself.

"Cut it off mother-fucker! Go on cut it off I said, or I'll cut yours off.", Bunny said slapping Larry hard across the back of his head.

Larry cried as he reached out and took hold of Doug's limp penis. He used the razor-sharp knife and in three sawing motions amputated it. He held it just a second before throwing it down; and when he gagged, he vomited watery green bile onto Doug's body and into the thickening blood now puddling on the floor around him.

"Naw, I don't think you ever gonna forget your old partner Dougy. Are you Larry?", Bunny whispered.

4:05 AM, SATURDAY, OCTOBER 15, 1966

Nick Patrokas loved his job. He could hardly wait to get to work each day. Nick was always early and never refused overtime. He didn't even like to take extended vacations – so he was never gone for more than a week. There were only two reasons why Nick felt the way he did about his night shift, computer operators' job at New York Guardian Medical Center – he had been married ten years and with six kids needed this well-paying job and the second reason was the forty-one-year-old nurse who visited him in the computer room each evening.

Nancy Barron loved this little Greek and saw him every night from 3:30 AM until 4:15 AM, sometimes for coffee, sometimes for conversation and sometimes for hurried, passionate sex on the computer manager's office couch.

Tonight had been for all three. It was now 4:05 AM and Nick and Nancy were intimately connected on the boss's couch and didn't know or at this particular moment care that there was an intruder in Guardian Medical Center's Data Processing Department.

It had been relatively easy for Bunny to gain access to the otherwise secure computer room. He had no problem entering the Hospital and just followed the signs that led to the Data Processing Department. He wore Larry Carson's security badge and used his plastic security card to open the computer room lock.

Bunny Ennis had never seen a computer before and was unsettled by the hospital computer center which looked like an IBM computer showroom with its wall-to-wall processing equipment. He had no idea where to find Larry's office and was wandering aimlessly until he heard Nancy Barron's loud climatic shrieking. He followed the sound and quietly entered the Director's office.

Nick saw him first – just standing at the door, watching. Bunny smiled and Nick's expression changed from ecstasy to outright fear in less than three seconds.

"Who the hell are you?", Nick shouted at the leering intruder and then demanded. "What are you doing here?"

Since he was lying on top of her, Nancy was having a difficult time understanding what was going on. Not having the slightest idea what Nick was screaming about, she thought he had added a new twist to their love making.

Nick pulled out of Nancy and awkwardly scrambled to his feet looking rather ridiculous with his shirt and tie in place but naked from his waist to his white socks. He also had an erection now at half-mast and sinking slowly. It was obvious that Nick was frightened, not of Bunny, but because of what he represented... the unknown. "Listen, I can explain, I ...", Nick began, stopping when Nancy loudly interrupted.

Now that she was free of Nick's body, she re-acted instinctively to Bunny's presence. He may have intimidated and cornered Nick, but not Nancy Barron. This leering intruder wasn't going to bully her. She got to her feet while at the same time pulling up her briefs and panty hose and fastening closed her uniform buttons.

"Who are you?", Nancy demanded in her Head Nurse voice.

She moved Nick aside and walked within a foot of Bunny. Nancy was his height and looked squarely into his black eyes.

Bunny stood his ground. "I'm looking for something lady. You work here?", he softly asked.

Not getting the expected reaction unsettled her. "Yes – I work here. How did you get in?". She noticed Larry Carson's identification badge clipped to his jacket but wasn't able to make out the name.

"I need to pick up some computer program code for Larry Carson. Where's his office?", he directed his question to Nick, who still hadn't put on his pants.

Nick wanted this guy out of the Computer Room and would have let him back up a truck and remove all the computer equipment if he had asked for it.

Seeing a way to get this guy out of the area he volunteered. "Yeah, sure. Come on, I'll show you."

Nancy couldn't believe that Nick was being so stupid. Putting her hand in front of his face she warned, "Wait a minute, Nick! We don't know who this guy is. You can't let him take anything out of the building."

Bunny shot her a menacing look. "Come on man. Larry's a friend of mine.", Bunny directed his appeal to Nick, ignoring Nancy again.

Nick was still unsure what to do but he had begun to overcome his fear of Bunny's presence.

Moving Nancy aside, he demanded, "Yeah? Well, why the hell did he send you to pick it up? He should have come himself. And why couldn't it wait till Monday?"

Ennis shook his head and sighed as if he were dealing with a disobedient child. "You're wasting my time Nick. You want to talk to Larry? I'll get him on the phone for you. You can ask him yourself.", Bunny then walked to the big grey metal desk, picked up the telephone and quickly dialed a number. Sal answered on the second ring.

"Hello, - put Larry on the phone —- Larry?", Bunny spoke into the receiver. "I got me a problem here. Talk to Nick. He don't want to give me the program man."

Nancy and Nick had listened attentively. "Here Nick,", Bunny handed the telephone to Nick. "Talk to Larry man."

Carson hadn't sounded too coherent and Bunny watched Nick's face closely for any reaction. He had been warned what would happen if he screwed up and Bunny was certain Sal was listening carefully to each response, ready to drop him if he fucked up.

"Larry, you sound like shit.", Nick began. "What the hell is going on? Why do you need a program at four o'clock in the morning?", he demanded.

Bunny gripped the snug pistol in his pocket and slipped its safety. He watched Nick for any sign. The nurse stood with her arms folded on the other side of the room glaring at him. Bunny smiled at her and she turned away.

Larry explained to Nick that he didn't want anyone to know he was taking a program out of the office, and that Bunny was Doug's brother-in-law. He also told him that there was a $100 for him if he helped out. The offer of $100 was all Nick really needed to hear. He was smiling when he hung up. He turned first to Nancy.

"It's OK babe. This guy is Larry and Doug's buddy. They're

working upstate this weekend and he's meeting them later at Albany Medical to do some freelance programming work."

"For god's sake put your pants on Nick!", was all Nancy said before leaving for her nursing unit.

Nick opened Larry's office and helped box up the 500 punched cards, printed source code list and all the documentation representing Carson's Single Action program.

"Larry says you have something for me.", Nick then reminded Bunny.

"Yeah my man, here's a taste for your trouble.", Bunny handed Nick five $20 dollar bills. "Preciate your help. Don't tell anyone that Larry and Doug are doin' some moon lighting on the side. It might get them in trouble. You dig?"

"Thanks. Yeah … I'll keep it on the QT. And tell Larry to call me if you guys need anything else.", Nick said opening the computer room door.

"Yeah, later."

Bunny was glad he didn't have to waste the little fucker. He liked him thinking, "He gets his self layed on the job and makes a quick $100 too, he be my kind of dude." Now the big mouth 'bitch' was another story… he would have enjoyed taking her apart.

Bunny reached the parked Caddy in five minutes and headed downtown to meet with his people and have the Single Action program code checked out before returning to the whorehouse.

"Fuckin' piece of cake.", he said aloud as he started the big engine. It had been a good day's work.

SIX

9:10 PM, THURSDAY, OCTOBER 20, 1966

The kitchen telephone had rung four times before Lydia Hayes answered.

"Hello?"

"Hello … is this Mrs. Douglas Hayes?"

"Yes. Who's calling please?"

"My name is John Dolan, Mrs. Hayes and I work for MBC Television News. I know this is a difficult time for you and I'm very sorry at the loss of your husband and I don't mean to intrude on your grief but if you don't mind, I'd like an opportunity to meet with you tomorrow if possible."

"I'm sorry…eh, Mr. Dolan, but I don't wish to meet with anyone at this time. Especially reporters.", she answered curtly.

"Our interview would be off-camera.", Dolan came back quickly. "And everything discussed would be kept in complete confidence."

"Mr. Dolan, I am devastated by Doug's death but he and I were divorced three years ago and I haven't seen him for over a year. I've already spoken with the Police Department and a number of your colleagues from the press, whom I might add, were both rude and insensitive.", her voice took on an angry tone. "I don't think an interview with you would serve any meaningful purpose whatsoever. I knew absolutely nothing about Doug's current life."

"I understand how you feel right now Mrs. Hayes, so perhaps we could meet some other time… but might I ask just one question?"

"What's your question Mr. Dolan?", she answered with an audible sigh.

"Was Doug a homosexual?"

"What? How dare you ask that?"

"Please Mrs. Hayes… I'm sure that question must seem insensitive but I'm an investigative reporter and from the circumstances surrounding your former husband's death I have reason to believe that Doug may have been murdered by organized gay haters."

She kept silent for what seemed like a long time.

"Hello, Mrs. Hayes?", Dolan finally asked, breaking her silence.

When she spoke, she sounded weary. "I… I don't know why I should answer your question but… I'm not sure Mr. Dolan. Doug may have been gay, but I'm not sure."

Johnny considered her answer; it sounded honest.

"Mrs. Hayes, I understand your concern about Doug's reputation and I promise anything you've told me or will tell me is completely off the record."

She continued. "Doug and I had many problems in our marriage, including sexual ones. He wasn't deviant but he had become sexually passive. I thought that he might be seeing other women and when I confronted him, he denied it."

"Did you know Larry Carson?"

"Yes, I did."

"Do you think that he might have been a homosexual?"

"No, I don't think so. Larry's married and has children – I guess that doesn't mean anything but I don't believe he was gay and I told you I'm not sure that Doug was either."

"I understand Mrs. Hayes. Thank you. I appreciate your candor."

"I hope I've been some help Mr. Dolan. I want Doug's killers found. Please contact me in a few weeks, perhaps we could talk should you have any other questions."

"Thank you again Mrs. Hayes. If you have a pencil handy, I'll give you my telephone number in case you think of anything important."

She took his number and Dolan hung up. He considered what Lydia Hayes told him – not much really – a wife might not know if her spouse was homosexual, but she didn't even suspect it. She thought Hayes might be fooling around with other women and from her comments, hadn't seriously considered other alternatives.

Lydia listened for Dolan's telephone click indicating that he had hung up. When it came, she still waited a few seconds before speaking.

"What do you think?", she asked her lover listening on the bedroom extension.

"I think you better fix me my drink and get your black ass back in here.", he roughly answered.

"Or what will you do to my black ass?", she answered, a jolt of passion heating her naked body and thickening her voice.

"Or I'll beat it till it bleeds before I fuck it."

Lydia hurriedly mixed his double Jack Daniels and Pepsi and carrying it into the bedroom found him as she had left him, naked, lying on her bed still stroking his cock.

She stood watching – her eyes now wide with lust and fixated on the up and down movement of his big hand on his fully erect penis.

He took his drink and sitting up with his back resting on the bed's head board, sipped it slowly. "Play with yourself.", he commanded, his green eyes boring into hers, now unfocused with lust. He could smell her musky scent mixing with her expensive perfume.

Obeying his order, she rubbed her right hand up and down between her legs and felt the sticky wetness. Lydia then slowly moved it up her body, brushing her breast, leaving a shiny wet smudge and then moving her hand onto her lips, where she licked and sucked her fingers. She felt her body begin to tremble and a lightness in her head.

"Stir my drink with your pussy finger.", he ordered.

She came to the side of her bed and stood staring down at him. "Only if you promise to beat my black ass.", she answered huskily.

He looked up at her and at the same time roughly grabbed her breast, his thumb and index finger pinching her erect nipple.

"Oh… I'm gonna beat it good bitch.", the Bunnyman promised.

SEVEN

6:25 AM SATURDAY, OCTOBER 15, 1966

Larry's pain was almost more than he could stand. His foot still burned from the acid, his mouth from broken and loosened teeth and his entire body throbbed from the kicks and punches he had received. But the worst pain came from flashes of Doug's death that played over and over again in his mind.

He knew it was morning. Sal had left him in a room with an opaque glass sky light. He was naked and shivering with cold. There was no warmth from the meager October sunlight filtering through the dirty source twelve feet above him. The room was barren and there was nothing that could be fashioned into a weapon, not that it really mattered. He had resigned himself to death and only hoped it would be quick.

His heart ached when he thought about his wife Pauline and their three kids. He had been a bastard the last few years and not being able to make amends for past sins hurt most of all. Larry Carson began to sob, softly at first and then loud enough to be heard outside the locked room.

Sal came in after a while, told him to "shut the fuck up!", and left. Larry was still crying an hour later when Bunny and Sal returned.

"Aw man, what's your problem? You alive ain't you?"

Larry stopped crying when he saw the contempt in Bunny's face. "Did you get what you wanted?", he asked.

"Yeah and you a lucky mother… the Preacher's genius says your Single Action program check out. Come on outta here, we gonna fix you up.", he ordered.

Sal helped Larry to his feet and then half carried, half dragged him to the office next door. He gave him his undershorts and let him use the office bathroom.

Carson was shocked when he saw himself in the cracked mirror. His face was swollen and bruised from the beating and his bloodshot eyes held a haunted look which frightened him. Cleaning up as best he could, he put on his shorts and limped back into the office.

It was empty. Larry saw the telephone on the desk and realized this would be his only opportunity to speak with Pauline. He decided to take his chance and had just picked up the receiver when Bunny entered.

"Who you calling Larry? The cops?", he didn't sound concerned. Bunny removed the pistol from his pocket and pointed it at Larry.

Larry Carson was calm – at peace. He couldn't be hurt anymore.

"I know you're going to kill me Ennis. I'm going to call my wife now.", he said quietly.

Bunny smiled and nodded. "Yeah, good idea. Go ahead, call her Larry."

Carson then dialed his home telephone number knowing that he would be dead before he had a chance to speak with Pauline. It didn't matter, just hearing her voice would be enough to take into eternity.

The telephone rang twice before she answered.

"Hello.", she said simultaneously with Sal's abrupt entry into the office – enough to distract Bunny for an instant.

"I love you Pauline.", Larry whispered as Bunny's .22 flashed.

She never heard the sound of the shot that killed her husband, only the telephone falling to the floor and then white silence.

Bunny Ennis made certain Larry Carson was dead.

"Dress this shit up like that other piece of dead meat Sal and toss them out with the garbage.", he ordered.

EIGHT

6:20 AM FRIDAY, OCTOBER 21, 1966

This would be the third time Dolan screened Mike Denton's video of the Carson/Hayes homicide. It was obvious that Denton was a pro – he included all the elements needed by a TV news editor putting a story together.

There were both long shots and close ups of bodies, cops, coroners' people and the few curious onlookers who had gathered at two o'clock on that early Monday morning of October 17th.

Johnny reviewed it all in minute detail until he had the scene firmly fixed in his mind. Dolan was a good detail man – developed through a combination of excellent natural powers of observation finely honed by his years of military training.

He noticed that neither corpse wore shoes and they were lying neatly, side by side. He also noticed the lack of blood on their clothing and the street and concluded much as Denton had earlier, that they were either naked or wearing something else when killed at a different location where they bled out.

3:20 PM FRIDAY, OCTOBER 21, 1966

Later, as Dolan completed his daily jog around his East Side neighborhood, he worked out the problems with the Carson/Hayes murders. His thoughts went "stream of conscious".

"Why would the killers – had to be killers because of the nature of the crime – the torture, body movement, etc., why would the killers go to the trouble of changing their victim's clothes – couldn't have – Carson and Hayes weren't wearing different clothing when they were killed – so they had to be naked.

Why were they naked? Were their clothes ripped off? No... not likely, nothing appeared torn in the video, their shirts were neatly buttoned, ties in place. Did they willingly remove their clothes for their killers? That's possible... Why? For sex-maybe. Because they were ordered to undress? Maybe. Then why did the killers dress them after they were dead? Probably because they had to. Why? Less conspicuous when moving the bodies from where they were killed to where they were dumped. Possible... why no shoes? Fingerprints on shoes? ... Carson's left foot had noticeable acid burns and was badly swollen; probably couldn't get his shoe back on. Did the shoes get thrown away... maybe they were stolen from their bodies – before the Police arrived. Possible. Dolan's jogging pace increased – matching his mind's activity.

"Was there any significance to where the bodies were dumped? Why not in New Jersey's Meadowlands or some remote place? Because either the killers wanted them found in a hurry or didn't care to go to any bother in getting rid of the bodies. Why? Were they setting an example? – the reason for most mob hits – were the murders gay bashers warning gays ... or maybe they were just too lazy to go to the trouble of dumping them out-of-town? Probably not... these guys seemed to know what they were doing; they even dressed the bodies after they were dead ... these guys weren't lazy.

The bastards didn't panic; they were pros. Then why were the wallets taken and not jewelry? – I'm sure I saw a wrist watch on Carson. Were their wallets lifted so they couldn't be immediately identified?

No, that didn't make sense; if the killers didn't want the bodies identified they would have dumped them in the ocean or the woods, burned them, whatever.

Maybe some passerby stole their wallets before the cops arrived ... the same people who took their shoes? Bums – street people? Now that could be possible.

Were there any witnesses to the dumping? What about the spectators in Mike Denton's crime scene video; anything interesting about them? Al Miller said that Carson and Hayes had left the bar with a black man and there was at least one black man in the crowd at the scene.

"And who called the police?"

About two miles into his three-mile run, Johnny Dolan began forming a murder theory and an approach for his follow up.

"Carson and Hayes were killed by pros.", he concluded.

"They may have been killed because they were gay but it was just as likely they died for some other reason. Their wallets and shoes may have been taken by street people who could have witnessed something important.

The key to the puzzle was to identify the black man they "willingly" followed to their deaths.

"First order of business – locate their Friday night hang-out!", he thought.

The people they worked with, maybe their wives, certainly Miller, knew the name of the bar. He decided to call Carson's wife and then check in with Miller and see if he had anything new. He would also call Mike Denton and get his first-hand impression of the crime scene.

Dolan realized he had a lot to do and after returning to his apartment, took a quick shower, had two cups of black tea and made his first call to Police Headquarters.

He was told Detective Miller was off-duty and would be back in two days. Dolan left his name and asked that Miller get back to him as soon as possible. He then called Mike Denton and set up a meeting at the News Center where they could review Mike's video together.

Before he could make his next call, his telephone rang.

"Hello?"

"Hello John. It's Brian."

"Bri... Hi, what's up?", Dolan answered already knowing the reason for this call.

"I'd like to see you John."

"Bri, I don't think we need to see each other. It just didn't work for us. Let's move on with our lives." Johnny said softly.

"John, I need to see you. I want to talk. I promise I won't call again if you'd see me. Please Johnny."

Dolan still cared for Brian Toth; he didn't want to hurt him anymore than he already had. He considered what he was about to say. "Brian, I hope it's not a mistake, but alright, I'll see you tonight at eight."

"Oh, that's great John. The Club?"

"Yes. We'll talk Brian – but only for an hour. I have to work tonight."

"Ok, thank you. I'll see you at eight. So long."

Dolan knew that this meeting might be a mistake, but there was a chance that he could finally end their more intimate relationship without losing Brian as his friend.

He then checked with his office for messages and his evening assignments. Gil Peterson had kept his word and Dolan's schedule was light tonight so he could devote as much time as needed to the Carson Hayes story. Dolan and Peterson were scheduled to meet on the following Tuesday and Johnny would need to demonstrate he was making real progress if he was going to continue on this assignment.

He now made his most difficult telephone call.

"Hello?"

"Hello, is this the Larry Carson residence?"

"Yes, it is. Who's calling please?"

"My name is John Dolan mam and I'm with MBC TV News. May I speak with Mrs. Carson please. It's important."

"This is Mrs. Carsons' sister and she can't come to the telephone. You understand that we buried her husband today and this is not the proper time for you to call sir. Goodbye.", she said indignantly.

"Wait – please wait.", Dolan pleaded, his tone somehow holding her.

"Yes, what is it.", She was rightfully annoyed with him.

"I truly apologize for my intrusion at this difficult time, but I have been assigned to investigate Mr. Carsons' death with the hope that my efforts will lead to the capture of his and Mr. Hayes' killer. I realize that I am being rude and inconsiderate but could I leave my name and number and perhaps at a better time when Mrs. Carson feels up to it, she might be kind enough to see me."

The "sister" hesitated. "Pauline wants to leave this terrible place and come home to her family in Virginia."

There was anguish in her voice.

"I understand; thank you. My name is John Dolan, that's D O L A N, … .. I'm a reporter for MBC News."

Johnny gave her the rest of the contact information and when he hung up, was reasonably certain that he would never hear from Mrs. Larry Carson.

5:20 PM FRIDAY, OCTOBER 21, 1966

On his way to his office meeting Johnny stopped in his local donut shop. Mike Denton loved his donuts and Johnny planned to reward him for taking time to meet with him.

"Hi,", Johnny greeted the new counter girl. "Could you box me up a dozen? I'll have four jelly's …

"She held up her hand and stopped him. "I'm sorry, don't tell me what you want, I'll forget."

"What? You don't want me to tell you what I want? Then how can I give you my order?"

"Let's start again sir.", she seemed annoyed.

"Ok, I want four jellies …"

"I asked you not to tell me …" The counter girl actually stamped her foot in anger.

"This is crazy. Am I going nuts or what?", he thought.

Finally, the store manager who had been listening to their conversation, came over. Johnny placed his order and left, still shaking his head.

"That was like something from a Kafka story. But kind of funny too.", he thought.

A few hours later he was seated with Mike Denton in one of MBC's editing rooms viewing the Carson Hayes video.

"I do nice work Johnny ... damn nice work. Don't I?"

"The best Mike. Here's your reward." Johnny patted Mike's back and handed him two sugar packets for his coffee.

"Look at that angle. What focus, Thanks. Got any donuts?"

"Over by the coffee pot.", he answered, pointing to the box of fresh donuts he'd brought in.

"Yum yum. Chocolate cream.", Denton licked his lips taking two of the donuts and returning to the viewing screen.

"Mike, I've looked at your work of art half dozen times and I still feel there's something there I'm not seeing. What is it?"

"Not enough blood on their clothes Johnny.", Mike answered, his mouth now full of chocolate donut.

"I know that.", Dolan answered sharply. "What else?"

"How the hell do I know! Let's look at it – slow."

So they looked at it again – frame by frame. Things they hadn't noticed began to appear. The neckties each corpse wore were poorly knotted and would have looked better with the other man's suit. Hayes body was further along in rigor. Carson's wrist watch was facing the wrong way.

Other things also seemed to materialize – there were eight spectators in the crowd that had gathered that early Monday morning, all were men. Two actually seemed amused by the gruesome scene – a young black man and a smiling moon-faced middle-aged, heavy-set man who looked either Spanish or Italian.

The cops appeared bored except for one young officer who was off to the side, talking excitedly to his sergeant.

They watched in slow motion as the coroner cut open Hayes' shirt and exposed a pattern of small, ugly upper body puncture wounds on his chest, each surrounded by congealed black blood.

"Look at that shit.", Mike commented excitedly. "What did he get shot with? A staple gun?"

"Christ, what did they do to Carson's foot Mike? Look how swollen it is.", Dolan added.

When the film ended, they re-ran it. They didn't see anything else worth noting so Johnny called it a day and thanked Mike Denton for his help.

"Any time Johnny. See you later buddy."

Mike grabbed the coffee pot, filled his thermos and lifted a donut "for the road" and headed out to his night shift.

Johnny then asked one of the MBC News editors to make him a blow up of the spectators and the young cop and sergeant from Denton's film. He'd carry the photos with him and who knows, maybe somebody he interviewed would be able to ID them. The young cop would be easy to locate.

He was completely convinced that Carson and Hayes were naked when murdered. Sex probably had something to do with the crime and he'd use this angle during his investigation. "You had to start somewhere.", he thought and this was as good an approach as any at this point.

It was almost 6 PM when he called Guardian Medical Center and asked to speak with the Director of Computer Center. He left his name and number when informed that Mr. Barnes had already left.

"Figures. This is not my day.", Johnny thought. He was getting a headache.

He got lucky on the next call. The archivist at the Daily News told him that he had located a morgue copy of the 1963 Douglas Hayes and Mayor of Nyack scandal story. He was sending a copy over to MBC by courier. Johnny thanked him and told him that he owed him one.

Dolan finished some paperwork and left the Newsroom for his eight o'clock with Brian Toth. He was seated in the Club's Reading Room sipping a coke at 7:45 PM.

The Club was a professional gay men's club. You only became a member by invitation and with acceptance from the entire membership. Dolan had been a member for nine years and had successfully networked himself within the top echelon of the gay community. The Club was always discreet, had an unlisted telephone and used a post office box. It occupied a handsome three-story brownstone on West 77th Street. was tastefully decorated and would probably pass muster as a business man's club to any straight who happened to stop in. But of course, no "straight or non-member" ever got pass the muscled secretary stationed at the front door reception area. Johnny had only casually known Brian Toth, another Club member, some years before they became intimate. The Club was definitely not a "gay bathhouse pickup hangout". Its membership were top New York City professionals and they frowned on the stereotype image of gay meeting places. Instead, they strove to create a gay consciousness and provide de facto leadership for the gay community in a very straight world.

Brian Toth was a successful Wall Street lawyer and a gay rights legal activist. He moved within all community segments and had defended gays on housing and employment issues. Toth was 38 years old, kept in shape and had a wide variety of interests.

Johnny stood as Brian entered the Reading Room. They embraced and moved to a quiet corner, ordering drinks from the black suited waiter.

"I guess I have to admit that I am glad to see you again Brian.", Johnny began.

"Johnny, let me begin by saying I will … will always love you."

Dolan made a face and bent his head.

"I can tell you don't want me to say that and I know why, but I can't help myself. Johnny, I'm not trying to get us back together – I know that won't happen. I just want to be your friend and see you socially from time to time."

"Bri … I really want to be your friend too, if we can just be friends, you will have made me very happy.", Dolan responded softly.

Brian Toth smiled and continued:

"I guess we said all that needs to be said on that subject didn't we Johnny?"

The declaration of continued friendship pleased both men and they spent the next twenty minutes talking about future gay rights projects.

When they got around to discussing Johnny's current work assignment, Brian seemed concerned.

"John, you're taking a big chance on this one. Do you know what might happen if you should get too close to these bastards? You could get hurt or killed. Have you considered the possibility?"

"I can take care of myself, and I don't intend to get that close. If I should get lucky and uncover anything, I'll just pass it on to the cops."

"Is it because of what happened to Jerry?", Brian asked. "Is this really your reason for working this story?"

Jerry Coyne had been Johnny Dolan's lover for many years. He was a bright, articulate TV script writer who had been on the brink of major recognition. He and another of Dolan's friends had been brutally beaten to death the year before by a gang of youths out gay bashing. Johnny was still suffering Jerrys loss.

"That probably has something to do with this thing Brian."

Brian placed his hand over Johnny's.

"Promise me that you'll be careful. Listen, I have some mean mother biker friends who would be more than happy to run interference if you should need them."

"Brian, I'll be careful and if I need any muscle, I'll be sure to call you first for the "leather boy" brigade if I find myself over my head."

They finished their drinks and promised to get together with friends the following weekend. Dolan left for work. He had genuinely appreciated Brian's concern but thought. "Maybe he's on to something? Maybe I'm going overboard on this? Am I in any danger?" What had happened to Jerry the year before had almost destroyed him. He knew if he lost objectivity as a reporter, he was next to useless. But he also knew that he had to follow the story where ever it took him. He had been deeply depressed for a long time and somehow following this story was helping him return to his former self ... end his depression.

NINE

11:15 AM MONDAY, OCTOBER 24, 1966

From the floor of the United States House of Representatives:

"The poor people of America deserve better."' The speaker paused for effect as said this as if he was personally offended for the condition of America's poor people.

"It has been their unselfish toil that shaped these United States into the great Country it is and we, the Congress of the United States, have a sacred duty to ensure that their sacrifices are not forgotten. Therefore, I ask each of you, my fellow Congressmen, to consider carefully this debt to the poor of our Nation as you decide your vote for HR 4800 which will be made later this week."

He closed his leather-bound notebook, paused for effect then nodded toward the gallery, loaded with his supporters who broke into loud applause.

"Thank you and I relinquish my remaining time to the gentleman from Georgia."

Congressman Fredrick Douglass Summerfield, representing the eighth congressional district of New York, essentially Harlem, was justly pleased with himself. He had just given one of the best speeches of his congressional career which was sure to be noticed by the leadership of his Democratic Party, his constituents and most importantly, the National Press. He graciously accepted the congratulations of his colleagues and their staff members as he left the House floor for his office in the Rayburn Building.

Summerfield was a vigorous fifty-five years old, six foot two, with sharp, striking facial features surrounded by perfectly coifed white, lionized hair. His good looks, intelligence and oratory skills assured him continued support from his Party and constituents. If he had been born white, he might have been considered as a possible running mate for JFK. As it was, he continued to be a leading national spokesman for middle ground blacks and was consulted and sought after by every politician who coveted the "negro vote".

"Great speech Mr. Congressman.", one of his colleagues said patting his shoulder.

"Thank you, Thomas. Now don't forget I need your support for the vote on Friday."

"And you'll have it Sum."

"Good man! I'll count on it."

Summerfield continued making his way toward the exit and noticed Congressman Charles Sadler approaching. He was obviously agitated and wanted to talk. Sadler followed him into the corridor.

"Sum … I need to see you later today. It's important."

Sadler was sweating and had a haunted look. Although both Summerfield and Sadler were Democrats, they were most always at opposite ends of any issues. Summerfield had a good idea why Sadler needed to see him and sensed an opportunity for an advantage.

"Certainly. Please come by at four Charles; we can talk then. Mrs. Hayes, please make a note that Congressman Sadler will be stopping by at four for a conference.", Summerfield instructed his aide, Lydia Hayes, who had just joined them in the corridor.

"Congressman Summerfield is available from 4 until 4:15 this afternoon Congressman Sadler. Will that be adequate?", Lydia inquired in her educated, well-modulated voice.

"Yes – that will be fine Lydia. Thank you. I'll see you later Sum."

She noted the appointment and briefed Summerfield as they continued toward his Ways and Means Committee meeting already in progress. They made a stunning couple and drew stares from even the most cosmopolitan bureaucrats they passed along the way.

Lydia, at five eleven, moved with a confident, athletic grace that almost seemed regal. Her perfect brown body was dressed in elegant business attire and she made a fitting consort to Congressman Summerfield.

Fredrick Douglass Summerfield was genuinely proud of his aide and relished the reaction they received when they were together. She was as intelligent as beautiful and thrived like a predatory animal within the Washington jungle of political intrigues surrounding Summerfield.

"Do you have any idea what Congressman Sadler might want of us Mrs. Hayes?"

"Yes sir – I think we both do.", she answered, smiling at this question.

"Then HR 4800's passage on Friday is a certainty, isn't it?"

"Like fucking on a wedding night Congressman Summerfield.", she responded.

4:00 PM MONDAY, OCTOBER 24, 1966

At four that afternoon Congressman Charles Sadler visited his colleague, Congressman Frederick Douglass Summerfield at the latter's office in the Rayburn Building.

"Can I offer you something Charles?"

"No ... nothing thanks.", he paused. "Sum – I need your help."

Congressman Summerfield fixed Congressman Sadler with his most kindly expression and folded his hands so that his index fingers formed a steeple before his now pursed lips.

"If I can ... I'd be pleased to help ... what's your problem?"

Sadler continued. "I'm in deep shit so I'll get right to the point. Doug Hayes is dead."

"Yes. Very unfortunate, very unfortunate.", Summerfield interrupted, his comment ignored by an agitated Sadler.

"Sum, I've been indiscreet with Hayes and I believe that there may be certain material among his personal papers that would compromise me."

"I see Charles, but can you tell me how I might be able to help. Could you tell me what papers could compromise you?", Summerfield voice and demeanor remained calm.

" Photos ... I don't know ... for god's sake Sum, the man's wife works for you! Couldn't you ask her to help? Go through his apartment collect all references, photos, whatever he may have on me."

"Lydia is Doug Hayes ex-wife Charles. He's dead. I'm not certain whether she has any access to his personal effects. On the other hand, I am sure she would not want to put herself in any legal jeopardy on this. Remember, her former husband was murdered. Removing these items would be considered an obstruction of justice."

"Yes, and if they find those photos, I'll be their number one suspect Summerfield! Could you ask her to help? Please. Ask her to look. Think of the effect on the Party.", he paused. "Forgive my outburst Sum, I'm at wits end on this thing."

"No apology necessary.", Summerfield responded – his hand held before him, palm facing Sadler. "What exactly would you like Lydia to try to secure?"

"Get all the letters, photos, anything that has my name on it.", he paused a second. "Sum please help me with this and I'll throw my complete support behind your HR 4800."

"Charles, now I am surprised. I already believed that I had your complete support on the Bill. You know what its passage will mean to the poor of this Nation."

"Yes, yes. Of course, I do – certainly you'll have my full support in any case Sum."

"Thank you Charles. By the way, I'm holding a press conference on the Bill tomorrow morning at ten. Can I count on you being there with me?"

Sadler hesitated before answering; it was well known that he didn't want any part of HR 4800.

"Perhaps I'll be able to give you a preliminary report on this other matter afterward Charles.", Summerfield said breaking the silence.

Congressman Sadler smirked and replied. "Have your people contact my aide with the particulars for your press conference.

I'll see you then Sum, and thanks for your help with this other thing."

Sadler rose, glanced at his watch and shook hands with Summerfield.

"That's not a problem Charles.", Summerfield assured, taking his colleagues arm as they walked to his office door. "I only hope that we can be of help during this difficult time."

After Sadler left, Summerfield opened his safe and removed a large manila envelope. Spilling its contents over the desk he said aloud: "Tsk, tsk – disgraceful. Oh my, look at that will you." He scowled while slowly viewing each of the photos laid on the desk top.

After studying them for a while, he picked up his telephone and asked Lydia Hayes to come into his office.

"Close the door Mrs. Hayes and would you lock it please."

Lydia did as she was asked and when she sat noticed the envelopes contents and his stern "you've been a bad child" scowl she timidly asked: "Congressman Summerfield, is there some problem?"

"Yes, there is Mrs. Hayes. I've just reviewed these disgusting photos of Congressman Sadler and your late husband in very disgusting sexual activity."

"Yes sir? But I thought you'd be pleased in having them.", she seemed hurt by his comment. "I thought that they would strengthen our position on HR 4800."

"Most certainly Mrs. Hayes and I am pleased that you brought them to me but it seems after careful review, something has developed that I need to bring to your attention."

"Yes sir, and what might that be?"

Summerfield smiled and pointed to his noticeable erection.

4:30 PM MONDAY, OCTOBER 24, 1966

Dolan decided he needed glasses because he couldn't believe what he was reading. He re-read for the fifth time the copy of the Daily News press clippings he'd received from the newspaper's morgue archivist.

It was a 1963 story concerning Douglas Hayes and Wilson Arno, the former Mayor of Nyack, New York. It described how they'd been arrested after being observed performing an un-natural act in the men's room at Grand Central Station. Johnny knew if a political figure hadn't been involved this story wouldn't have made the papers.

What surprised him were the two Daily News photos that accompanied the initial story and its brief follow-up article. Both showed the participants to the "crime". The Mayor was grim faced and obviously humiliated and he was accompanied by a young black man identified in 1963 as Douglas Hayes who didn't look one bit like the 1966 corpse of Douglas Hayes.

At first Dolan assumed that a few years and twelve hours of rigor mortise accounted for the physical differences but after comparing the images for over an hour he was certain that these were two different men.

Since the second Daily News article noted that Hayes was accompanied in Court during his arraignment by his wife "Lydia", it seemed likely that this was his "Douglas Hayes".

"Who was the guy who was murdered – the real Douglas Hayes or an impostor?" he thought.

Picking up his telephone he dialed Lydia Hayes home number and reached her answering service. He was informed that Mrs. Hayes was in Washington and would be out of town until the following Monday.

"It's important that I speak with her. Could you give me a number in Washington where she could be reached?

"Excuse me?", the operator answered.

"I need to speak with Mrs. Hayes immediately.", Dolan used his military command voice and as usual, it worked; he was given her Washington telephone number.

He then placed a call to Washington.

"Good afternoon. This is Congressman Summerfield's office. How may I help you please?", came the crisp answer after only one ring.

"Congressman Summerfield's office?"

"Yes, it is, how may I help you please?"

"Yes, sorry – may I speak with Lydia Hayes please."

"May I ask who's calling please?"

"This is John Dolan from MBC TV News in New York."

"I'm very sorry Mr. Dolan but Mrs. Hayes is not available at this time. May I take a message? Perhaps you would like to speak with the Congressman's "Press Secretary.""

"No thank you. When will Mrs. Hayes be available?"

"She's in conference and out of the office. She probably won't be returning today."

"Will she be calling in for her messages?"

"Yes, she will. May I take your message sir."

"Would you please tell her I'd like to discuss the Mayor of Nyack with her."

"Excuse me? Did you say the "Mayor of Nyack?""

"Yes, that's correct. I'm sure she'll understand."

Dolan left his number and thought as he hung up. "Well, that should give Mrs. Hayes something to think about." He then considered calling Al Miller with his discovery but since Miller hadn't returned his telephone call from the previous week, he decided to "sit on this" for a while … "screw him.". he thought.

Johnny put the 1963 Daily News photos and the picture his editors made of the crime scene spectators from Mike Denton's video in an envelope, stuck it in his pocket and left for his appointment made earlier with Mr. Barnes, the Data Processing Director at Guardian Medical Center.

He grabbed a cab and headed uptown to the East Side. The brisk October weather gave the City a healthy autumn glow. People were wearing light coats and sweaters and there was an extra quickness as they moved through the crowded New York City streets. It would be Halloween in a few days and Johnny was eagerly looking forward to the annual major gay event held in Greenwich Village. Here would be an outlandish costume parade and many parties held all over the City.

Guardian Medical Center was an imposing and renowned research complex in the middle of "hospital row", a conflagration of specialty hospitals and medical centers on the East Side of the City. Thousands worked in these facilities and there was a special purposeful bustle all over York and First Avenues. White uniforms were de rigor and the from the faces of the ordinary man on the street, it appeared as if a United Nations General Assembly meeting was being held nearby since so many different nationalities populated this area.

The neighborhood was also the home of many bars, clubs and Up-scale restaurants serving a variety of ethnic cuisine. The "Swinging 60's" had many new high-rise apartments and was a Mecca for airlines stewardess and nurses which in turn brought an army of horny guys to the local bars.

Dolan's cab left him in front of the building that housed the Computer Center. He entered, identified himself to the receptionist and was escorted into a small, tastefully furnished conference room. There were framed photos of Computer Center staff and service awards hanging on the walls. The receptionist returned with his tea and told him that Mr. Barnes and Miss Gibbons would be in momentarily. He thanked her and wondered who Miss Gibbons might be.

A few minutes later a couple entered. Mr. Barnes was fiftyish, overweight with large circles under his eyes. He had a furtive look about him and spoke with a speech impediment; he pronounced his "s's" with the "th" sound.

Miss Gibbons on the other hand, was as pert and bright as Barnes was dull and reserved. She was introduced as a senior assistant in the Center's Public Relations Department and had been asked by Mr. Barnes to sit in on his meeting with the "media".

Dolan got right to business. He started off by thanking them for their time and described his assignment. He asked about Carson and Hayes' work, avoiding any references to homosexuality. Barnes didn't offer any real information until Johnny asked him if he had any theory as to why they had been murdered.

Barnes dull face lit up and his gestures became animated.

"Of courth – ith thimple; they were killed because of their knowledge of the Center's computer programths. Their murderer even had the gall to come to the Center and theal program code uthed for a number of our moth thecret cancer rethearch projechs. Our Thecurity Department and – ah – thince we receive funding from the National Inthitute of Health, reprethentatives from the Federal Government are coordinating programths, I am certain they would be better able to give MBC Newths all the detailths of their invethigation."

It took a few seconds for Barnes' "Elmer Fudd" analysis to sink in and since it added a new twist, Johnny couldn't immediately recognize the implications. Miss Gibbons picked up on Dolan's confusion and took charge of the interview.

"Mr. Barnes believes that the international drug manufacturing industry would pay handsomely for our research findings."

"Oh. I see; very interesting. Thank you.", Dolan responded.

"Well Mr. Dolan if you have no further questions Mr. Barnes and I have another appointment.", she concluded.

"Yes, I do have one more. Do you know where Carson and Hayes usually went for a beer after work?"

"I am thure I wouldn't know.", Barnes quickly answered. He rose and shook Johnny's hand with his limp, clammy hand.

"Nice meeting you Dolan. Are you coming along Janet?"

"Yes, but why don't you go ahead. There are a few public relations technicalities I need to discuss with Mr. Dolan.", she answered. After Barnes left, she closed the door and sat back down.

"Why do you think they were killed Mr. Dolan?"

"Call me Johnny. Frankly, this research business is an angle I hadn't considered. My theory was a good deal more pedestrian I'm afraid. I was working on the premises that Carson and Hayes were the victims of a gay bashing attack Miss Gibbons."

She considered his answer a few seconds, smiled and looking him in the eyes said: "And please call me Janet. You know – your theory might be closer to the truth. May I speak off the record Johnny?"

"Sure. What have you got?", Dolan flashed one of his winning smiles.

"There's a lot of talk around here that Barnes is the computer industry's leading ass-hole and the research projects he's responsible for supporting are so far behind schedule that he grabbed a brass ring when a black guy came in here the night Carson and Hayes were murdered and walked off with some program code. Barnes' is covering his ass with "missing research project code" that nobody seems to know anything about. We're going along with his story until we can get the IBM experts in here to check it out."

"Will you keep me posted?", Dolan asked.

"As long as it's all background – off the record, no problem. The Center may need a favor from MBC News someday and I want you on the hook."

Dolan liked Janet Gibbons.

"You make sure that you call me or my boss Gil Peterson anytime you need a favor Janet."

"Thanks. Oh and by the way – check out a bar on First and 62nd street, it's called the Keg. That's where the guys hung out. You play darts?"

"No, but I can learn. Why?"

"The Keg is known for its cold beer and hot darts. Are you going up there now?"

Dolan checked his watch.

"Yes, I think I have time."

"Good. Well maybe I'll see you there later. You can buy me a beer Johnny."

"I look forward to it Janet."

Dolan had no problem finding the Keg. It was a short walk from the Computer Center and he enjoyed the crisp invigorating autumn air. He could smell chestnuts roasting. Johnny didn't particularly care for the taste of roasted chestnuts but he relished their aroma.

The Keg on the other hand, did not smell like roasted chestnuts. It smelled like a saloon – beer and popcorn – which Johnny also enjoyed. He telephoned the office for messages and learned that Al

Miller had finally gotten around to returning his call. There was a message from Gil Peterson reminding him that they had a meeting later and a call from Pauline Carson. Things were picking up.

The Keg wasn't all that crowded and there was plenty of room at the bar. He was greeted pleasantly by an attractive bar maid.

"What can I get you?", She had a "don't I know you " look all over her pretty Irish face.

"Well among other things – let's start with a Jack Daniels on the rocks."

She fixed his drink and placed it before him ignoring the ten dollars he placed on the bar.

"My name is John Dolan and I'm a reporter with the MBC TV News."

"I knew it. I knew it the minute I saw you. I really did. You're on the FIRST LIGHT show, I see you every morning.", she answered excitedly, "Hi John, I mean Mr. Dolan. My name is Rosemary Cusick. I'm a communications major at NYU."

"God bless NYU.", he said, raising his glass.

He took a lip wetting sip and placed his glass on the bar.

She looked at him as if he were a rock star. "Is Chuck Dawson really as nice in person as he is on the FIRST LIGHT show and how about Betty Waters; Is she a bitch?", she asked.

"Well, to tell the truth, one of them is wonderful, salt of the earth, but the other one stinks!", Dolan said solemnly and then began to laugh. Rosemary giggled along with his "inside joke". "Just kidding Rosemary ... you'd love them both ... salt of the earth.", he repeated.

"Now I have a question for you Rosemary, did you happen to know Larry Carson or Doug Hayes?"

"Yes, I did Mr. Dolan, both of them use to come in here all the time.", her tone becoming somewhat apprehensive. "I already gave a statement to the police and description of the man they left with the night they were killed. But you probably already knew that."

"No, I didn't Rosemary. The police are very careful not to release information about their witnesses until they bring in a suspect."

Now she really seemed nervous.

"Don't worry I'm like a priest. Seal of confession – never reveal a source. Didn't they teach you that at NYU yet?"

Rosemary smiled, "I guess I was out sick that day Mr. Dolan."

"Mr. Dolan is my father's name, please call me Johnny, and don't worry, anything you tell me is off the record. I'm doing background on a series. Could you tell me about that last Friday night they were here and maybe describe the man they left with?"

She told him everything she told the police which wasn't all that much.

"Is there anything else beside the $20 tip that stood out about him?", he asked.

"Well, I didn't tell the cops but you reminded me with your drink. He drinks your brand – Jack Daniels, but he screws it up with Pepsi."

"Pepsi?"

"Yeah – Pepsi.", she nodded.

"Put a little Pepsi in mine.", Johnny said pointing to his drink. She made a sour face and poured some into his drink.

He tasted it and found it was OK – but not exactly to his liking.

"Dump it Rosemary, I'll stick to my regular concoction."

When she returned with a fresh drink he went for broke and asked:

"Would you say this guy they left with was effeminate?"

"Effeminate?", she parroted, making a face.

"Oh no. No John, not at all. He acted like a jock: baseball player – fighter maybe.", she said emphatically.

"Could you hear anything he said to Carson or Hayes?"

"John at that time of night on a Friday the only thing I hear is a bunch of drunks yelling for refills. This place is a nut house."

"How are the tips?", he asked, noticing her blouse button which read

"TIP ME OR GO THIRSTY"

"Tips from this crowd? Not counting occasional killers that stop by, I did better working in the redneck joint over in North Brunswick, New Jersey. Cause I'd get punched out every once in a while."

Johnny laughed and then shifted gears.

"Rosemary could you take a look at this picture and see if you recognize anyone?"

He handed her the colored blow-up of the murder scene spectators and watched her face while she studied it.

"No.", she finally said. "I don't see anyone I recognize."

Dolan was disappointed – he had an unreasonable hope that the one of the black man shown in the small crowd had been the guy who had taken Carson and Hayes out of the Keg. Rosemary returned his photo.

"Here Rosemary, take a quick peek at these two, do you recognize either of the guys in them?", he asked, now handing her the 1963 Daily News black and white photos of the Mayor of Nyack trial.

She smiled. "Yeah, this is more like it. But I only know one – the black guy. He's or rather was, Allie Summerfield. He used to come in all the time before he died."

Dolan's stomach did a flip when she mentioned the name Summerfield.

"What did he die from?"

"A bullet in the mouth, self-induced. Allie was a sad case. Had a drinking problem, used LSD and other drugs – a half-assed hippie doper. But a nice guy."

"Did he know Carson and Hayes?"

"Allie and Doug Hayes were good friends; dart partners too for a while. I don't think he hung out with Larry. But he knows, eh, knew him though."

"When did Summerfield die?"

"Over a year ago. He was in a re-hab, upstate somewhere I think."

"Where did he work?"

"I don't know. I'm not sure he had a job; he was always in here. Allie had plenty of money; maybe he had rich parents."

"How about a rich girlfriend?"

"I don't think I saw Allie even talk to a girl. He didn't have a girlfriend, John. You know, come to think of it – he was kinda effeminate."

"Did you ever hear anything said about Congressman Summerfield, Rosemary?"

"No – hey was Allie related to Congressman Summerfield?"

"Maybe. I don't really know."

They chatted a little longer but when business began to pick up Rosemary had to work. Dolan was just about ready to leave when Janet Gibbons entered the Keg.

"I'll have that drink you owe me Mr. Dolan.", she said squirming her way in next to him.

"Hey Janet, sure you will. Rosemary bring this thirsty Legionnaire a cold one!" Johnny said pointing to Janet Gibbons seated beside him.

"Make that cold one a Dewar's rocks Rosemary.", she corrected.

"I thought you were a beer drinker?"

"Not when someone else is buying.", she responded.

"Your Mom didn't raise any stupid children.", he said smiling at her quip.

"Yes, actually she did; my brother Billy. He would have taken the beer."

Rosemary brought Janet's scotch and a re-fill for Johnny.

"God Bless.", she toasted Dolan with a healthy swig.

"Tell me about the guy who grabbed the Center's programs."

"God damn! You're all business aren't you Mr. Dolan. OK, you brought the booze – I guess you're entitled to some more "off the record" information."

Dolan liked this lady, a lot.

"Two days after we found out our guys were killed, one of the night duty head nurses reported that she was in Data Processing picking up patient census reports about 4 AM Saturday when a guy came in and convinced the computer operator that he was sent by Carson and Hayes to pick up some programs. We talked to the operator and at first, he denies everything. He was scared shitless. We got the nurse and the operator together and she pressures him to tell what happened. He finally gives in and corroborates everything she reported. It seems that this black guy even called Larry Carson while he was in the Computer Center. Some nerve, right? Well, anyway, Nick the operator packs up a program Carson called "Single Action" and the black guy takes off with it. That's all I know. We told the cops. Was that worth the price of a scotch Johnny?"

"It was worth a quart of "Pinch" Janet."

She smiled, "Keep the scotch, I'd settle for dinner."

"Deal, but not tonight.", he finished his drink and stood.

"Got to go to work Janet. By the way, what does "Single Action" mean?"

"Huh?", she answered with a confused smile. "Damned if I know— maybe it has something to do with masturbation. I'll think about it for you. Here's my number for your "owe them a dinner" file.", Janet reached into her purse and then handed Dolan her business card with her home telephone number penciled in.

"Thanks.", he said, looking at her card before placing it in his wallet. "I'll call you soon, and really … thanks again for everything Janet. I really appreciate it. You've been a major help."

They shook hands and Dolan shouted good-bye and sent a wave toward Rosemary working the far end of the bar. He left her a $5 tip.

TEN

5:30 PM MONDAY, OCTOBER 24, 1966

Don Carmine San Fillipo sat across the table from Bunny Ennis in his quiet office at the Friends of Sicily Hunting and Social Club in "Little Italy". Carmine was fifty-two, solidly built but growing flabby, which bothered him since it made his eight-hundred-dollar suits too snug and causing him to worry about his "image". He was not in good humor in any case and his current preoccupation with his "weight thing" didn't help matters.

"Ennis You're a stupid fuckin' moulin who doesn't have the brains of the fuckin' rabbit you were named after! Why the hell you kill those guys anyway? The fuckin' computer bullshit thing you grabbed ain't no fuckin' good to us without them – and you got that other nigger, Preacher, ready to start a fuckin' war and your asshole gumba Sal Caputo, gets his fuckin' picture in the fuckin' TV News no less, gaping at the two fuckin' stiffs he dumps in front of the Preacher's Club! What the fuck am I going to do with you Ennis?"

"Carmine you can start by calming down.", Bunny answered.

"Calm down! Calm down! Fuck you calm down!", he shouted back.

Ennis was used to San Fillipo's temper and wasn't much bothered by it.

"You want something to eat Bunny?", not waiting for an answer, Carmine shouted to his nephew in the next room. "Gino. Gino!"

"Yeah Carmine?", a dark, good looking man about twenty stood in the doorway. He bore a strong resemblance to Carmine accentuated by the almost identical suit and tie combination he wore.

"Bring me and Bunny some of that ziti your mother made; oh, and a stick of that bread Fat Jimmy brought in – heat it up with the ziti."

"Don't bring me none Gino.", Ennis interjected.

The young man turned in confusion to his uncle. "Bring him some.", Carmine said with finality.

Gino left them staring into space with the sounds of a Puccini's "Si, mi chiamano Mimi" wrapping itself around their thoughts.

Bunny finally broke the silence.

"We have the computer program don't we Carmine? Just get someone with the brains to figure the fuckin' thing out. The asshole you told me to give it to said he had every fuckin' thing he needed"

"I'm workin' on it.", Carmine responded, pounding on the table to punctuate an end to this topic. Bunny ignored the warning and said just as loudly: "I busted my ass and risked my neck to get it for you, didn't I? It's not my problem that you can't find someone who can make it work."

"I told you – I'm fuckin' workin' on it!", Carmine shouted now holding up his hand for silence.

The aria soared and even Bunny was trapped by its simple beauty. When it ended Bunny turned to Carmine and said: "Sal's an asshole – I'll take care of that shit and don't worry about the Preacher, he's my problem."

"You better take care of it and quick. We don't want no fuckin' war with the niggers. You understand what I'm saying to you?"

Bunny nodded his agreement.

"Answer me Ennis – you understand what I'm fuckin' saying?"

"I know what the fuck you're saying.", he responded.

It was obvious to San Fillipo that Ennis didn't like to be prodded so he continued. "Then don't forget it. Get these problems fixed!"

Gino brought in the hot food and more wine and Carmine smiled and played the gracious host for the next hour.

Before Bunny left the Club, he telephoned Sal Caputo.

"Sal, I want you to close early tonight, I got a special party coming in. Make sure Monica, Carol and Jackie are working."

"You got it Bunnyman. Anything else?"
"That's it my man. Later."

5:50 PM MONDAY, OCTOBER 24, 1966

The first thing Dolan did after leaving the Keg was to locate a nice quiet place to return his telephone calls to Pauline Carson and Al Miller.

He called Miller first since it was almost 6 PM and didn't want to miss him again. But he needn't have worried, Detective Al Miller usually came to work early and generally stayed late.

"Detective Miller, how are you. Thanks for returning my call."

"I'm doing fine Dolan. What's on your mind?"

"I like that about you Detective Miller, always getting right to the point. Let me try to emulate you ... is there anything new in the Carson Hayes case?"

"The media has been advised that the Coroner's report is available. There's now a Police artist drawing of our number one suspect and the wallets of the two decedents were recovered.", he reported in a bored monotone.

"Where were the wallets recovered?"

"From the mailbox on the block where their corpses were found. We're running a check on the fingerprints we lifted."

"Was there any cash in them?"

"No cash, but their credit cards and other personal effects were still there."

"Sounds like some civilian lifted the wallets from the stiffs and ditched them after removing the cash. You may have a witness somewhere out there, Detective Miller."

"That's out theory. But thanks for your suggestion; we'd probably never thought of that."

There was a long pause before Dolan broke the silence. "Is there anything else you might be able to tell me?"

"Not at this time Dolan."

"OK then, thank you for the information Detective Miller."

"I'm just doing my job Dolan.", Miller answered and then immediately hung up.

"Well have a nice day to you too Detective Miller", Johnny spoke into the dead telephone receiver. He was glad he didn't share his discovery of the "1963 Summerfield Hayes switch".

Dolan called his office and asked to have Congressman Summerfield's bio pulled and copied. He also requested a pickup of the Coroner's report and the artist's sketch of the suspect. He knew they would be on his desk before midnight – one of the advantages of working for MBC TV News.

He then dialed Mrs. Pauline Carson. When she answered, Johnny identified himself and expressed his condolences.

"Thank you, Mr. Dolan. My sister mentioned that you telephoned. How can I help you?"

"I explained to your sister that my assignment was to investigate your husband and Doug Hayes murder and I'd appreciate an opportunity to visit for an hour or so if you feel up to it."

"I would be willing to speak with you Mr. Dolan but I'm taking my children back to Virginia on Wednesday and I'm sure that I'll be much too busy these next few days."

"I understand Mrs. Carson. I am available this evening if you could see me."

Pauline Carson considered his request. "That would be alright, but after 8:30 and only for an hour or so."

"That's no problem. Thank you. Now if you could tell me where you live …"

8:35 PM MONDAY, OCTOBER 24, 1966

The Carson's lived in Bay Ridge, a pleasant section of south Brooklyn that overlooks the entry to New York harbor called the Narrows. It was now spanned by the Verrazano Bridge which had opened two years before linking Brooklyn to Staten Island and creating a land rush to Staten Island, the least populated of New York City's five boroughs.

Dolan knew this area of the City well having grown up in the neighboring section of Gravesend. These were neighborhoods of rounded brick row houses which were the homes of New York's solid middle class – the people who made New York City work.

Driving through these Brooklyn streets brought memories of growing up in an Irish Catholic neighborhood populated by churches and saloons. Dolan was the son of a boiler-maker who drank hard and died young. His Father was proud of his son's accomplishments – graduating from West Point and serving as a combat officer in Korea. Dolan was glad that he never had to tell his father that he was homosexual; he would have never accepted it. Pop had died suddenly while Johnny was recovering from wounds received outside of Seoul.

Seeing this neighborhood, Dolan suddenly felt an overwhelming sense of grief. Everyone he loved had died suddenly and sometimes violently.

"What has my life meant to anyone?" he thought.

Dolan sensed that he had somehow lost purpose and he was just marking time to his own eventual end.

The October night matched his black mood. It had turned cold and rainy as Dolan's cab made his way to Carson's Brooklyn home. He hardly acknowledged the cabby's "what's wrong with New York" lecture and stared silently at the shiny wet Brooklyn streets and the lights from the countless apartments passed along the route. The little raindrop rivers raced down the window pane and at times glowed red or green from the passing traffic lights. Johnny's mind drifted to a scene it had played over and over again these last six months. He was sitting at a below ground bar that had a view of the inside of an immense swimming pool. He sat there for a while, sipping a Jack and watching the swimmers lazily pass by his window. Then as it always happened, the water violently parted and he could see himself sink below the pool's surface. He was dressed in a dark business suit and wore shiny black shoes. He watched as his body floated before the bar's glass window, seemingly at peace. As his body sunk lower into the pool, his hair billowed out from his head and eyes remained closed.

After a while the image faded and Dolan refocused on the wet Brooklyn streets that glistened past him in the dark.

"Here ya go pal – that'll be twelve dollars.", the cabby announced.

The Carson's lived in a "parlor floor and basement" brownstone apartment next door to a girl's high school. There were kid's bicycles and miscellaneous toys in the vestibule that Dolan needed to step over to reach the doorbell. He could smell meatloaf and the aroma of fresh baked bread which made him realize he was hungry.

He waited about twenty seconds for Pauline Carson to answer the door; standing there, he listened to the muffled sounds of children's voices at play mixed with the musical sound of their mother's voice. Suddenly the darkened vestibule exploded with light as she opened the door and greeted him.

"Oh Mr. Dolan, you're right on time. Please come in. Sorry about the clutter out here; watch your step. Is it raining?"

She had the same soft Virginian drawl as her sister, which Dolan found charming. Pauline Carson was about thirty, attractive with long blond hair and a sad look about her otherwise pretty face. She had reached that point in life where she was neither young nor old – somewhere on the brink of her future appearance but still retaining most of the glow of her recent youth.

"Please have a seat in the parlor Mr. Dolan, while I put my pesky children to bed."

Dolan caught sight of a little blond headed girl in Dr. Denton's giggling as she playfully ran from her mother.

He found a comfortable chair in the parlor and listened to the music of young children going to bed. "Larry Carson had to be a lucky man.", he thought and hoped that Carson had realized his good fortune.

It was fifteen minutes before Mrs. Carson returned. By then, Johnny had begun to shake his earlier depression surrounded by the warmth of Carson's parlor and the Carson Family. He had almost forgotten that this also was a place that tragedy recently visited.

"Can I fix you something Mr. Dolan? Have you eaten?", she asked.

"No, I haven't Mrs. Carson. But please – I wouldn't want you to go to any trouble, I can grab …"

"Mr. Dolan it's really no trouble at all. Come on out to the kitchen and I'll fix you a sandwich and some coffee while we talk."

The kitchen was oversized. These "railroad flats" were built in the early twenties when families were large and ate all their meals together in the kitchen. Dolan took a seat at the rock maple table and watched Pauline Carson prepare his meal.

"This is very nice of you Mrs. Carson."

"It's no bother at all. I have meatloaf. Is that alright?"

"That's great.", he answered.

"There's plenty leftover; I guess I keep forgetting that Larry's not coming home.", she paused. "I'm sorry Mr. Dolan. Would you like coffee or hot tea?"

"Tea would be fine, thanks."

"Well, I finally met the only other person in New York who drinks tea."

"Oh, there are lots of us tea people in New York."

Smiling, she placed an oversized meatloaf sandwich before him. She filled the kettle and organized two cups and saucers on the drainboard and then spooned two measures of loose tea into a steel "tea ball" hanging it from its chain in a pretty white ceramic tea pot.

She sat across from him, "It will be ready in a bit.", she said causing Dolan to look toward the kettle.

"Now please don't watch that pot or it'll never boil. How's your sandwich? Oh, I'll get the salt and pepper for you.", she said, standing.

He motioned for her to sit. "It's fine. Great meatloaf and is this homemade bread?"

"Yes."

"It's delicious Mrs. Carson."

She beamed at his compliment. "Thank you. I'm pleased you like it."

"Thanks again for seeing me on such short notice. Mrs. Carson – now, can you think why anyone would have wanted to hurt Larry?"

She shook her head and quietly answered with a sigh. "No and I've thought about that a lot. I still don't understand it. Larry didn't have many friends but I could never believe that anyone hated him or anything."

"How about Doug Hayes? Did he have any enemies?"

"I really don't know – I don't think so; Larry would have said something to me."

"Was everything going alright for him at Guardian Medical Center?"

"Yes, very well. He had been promoted last year and he enjoyed programming."

"Did you know Doug Hayes well?"

"No … not really. He was one of Larry's work friends. Larry got him his job at Guardian."

"When was that?"

"Two or three years ago I think."

"What did you think of Doug Hayes?"

"Oh, he was alright. I didn't see him that often.", she added.

Dolan detected some slight uneasiness in Pauline Carson's Doug Hayes response.

The Kettle began a soft whistle and she poured the boiling water into the tea pot.

"We'll just let that steep for a bit.", she said sitting back down.

"Did you feel that Doug may have been a bad influence on Larry?"

She smiled. "You must have antenna coming out of your head Mr. Dolan. Yes, there were times I felt that Larry was being manipulated by Doug. This business thing they were into didn't sit too well with me. I think Larry did all the work and Doug just wanted to get rich from it."

"What kind of business were they in?"

"You might say it was a peculiar one Mr. Dolan, it had something to do with picking numbers with the computer."

"Picking numbers? You mean like gambling, ah – the number's racket – policy?"

"Well, I don't know what you'd call it but Larry wrote a computer program that picked numbers for the people who bet on them. They sold lists for five dollars a copy.", she smiled at the memory. "I helped open the envelopes and mail the lists. The guys made almost $3,000."

She poured them each a cup of tea. "Like a cookie? Chocolate chip, homemade."

"Ah, I'm tempted but no thanks. This business sounds intriguing. How did they get into it?"

Pauline sat back down after placing a steaming tea cup before each of them. She stirred in two spoons of sugar and added some milk to her tea. Johnny followed suit.

She answered his questions. "The business was Doug's idea. He told Larry that people would pay money for suggestions on what numbers to play. I guess I learned something about the business too. Well anyway, Lydia, that's Doug's ex-wife and Doug were over one night a few months ago and somehow, we got talking about it. I didn't think anything more until Larry announced that he was writing a program to select the best numbers to play."

She jumped to her feet. "Wait a second, I want to show you something Doug did."

She left the kitchen and returned a minute later with a copy of the Amsterdam News, a Harlem based newspaper published for the Black community. She opened to the classified section and pointed out a crude sketch of a computer character with a caption that read:

PUT THE COMPUTER TO THE TEST,
AT PICKING NUMBERS IT'S THE BEST!

It then listed a company name, post office box number and requested five dollars for a list of ten numbers that were most likely to win over the next thirty days.

"Doug drew the little computer figure and thought up the ad. He brought it to the newspaper and set up the box number too. I was really surprised when we started getting mail. People would send letters with their five dollars telling what they were going to do with all the money they were going to win. Computers are still a curiosity and the people that sent money believed that a computer could really pick a winning number for them."

"Did Larry's program work?"

She smiled and explained. "Larry didn't believe his program was all that good. He knew that any number could win on any day, but the program calculated probabilities based on the previous playing history of the number, you know – over a period of time all numbers should win the same number of times. I was a math major and got a kick out of his "Mickey Mouse" algorithm.

It may have been a coincidence, but five of the numbers on the first month's list actually won. You should have seen the letters with the $5 bills come pouring in after that!"

She smiled at the memory of their success.

"Larry and I went out with Doug and Lydia for a night on the town to celebrate. It cost a fortune. We went to a real night club in the City."

"It must have been fun for you. Did Larry call his computer program Single Action?"

"Not that I remember. We always called it the "Numbers" program."

"Alright, that makes sense. Ah, from what you've said, it sounds like Doug saw his ex-wife quite a bit."

"He did, at least the last few months. I liked Lydia, but she and I were in different leagues. You might already know she has a good job with the Government. She's in Washington most of the time."

"Yes, I know; I tried to reach her earlier today. She works for Congressman Summerfield, right?"

Pauline nodded yes to Johnny's questions.

"What happened to the guy's business; did they keep it going?"

"They did, but it changed. They dropped the newspaper ad and started doing some kind of consulting work with the numbers program.

Larry came in one night a few weeks ago and had almost five thousand dollars in cash he had received from the company he and Doug were helping. We put it in the bank; you see we had planned to buy a house over on Staten Island next year."

She slowly sipped her tea, her eyes filling with tears.

Dolan was beginning to feel like an intruder. "I know this is hard for you Mrs. Carson, I don't have too many more questions.", he said softly.

"That's alright Mr. Dolan, it helps to talk.", she answered, dabbing her eyes with a paper napkin.

"Did you tell the police about Larry's consulting business?"

"No, I didn't think it was important. Do you?"

"It might be. I suggest that you mention it to them. Did you ever meet or hear of a man named Allie Summerfield?"

"I don't recall. Is he any relation to the Congressman?"

"Well, he might be but I don't know yet. I do know that he was a good friend of Doug's. Had you noticed any change in Larry recently?"

"How do you mean?" She answered, her tone becoming defensive.

"Well, I mean was he different to you and the children – you know, moody, nervous, unhappy?"

"We all change over time Mr. Dolan. I believe Larry was happy but I felt he was disappointed that he wasn't doing better financially. He was an intelligent man in a very new field. He believed he was underpaid as a programmer at the Guardian Center. Larry loved his family, but sometimes I felt that he would like to be free."

"Please don't think I'm trying to get out of line, but do you suspect he might have been seeing other women? Did he gamble or did he have a drinking problem?"

"No, none of those.", she answered emphatically.

"I'm sorry, I didn't mean to offend you with that question."

Dolan then removed the two Daily News photos from their envelope and handed them to her together with the murder crowd picture.

"Do you recognize anyone in these?", he asked.

She studied them and shook her head and handed them back.

"Nope – would you like another sandwich, some more tea?"

"No thanks. I do have one last question – I understand you received a telephone call from Larry early on the morning he was killed."

She nodded and pursed her lips.

"Could you tell me what he said Mrs. Carson?"

There were tears in Pauline Carson's eyes as she answered his final question. "My husband told me he loved me Mr. Dolan."

11:30 PM MONDAY, OCTOBER 24, 1966

Dolan returned directly to the MBC Newsroom from the Carson's home. He was moved by Pauline Carson's courage and had promised to keep her posted on the status of his investigation. She gave him her family's address in Amherst, Virginia and said she would call if she thought of anything else that might be important for him to know.

Johnny now knew that Lydia Hayes lied when she told him that she hadn't seen Doug for over a year. He also uncovered another motive for the murders. Carson and Hayes may have been involved with organized crime through their computer program. They could have been working for a gambling interest and the competition felt using a computer to pick winning numbers gave them an advantage or perhaps they were marked because of the success of the computer pick list they sold through the mail.

Larry Carson was also emerging as a straight shooter and might just have been the innocent bystander in this puzzle. Doug Hayes on the other hand, remained a mystery. Broken marriage, best friend commits suicide, his get rich quick schemes, all added up to a guy who was out of focus with life.

After settling in at his desk, Dolan opened the thick file left for him and started reviewing Congressman Fredrick Douglass Summerfield's bio. It was a good one; very detailed. Summerfield's life hadn't been a "rags to riches" story. He came from money, went to the best schools, and married well. He had a son and although the bio didn't include the boy's name, he would have been about the same age as Allie Summerfield.

Dolan had heard him speak and knew he was effective in a preachy sought of a way. Summerfield was ambitious and definitely on the Washington fast track.

He made some notes and then began reading the Coroner's report. It satisfied his morbid curiosity and at the same time, revulsed him. During his time in Korea, Dolan had seen violent death first hand and had learned to view the blood and guts horror without impassion. But there was something creepy about reading a scientific report describing the results of physical torture. Dolan had begun to feel a kinship with Carson and Hayes and somewhere in his mind's dark recesses he could hear their screams and feel their pain at the ordeal to which they had been subjected before being viciously killed.

There was no indication that they had been sexually abused before death, notwithstanding the amputation of Hayes' penis. There had been no anal penetration or the presence of semen found anywhere on skin surface or their clothes.

They were each shot with the same .22 caliber weapon, probably a pistol, at very close range. Since this was the favorite weapon of professional hit men, it gave credence to the organized crime hit theory.

He remembered Janet Gibbon's description of the night visitor to the Computer Center. He walked off with a program called "Single Action" – maybe that was the computer program that picked the winning numbers. If it was, Dolan would have uncovered a genuine motive for the killings.

ELEVEN

Jackie Kaplan was a computer programmer and a horse player. He wasn't particularly successful in either endeavor but since most people had very little understanding of what computers were all about, many thought he was some kind of mad genius.

Kaplan was quick to brag about his computer programming skills and at this particular moment wished that he had been more judicious in who he had bragged to. The loan shark that he was in to for five "big" ones introduced him to some connected people who asked him to do them a favor. "Sure, sure, be glad to.", Kaplan told them. "They gave him documentation and a program called Single Action. Figure it out and you're off the hook.", they promised. That was over two weeks ago and he had been working on it ever since.

First, he ran an "80-80" list of Single Action and then did a pre-assembly of the program source code. Initially he thought that he was working with some pretty "bullshit" code but after a while discovered how elegantly programmed Single Action really was.

It was written in IBM Assembler code and every one of the two hundred mnemonics available to a programmer in this difficult computer language were used. At first, he thought it would never work but after studying the code for days, it became obvious to Jackie that the Single Action programmer knew his business.

He had set trap after trap within the program. Branching instructions were suddenly altered during program execution throwing off any "snoop" who might have put a trace in the object code to monitor what was taking place. There were all sorts of subroutines that used erratic combinations of the computer's sixteen machine registers so anyone trying to break the code could never be certain what was going on internally at any given microsecond.

In spite of all the technical tricks and hidden traps in-bedded in the code, given enough time, Jackie would have figured it out. But the son-of-a-bitch who wrote Single Action had pulled a trick that could never be mastered with just the available program source code. He had inserted three "CALL" sub-routines that "imported" code into the main computer memory from an external disk unit.

Jackie had no access to these sub-routines or the external disk they originated from, so he didn't have a clue as to what they did. It wasn't his fault, even the best programmer in New York City wouldn't be able to master Single Action.

But it was his problem none the less. Since he was the one who would have to tell the wise guys that Single Action could not be cracked, Jackie Kaplan knew he was in deep shit. Originally, he had told his "guy" that the program source code was good. Now he knew it wasn't, the important parts were missing and he would never be able to find or replicate them.

"It is what it is.", he thought as he made the telephone call.

TWELVE

4:00 AM TUESDAY, OCTOBER 25, 1966

Dolan began his progress report to Peterson promptly at 4 AM. At first, Gil only listened but began to ask questions when Johnny described the 1963 arrest of "Douglas Hayes" with the Mayor of Nyack. His interest peaked when he learned Hayes' ex-wife was an aide to Congressman Summerfield. Finally, after comparing Johnny's Douglas Hayes court photos, Gil agreed that these were pictures of two different men.

Peterson pushed his chair back to the wall and lifted his small feet to his desk top. "I don't know if you've been following what's hot in DC legislative circles right now Johnny, but Summerfield has been pushing hard to get passage of a civil rights bill, HR 4800 I think, that will open the national piggy bank to minority business. Background is that Summerfield has a personal interest in getting this Bill through – he's tight with a group known for their pushed in noses and it's likely they'll try to cut a nice big piece of the Federal money pie for themselves."

Dolan asked: "How the hell will they get away with it?"

"Easy, Lyndon Johnson has half a billion to spend on his Great Society legislation this fiscal year and you can be sure that nobody's watching too closely how it's spent. Besides, LBJ wants to go down in history as the "Civil Rights" President and HR 4800 will add another notch to his gun." Peterson finished his political analysis with a scowl which caused Dolan to smile and ask:

"Getting a little cynical in your old age aren't we Gil? Well get hold of your chair, here's the real bombshell. I have a preliminary ID on the "1963 Douglas Hayes", the one in the Daily News photo.", Dolan pointed to the photo on Gil's desk. "I think his real name is Allie Summerfield and he could have been Congressmen Summerfield son."

"Holy shit!", Gil exclaimed. "How good is your source on the kid's ID?" Peterson dropped his feet back on the floor and studied the photograph with renewed interest.

"Probably accurate. Summerfield's bio notes that he has a son the right age and I got a positive verification on the Daily News photo from a barmaid who knew him as Allie Summerfield. She saw him every day for a couple of years. Said the kid had money and was best friends with Doug Hayes. She also told him that the Summerfield kid blew his brains out last year at a "drunk farm" somewhere Upstate."

"So, we may have a congressman's kid who gets arrested and then uses the name of a guy who's married to his father's top assistant – probably to protect his old man. Who knows – maybe Congressman Summerfield was getting blackmailed by Mr. Doug Hayes and had him smacked by his Mob friends.", Gil surmised?

"Maybe Gil, but here's another angle for you." Dolan then told Peterson about the computer program Larry Carson had designed for picking numbers and the intruder who grabbed it from Guardian Center the same morning Carson was killed.

Johnny also reviewed the highlights of his interview with Pauline Carson, mentioning what she had told him concerning Lydia Hayes' participation in the development of the idea to create the numbers charting business using the computers, and the "consulting work" that brought in big cash for Carson and Hayes.

Gil listened attentively until Dolan finished. He then asked: "The numbers program angle gets us back to a mob related hit. What do the cops know about the numbers business Carson and Hayes were into?"

Dolan shrugged and sighed. "From what they've released so far Gil – I doubt that they even know about it. Oh, here, take a look at this. It's a police sketch of their primary suspect."

Dolan handed Peterson the composite sketch of the Carson Hayes murder suspect.

"Looks like something my kid drew.", Peterson commented, throwing the drawing of the non-descript black man on his desk.

Dolan laughed and asked: "Do you know anything about playing the numbers Gil?"

"Are you kidding? I play a dollar everyday with Sammy downstairs at the coffee shop."

"How does it work?"

"What? I thought you grew up in Brooklyn Dolan? You don't know how to play the numbers?", Peterson was shaking his head in disbelief. "You pick three numbers from triple zero to a nine hundred ninety-nine and bet on how they will play."

"What do you mean "play"?", Dolan then asked.

"Pay attention and you'll learn something. The last three numbers of the total gross dollars bet at Aqueduct Race Track each day are the winning numbers. They're published in the sports section of the paper. The numbers you bet have to either match them "straight", that's in the same sequence you played them, or you can "box" your bet, meaning you win if you have any combination of those numbers. Oh, and there's also a single action bet you can make on anyone of the three numbers. Pays nine to one if you win and you get 600 to one if all three come in straight."

Johnny jumped to his feet ran around the desk and smacked Gil on the arm. He was beaming from ear to ear.

"What did you say Gil? Did I hear you say you can bet "single action"? That's Carson's computer program – he called it "Single Action"! That's the program that was taken from Carson's office at the Hospital Computer Center. Gil these guys were killed because somebody wanted their numbers program!'

Gil became equally excited by Johnny's deduction.

"All right, all right, let's calm down.", he cautioned. "Did their program work? I know computers can do involved calculations but picking numbers?"

Dolan returned to his seat. "It worked well enough to pick five winners on the first list of ten that they sold. Carson's wife told me that she didn't have such faith in it but most people who bet numbers would probably be happy with five winners out of ten picks. What do you think?"

"I would have killed for a copy of that list.", Gil quickly answered.

"Somebody did Gil.", Dolan added.

Peterson abruptly stood and began to pace.

"Johnny, we have at least three angles on this story.", he concluded as he continued pacing. "They may have been killed by the Mob for the numbers program, or because Hayes had something on Summerfield or because they were gay – which was your original theory."

Johnny shrugged his shoulders. "Being gay is a possible reason why they were tortured. A lot of people don't like gays."

"Right.", Gill continued. "So that angle is still valid especially when you consider young Summerfield's problem with the Mayor of Nyack and his close relationship with Doug Hayes. But everything points to a Mob connected hit. The .22 used to smack them, the program taken from the hospital computer center, and you mentioned that Carson told his wife that he was doing some numbers consulting – and didn't you say he was paid in cash?"

"Yep – five thousand dollars' worth of consulting. The Mob doesn't have a checking account, does it?", Johnny confirmed.

Gil sat down and thought for a moment.

"OK. Here's what we're going to do. First, from now on this is your only assignment. Second, you're getting on the next plane to DC and visit with Mrs. Hayes and if possible, Congressman Summerfield. Third, you mentioned Hayes ran an ad in the Amsterdam News; I have a friend up there who may be able to give me some help on who would benefit from owning "Single Action".

"Can you think of anything else?", Gill looked at Johnny.

"Yeah, but what about the cops? Do you think we should bring them into this?", Johnny asked.

"Not yet. I'll handle it, but only when we have more to give them. Now get the hell out of here, you've got a lot of work to do to get ready for Mrs. Hayes and Congressman Summerfield. We'll talk tomorrow night."

Johnny packed up his notes and called Eastern to get the departure times for the morning DC shuttle. He would have time to go home, shower change and grab something to eat, but no time for bed. He would try to catch some sleep on the short flight.

Before he left the Newsroom, Gil called and asked if his Congressional Press Pass was current.

"Yup, it is.", Johnny answered after checking the expiration date on his card. "Why?"

"Because you are going to Congressman Summerfield's press conference at 10 this morning. I'll call our Washington Bureau and let them know you'll be joining them. You should be able to get to Lydia Hayes and her boss a lot easier after the conference. What do you think?"

"I think we may want to begin getting this story ready for air time depending on what I find out."

"OK Johnny. Let's see what you get."

THIRTEEN

1:15 AM, TUESDAY, OCTOBER 25, 1966

Sal Caputo was seated at his table in the little foyer outside the whorehouse entrance when Bunny arrived. He closed the book on astrology he had been reading and stood to greet his boss.

"Hey Bunnyman, what's shaking?", he said loudly.

"Sal my man! My Ladies here?" Bunny slapped Sal's outstretched hand in greeting.

"Yeah Bunny, but eh … Monica's on the rag. I … a … gave her the night off. But I got Tammy for your party instead. Hey where's the Johns?"

"They be here in a bit.", Bunny's voice began to rise. "Sal, I thought I told you I wanted Monica here."

"I know Bunny, but … ", Sal pleaded.

"I don't give a shit what that bitch's raggedy ass problem is. You get on the phone and tell her to get the fuck in here now. You capish me Sal?"

Sal knew Bunny would be pissed about Monica and also knew it wasn't a good idea to fuck with him at this particular moment.

"Sure Bunny.", he reassured, "I'll get the bitch here right away."

The two men then entered the dimly lit bar room. Sal locked the front door after them and then headed for the office to call Monica at home. The three-half naked "ladies" greeted Ennis warmly and Jackie, a buxom red head, fixed his Jack Daniels and Pepsi; after a minute or two, Sal returned.

"Monica will be here in a little while Bunny.", he announced sitting by his Boss at the little bar.

When Bunny scowled, Sal changed the subject.

"You remember Tammy don't you. She's Carmine's cousin's friend.", Sal said pointing to the shapely brunette.

"Yeah, I know Tammy. You lookin real good tonight mama. Fuck! Ain't she lookin' good ladies? All my ladies is prime."

The girls beamed at his compliment.

"When are your friends coming Bunny?", the new girl Tammy asked.

"They be here by and by. You anxious to go to work baby?"

"What kind of action tonight Bunny?", Carol asked.

"Ain't no secret what makes the Johns happy.", Bunny responded and then turned to Sal and announced:

"Sal, I got a little taste of nose candy that gonna make my ladies ready to party all night. Come on over here ladies for a snort."

Bunny removed a vial of white powder from his pocket and spread three fat lines of cocaine on the bar. The girls eagerly came to him to take a toot and Bunny then drew each a second line. He moved behind them as they stood, their faces close to the bar top, his hands sensuously roamed over their bodies – caressing and squeezing each in turn.

He finished behind Tammy, who responded by pressing her ample ass tightly into his groin as she bent to snort her hit from the bar's surface.

"You know, I got me an idea while we be waiting for the Johns. I think it be good if you two ladies got to know Tammy better – you know, let's loosen her up some.", Bunny continued stroking Tammy's breasts as he spoke to Carol and Jackie.

"Sal shut off that fucking Beetle's bullshit and put on that Sam Cooke album.", Bunny ordered.

A minute later Sam Cooke began to wail "Twistin' the Night Away."

Bunny and Sal clapped their hands in rhythm with the music.

Carol and Jackie needed no further encouragement and dancing over to the bar, took Tammy's hands and led her to one of the couches. They then removed her top and panties and began to kiss and caress her. Tammy welcomed the attention and before long, all three were naked and totally preoccupied with each other. Sal and Bunny remained at the bar, sipping their drinks and watching the passionate performance.

"You like watching that shit Sal?", Bunny softly asked.

"I love it. It's the greatest thing I ever seen."

"It really make you happy Sal?"

"Couldn't be happier." Sal half turned to face Bunny. "What's the matter Bunny – is something the matter?", Sal was suddenly anxious, he knew that Bunny Ennis never gave a fuck if anybody was happy.

"I saw Carmine today Sal.", he answered in the same soft sounding voice.

"What's that hard-ons problem?", Sal roughly answered. He hated Carmine San Fillipo.

"He didn't like your picture on the TV News show – you know, the one with you gappin' at the stiffs."

"Well fuck him!", Sal angerly responded.

"Sal why the fuck you hang around there and get your picture on the TV and why the fuck did you dump the stiffs in front of the Preacher's place. That ain't too swift my man. The Preacher is lookin' to start a war with the Family."

Sal was getting nervous. It wasn't very smart or safe to be the cause of a gang war.

"I ... eh ... was just havin' some fun. I figured eh ... since the stiffs thought we worked for the Preacher; it would be a blast to dump 'em in front of his place. And what's with this shit anyway Bunny? Didn't I already tell ya I was still lookin' for the bum that seen me dump the stiffs when the cops showed up. I didn't know that somebody would be taken pictures for the TV. But what the fuck, I was only on the TV news once and who the fuck is gonna recognize me?"

"Carmine did, and he thinks we fucked up bad Sal."

"Fuck him!", Sal paused. "What do you think Bunnyman?"

"I think Carmine be right. Good bye Sal."

Ennis had removed his pistol and had held it unseen behind his back during his brief exchange with Sal. At a distance of less than three feet it was impossible for Bunny to miss his target – the hair that grew thickly on the bridge of Sal's nose between his dark brown eyes. The single shot dropped Sal like a brick from his bar stool, and the shocked expression stayed frozen on his fat face. He was dead before he reached the floor.

The entangled girls were too preoccupied to re-act to the pistol's soft sound. Bunny now stood above them, quickly and efficiently emptying the remaining nine rounds into their naked, sweaty bodies, linked together forever in an erotic tableau.

They never really understood what was happening to them. There were no protests, no screams and very little sound except for the quick pop, pop, popping of his Colt "Ace" .22 and its blowback bolt action.

When it was over, the room stunk of cordite and was misted with a cloud of blue, hazy gun smoke. The mosaic tiled floor was covered with a running river of hot, sticky blood and Bunny had some splashed on his pants and shoes. "Shit!", he cursed, wiping his shoes clean on Sal's shirt. He returned to the bar where he dropped the empty clip and began reloading his piece. He would wait until Monica arrived. But he needn't have since Sal hadn't been able to reach her when he called. Sal had lied when he said Monica was coming to the "party".

Sam Cooke continued singing "Twisting the Night Away" until Bunny gave up on Monica and left the whorehouse massacre at five that morning. Before departing, he removed Sal's switch blade from the dead man's pants pocket.

"Fine cuttin' blade you got here Sal and you sure as hell don't need it anymore. You must have fucked with me about Monica coming.", he said looking into Sal's dead "fish" eyes.

He then kicked Sal viciously in the head causing the congealed blood to briefly flow once more.

"Later.", he said imparting to the four corpses already stiffening on the cold mosaic floor.

Bunny wiped his finger prints from anything he might have touched, locked the front door after himself, and headed out onto the still empty, early morning City streets. It was cold this October morning and Bunny enjoyed the crisp air as he jogged to his Cady parked four blocks away in a 24-hour lot.

He'd never be back here, so he wasn't concerned. There was nothing to connect him to the whorehouse. Everybody thought Sal was the "Man". Sal had made all the payoffs to the cops and he paid the girls and kept everything in line.

When the Preacher heard about these hits, he would be appeased at the Family's partial restitution for its take out of Carson and Hayes, his computer "consultants".

Carmine had the useless Single Action program for the Family and would be sending an apology to the Preacher for the action of the "renegades" in his organization. Since the Preacher hadn't been able to secure the original program from Hayes, he was no worse off and Carmine's organization now had a version that didn't work but they'd get someone to figure it out eventually. But the Preacher wasn't stupid; he would guess that Carmine probably had his copy and it was just a question of time before the Family mastered its uses.

Killing Sal temporarily restored the fragile balance that had existed for over twenty years; there would be no all-out war. For the time being the Preacher was still "master of policy" in New York City's ghettos and it was still up to Bunny Ennis to snatch the crown for the San Fillipo Family, at least that's what his Mafia associates thought.

"Carmine", Bunny spoke softly into the telephone receiver at 5:30 that morning. "I took care of our little TV star."

"I hope so.", he answered. "But don't forget, it was your fuckin' problem you took care of."

Bunny then made a trip to a deserted Hudson River pier. He had already wrapped the Colt "Ace" .22 and added some extra weight before tossing it into the river just as he had the piece used to smack Carson and Hayes. The Family seemed to have an ample supply of

"Ace" .22 pistols, little brother to the more familiar Colt .45 automatic and it was a Cardinal rule that a "hit" weapon was never used more than once.

7:35 AM TUESDAY, OCTOBER 25, 1966

When Bunny returned to his apartment, he stripped naked and folded everything he had worn into a pillow case. Later, he would take this bundle to the building's incinerator. Now he was going to take a long hot bath then sack out, take it easy for a while. He had worked hard and since he planned to visit Lydia in Washington, Bunny needed to rest up.

He wasn't worried about losing Monica. She'd probably bolt when she heard about Sal and the girls but Bunny knew that Monica wasn't going anywhere that he couldn't find her; not with her heroin habit. When he caught up with her, he'd take care of that business too. He was the "Bunnyman" and didn't leave loose ends.

FOURTEEN

10:45 AM TUESDAY, OCTOBER 25, 1966

The press conference had been a roaring success. Congressman Summerfield articulated the great social benefits that would accrue to the Country's minorities as a result of the passage of HR 4800 now called the Summerfield-Cain Bill since it was being co-sponsored by Senator Howard Cain of California.

Having Congressman Sadler appear with him at this conference added greatly to Summerfield's congressional support. Even the softball questions from the Press Corps seemed enthusiastic and almost "leading" at times – giving him opportunities to "sell" the benefits of the Bill.

Summerfield was in his element. He was masterful in his handling of the Press. Many of his colleagues watching were convinced that his chances of becoming House Speaker were greatly enhanced by his performance today.

Johnny Dolan sat in the back of the room listening to Summerfield's precision presentation. He could be stern, folksy, honest, the big city politician, a statesman and even humorous in answering the many questions thrown at him. The Washington Press Corps were a cynical bunch but they were being charmed by a master. They understood what was being done to them but they loved him for it.

Dolan wished that Summerfield was not what Gil Peterson said he was – a front man for the Mob. The United States Congress needed black leaders who could articulate reasons for equality and equal opportunity and help mold civil rights legislations that would make a difference.

If Summerfield was an imposter, he was committing the greater sin. He was ultimately increasing race alienation that would make whites more cynical while keeping black Americans frustrated.

After the conference ended, Dolan made his way to the front of the room.

"Congressman Sadler", he called. "Congressman Sadler over here."

Charles Sadler saw Dolan, waved and excused himself from the knot of reporters and congressional aids surrounding him.

"Johnny what the hell are you doing here? MBC transfer you to Washington?", he said, genuinely pleased to see Dolan.

They shook hands and stood together as old friends – no one intruding. They had known each other from the Club and although Sadler kept in the background and "stayed in the closet", he was a major supporter for the Gay Rights movement in New York City.

"No Charles, I'm only down for the day. Summerfield did a masterful job didn't he?"

"There's no denying his charismatic articulative skills."

Dolan laughed. "Is that a nice way for saying he's full of shit?"

"I guess you could say that too.", Sadler laughed. "Seriously, what are you down here for anyway?"

"I need to meet Summerfield's assistant, Lydia Hayes. I'm doing a project and her late husband is one of the key ingredients."

Sadler blanched.

"Is there something wrong Charles?", Dolan asked gripping Sadler's arm in support.

"There's a problem, but I can't discuss it here Johnny. We'll talk later, I have a committee meeting to attend."

"Are you alright Sir?", Sadler's aide had seen his chief's face and rushed to his side.

"Fine, fine. Where will you be this afternoon?", Sadler asked, regaining his composure.

"Probably back in New York.", Dolan responded.

"Call my office. Speak with George here.", Sadler turned toward his assistant. "George, I'd like you to meet John Dolan from MBC

News. Take him over and introduce him to Lydia Hayes and when he calls the office later, tell Johnny where he can reach me tonight."

Johnny shook George's hand, said his good bye to Charles Sadler and then accompanied George over to the small group still surrounding Congressman Summerfield.

Johnny Dolan was very impressed with Lydia Hayes. Not only was she one of the most beautiful women he had ever seen but after speaking with her less than a minute, he recognized that she was exceptionally intelligent as well.

"Yes Mr. Dolan, I received your message this morning and I agree that we need to speak. However, you must understand that I am extremely busy today and we'll have to schedule something for later next week."

"Oh that's, eh ... that's too bad Mrs. Hayes. My Editor has scheduled me to go public with this story this week and it would have made sense to be able to discuss why the Congressman's late son used your husband's name when he was arrested in 1963." Johnny decided to flush out what

he could with the un-substantiated report that Allie Summerfield was Fredrick Douglass Summerfield's son and his tactic worked.

Mrs. Hayes didn't show it on her face, but she needed help.

"Please excuse me for just a moment Mr. Dolan.", Lydia politely requested.

"Certainly.", Dolan answered.

She turned and walked the twenty steps to the group still surrounding Summerfield. Taking him aside, she whispered close to his ear. He raised his head, looked over at Dolan nodded in agreement and returned to the knot of reporters still waiting.

Lydia smiled as she asked: "Would four this afternoon be convenient for you to meet with myself and the Congressman? We have twenty minutes available in our schedule for your interview."

"Thank you. That will be fine. I'm sure we can get this matter cleared up in twenty minutes. I look forward to meeting with you and the Congressman this afternoon."

2:46 PM TUESDAY, OCTOBER 25, 1966

Dolan had no problem locating a cab outside Arlington National Cemetery. "Please take me to The Rayburn Office Building."

He stared out the cab window and thought about the dozen years that had passed and the kid soldier resting so long in the grave he had just visited.

Korea … hot Sherman tank, the kid driver. The North Korean T34 tank shell exploding and him flying out the commander's hatch and leaving the kid and the rest of the crew dead or dying in the burning hulk.

3:45 PM TUESDAY, OCTOBER 25, 1966

"Congressman Summerfield, President Johnson is calling.", Lydia Hayes announced from the office doorway.

"Please put the President through immediately and I want you here during our call Mrs. Hayes."

Summerfield composed himself, waited a few seconds for Lydia's return and then picked up the telephone receiver.

"This is Congressman Summerfield speaking."

"Please hold for the President.", was the crisp response.

"Son of a bitch one upped me.", Summerfield thought.

The nasally baritone of Lyndon Baines Johnson boomed loud over the receiver.

"Sum, I saw your press conference this morning. Great job son. Get that Bill through on Friday and you'll have my signature on Monday."

"Thank you, Mr. President, I was certain I could count on your support."

"You know this legislation ties in nicely with my Great Society plan and compliments my Medicare program. So, keep me posted Fredrick. I don't want any problems on Friday. How does it look?"

"From where I see it, I believe we have all the votes we need Mr. President.", Summerfield shot a wide, toothy smile at Lydia, who had a "hero worship" glow all over her face. As he looked across at his beautiful aide, a flash of overwhelming desire surged through Summerfield's guts. He never experienced more sexual energy with any other woman than with Lydia Hayes. Her appetite was insatiable and at 55, he sometimes had trouble matching her spontaneous passion.

LBJ's voice shocked him back to reality.

"Well let's get that son of a bitch passed Summerfield! I'm counting on you."

"I won't let you down Mr. President."

Johnson had already hung up even before Summerfield completed his assurance of HR 4800's passage.

He handed Lydia the telephone and they both began laughing. She came around the desk to him and sat on his lap. Putting his arms around her and roughly seeking her mouth, Summerfield kissed her with a devouring passion. After a minute of running his hand over her manicured body he realized that the office door was unlocked and anyone could surprise them.

"We'll stay together tonight Lydia – at your apartment.", he said huskily removing his hand from between her legs.

"Oh yes Fredrick. That will be wonderful."

Their intimate interlude ended with the sound of a buzzing intercom and secretary's voice announcing the arrival of a "Mr. Dolan from MBC News".

"Please ask him to wait Mrs. Dawes.", Lydia promptly responded.

She stood, straightened her clothing and took a seat across from Summerfield who remained behind his desk.

"I told you about his message Fredrick. He knows that Allie used Doug's name when he was arrested. What should we tell him?". Lydia was concerned because they hadn't had time to prepare for Dolan's interview.

"Tell him the truth – but we'll tell him, "Off the record", so he can't use it.", Summerfield answered matter of factly.

"Please show Mr. Dolan in, thank you Mrs. Dawes.", Lydia called to the receptionist as she stood waiting by the now open office door.

Summerfield stood to meet his guest. "Mr. Dolan please come in. Thank you, Mrs. Dawes. Lydia, please offer Mr. Dolan some refreshment. Very nice to finally meet you Mr. Dolan."

Shaking his hand with a firm grip, Summerfield graciously escorted his visitor to a small conference table in the corner of the office. Dolan recognized the power of Fredrick Douglass Summerfield by the look of his office. Autographed pictures of three Presidents hung on his walls together with many other national and international personalities; there was Reverend King's photo, over there, Bobby Kennedy's. The furniture, the decor and the magnificent view of the Capitol Building emphasized that this man was a congressional leader and all who entered his domain must pay homage.

"What can I offer you Mr. Dolan?", Lydia asked.

Dolan felt Lydia Hayes sizing him up. He rather liked her very direct and positive manner. She reminded him of the "up and coming" junior officers he had known during his time in the Army.

"Hot tea would be fine, thank you Mrs. Hayes."

"Congressman would you care for something?", she asked.

"Coffee – thank you."

Lydia instructed Mrs. Dawes to bring coffee and then took a seat at the conference table to Summerfield's right.

Summerfield began the interview. "Well now, I understand you have some questions about my son Albert, Mr. Dolan."

"Yes, I do sir, as well as a few other topics I'd like to cover. I know you're busy, so if it's alright I'd like to get right to business.", Dolan responded.

"That'll be fine. By all means – please ask your questions Mr. Dolan, I'll answer as best as I can."

"Actually, my first question is for Mrs. Hayes."

Johnny turned and faced Lydia. She challenged his gaze, a vague smile played across her full lips.

"Mrs. Hayes, what did you know about Doug's business venture with Larry Carson?", Johnny maintained his disarming Irish smile. "Surprised her with that one.", he thought noticing her body language reaction.

Crossing her legs, she leaned slightly forward. "Do you mean their work at the Hospital's Computer Center?"

"No, actually I'm more interested in the computer program they had to pick numbers. You know ... Policy. I believe they were selling lists of numbers each month. Did you know about that?"

She didn't hesitate in answering. "I was only vaguely aware of their little venture, which was perfectly legal I might add. Doug was excited about their little business and told me of course, but I didn't learn much about its workings. Frankly Mr. Dolan, I wasn't very interested in anything Doug did."

"Touché!", Johnny thought. "She's quick."

"I see.", Dolan nodded. "Perhaps you might know for whom they were providing consultant services? Mrs. Carson mentioned that Doug and Larry were consulting for some organization using their special numbers forecasting computer program.", Dolan then paused for effect before continuing.

"By the way, you might already know that there's some official thinking that this may have been the reason for their murders. They could have had a business relationship with an organized crime group that went bad. There's some thought it might be the San Fillipo crime family."

Out of the corner of his eye, Dolan noticed that Summerfield winced at his "organized crime" comment.

"I have absolutely no idea what Pauline Carson was talking about Mr. Dolan. I very rarely saw Doug and as I already said, knew even less about his business dealings. Do the Police have any evidence to support this theory?"

"Yes, I believe that they might.", Dolan lied. "When we spoke last week, you mentioned that you hadn't seen Doug for over a year, but a ... Mrs. Carson indicated that you and Doug were recently at the Carson's home and had even gone out together to celebrate the success of their new business. Could I have misunderstood you Mrs. Hayes when we spoke?"

"Perhaps you did Mr. Dolan. I recall that when we spoke, I was very upset about Doug's death."

"I see. Certainly, I misunderstood you then.", Dolan now turned toward Summerfield. "Congressman Summerfield, it appears that your son Allie, excuse me Albert, and Doug were close friends. Is that true?"

"Yes, they were. They had become acquainted through Lydia. They shared many common interests didn't they Lydia?"

"Yes Mr. Dolan", Lydia agreed "Doug and Allie became very close."

"Mr. Dolan you are aware that Albert is also deceased."

"Yes, I am Congressman, and I'm sorry for your loss."

Mrs. Dawes entered the office with a coffee and tea service tray and an assortment of cakes. She fixed each a cup and then left the office closing the door.

"Now about Albert, Mr. Dolan.", Summerfield continued, "I am most concerned about his reputation and would expect that anything you should learn here today would be kept off the record."

"I have no problem maintaining that confidence sir."

Summerfield believed that Dolan already knew about Allie's arrest and decided to acknowledge it. "Thank you. You likely have knowledge that Albert was arrested and charged with an offense I doubt he committed considering the circumstances. Simply stated – the boy panicked – didn't keep his wits about him. He was afraid that somehow, I'd suffer if it were known that he was my son. That's why he incorrectly identified himself as Doug Hayes. I might add that this mix up was corrected in judge's chambers and the morals charge was reduced."

"I understand that Albert took his life.", Dolan softly asked.

Summerfield briefly hung his head and signed. "Yes, unfortunately he did. Albert had many emotional problems which professional help could not solve. I regret that I might have contributed to his problems. Perhaps if I had only ..."

Lydia interrupted. "Congressman Summerfield you must stop blaming yourself for what happened.", turning to Johnny she asked impatiently, "Mr. Dolan is there anything else you would like to discuss?"

"No Mrs. Hayes that's it. I appreciate the time you've given me. Congressman", he nodded as he stood. "Thank you, Sir and Mrs. Hayes for taking time to speak with me and good luck, with your Bill vote this Friday." Dolan extended his hand which Summerfield took in his.

"Are you interested in politics Mr. Dolan?", Summerfield asked, switching quickly from remorse to interest.

"As much as anyone else in the news business sir."

"I noticed that you're a West Pointer.", Summerfield gestured toward Dolan's oversized class ring.

"Class of '46.", he answered.

"Missed the big one eh?"

"Korea was big enough for me, thank you sir."

"Of course, of course." Summerfield returned to his desk and Lydia escorted Dolan to the outer office door.

"Oh, I almost forgot.", Johnny removed the photo of the murder scene spectators from his jacket and handed it to Lydia. "Do you recognize anyone?"

She scanned it quickly and handed it back to him.

"No, I don't recognize anyone, and please feel free to contact me should you have any more questions Mr. Dolan. Good-bye."

It was obvious that Lydia Hayes wanted him gone.

"Thank you, and yes I'll be sure to call should I have any further questions for you or the Congressman. Good-bye for now Mrs. Hayes."

Lydia returned to the inner office where Summerfield waited. As soon as she had closed the door he angrily demanded: "What the hell was Dolan talking about – picking numbers with the computer? Was Doug involved with Policy? What do you know about this Lydia and why didn't you tell me?"

"Frederick all I know is that Doug and Larry Carson were doing something with the computer for the Preacher."

Summerfield's eyes bulged.

"They were working for the fucking Preacher and you didn't think to tell me? What the hell is wrong with you Lydia? Don't you know that I can't afford to be linked with that man in any way, shape or form and if it became known that the former husband of my senior aide was working for him, I'd be crucified. I'd lose everything I've been striving for all these years!" He was now shouting at her.

"Fredrick, please!", she pleaded coming to him. "Calm yourself – there's no danger to you. Doug was playing with some stupid little computer program and selling mail lists of numbers through an ad in the Amsterdam News for five dollars a copy. How could that hurt you?"

"Then why did you say he was working for the Preacher?"

"Doug liked to brag. He made some money from his mail list and he lied when he told me that the Preacher was interested in his business. He was always jealous of our relationship and he wanted to act important. I'm sure he was lying to me."

Summerfield shrugged off her hand now resting on his shoulder. "I can't afford to take any chances on this Lydia, there's too much at stake. I'm going to contact San Fillipo tonight. Make a call to your "rabbit" friend and have him arrange the details. Do you understand Lydia?"

She backed away and returned to stand on the other side of the oversized desk. "I understand Fredrick. I'll take care of it right away.", she promised in soothing tones. "Are we staying together this evening?"

"I'll have to get back to you on that.", he abruptly responded.

4:55 PM TUESDAY, OCTOBER 25, 1966

The first thing Johnny Dolan did after leaving Summerfield was to place a call to Congressman Sadler's office using his private number. He spoke with George who gave him a second number where the Congressman could be reached until six. Dolan called and was immediately connected to Charles Sadler.

"Johnny, thanks for getting back to me. Did you see Lydia Hayes? Was she helpful?"

"I saw both her and her boss Charles, but they didn't tell me anything I didn't already know."

"Really? What do you know about Doug Hayes, Johnny?"

Sadler sounded panicked.

"I'm learning more everyday Charles.", Dolan answered non committedly. "What do you know about him?"

"It's difficult for me to talk right now. Are you going back to New York tonight?"

"I'm leaving for National as soon as we hang up. Do you want to call me later?"

"Yes. It's important we speak. Will you be home by nine Johnny?"

"If my flight is on schedule, but I have a conference with my boss at midnight, so don't call too late."

"I'll plan to call you at home around nine. Good bye Johnny."

Johnny was tired, dog tired and had a splitting headache. Lack of sleep and pressure from trying to unravel this puzzle were beginning to take their toll.

"Why would Charles Sadler be so concerned about my Doug Hayes assignment? Did Charles know Hayes – was he involved with him?", he thought.

FIFTEEN

5:40 PM TUESDAY, OCTOBER 25 1966

At the precise moment Dolan felt as if his head was about to explode, Bunny Ennis couldn't have felt better.

He had rested all day and eaten his late breakfast of steak and eggs at five that afternoon, just about the same time Dolan's cab was dropping him off in front of the Eastern Terminal at DC National Airport.

Ennis enjoyed cooking. It was a skilled learned when he was a kid at reform school in Elmira, New York. He had a well-stocked kitchen and kept an excellent wine rack. His tastes ran simple but he was expert at various regional dishes like Cajun gumbo. He was finishing his second cup of rich Columbian coffee mellowed with Carnation evaporated milk when the telephone rang.

"Yeah?", he answered.

"Bunny it's Lydia."

"What's happening baby?" his tone softening.

"Bunny I think we're in trouble. I have to talk with you but not right now. Can I call you back in an hour, about six thirty?", Ennis checked his watch. "I'll be here. Later.", he said hanging up.

"What the fuck is the bitch's problem now? Lydia's a hot piece of ass, but she's getting to be a real pain in the ass.", he thought.

He finished his coffee, poured himself a third cup and began cleaning the kitchen. Bunny was a very neat cook and never left a mess. When he was finished, he threw on some clothes and went out to buy an afternoon newspaper – to see if Sal and the girls had been discovered. There was nothing in the paper and nothing on the radio or TV news.

"They'll probably stink before anybody finds them.", he concluded.

He was wrong. Their bodies had already been discovered. There had been a small, smokey grease fire in the Pizzeria downstairs and the firemen broke down the whorehouse door because choking smoke had circulated throughout the building. At first, they thought that the four bodies lying on the floor had been overcome, but on closer inspection even the least experienced fireman knew that sucking burnt pizza smoke doesn't put small round holes in your head and chest.

"Hey Captain! There's three naked women and a guy shot dead upstairs.", Quickly running down two flights of stairs, Fireman James Martin reported to his boss, Fire Captain John Cassidy standing outside the building directing the efforts of his Company.

"No shit Dick Tracy!", Cassidy exclaimed, double timing it into the still smoking building.

"That's the fastest his fat ass moved in years." Martin commented to one of his partners working the truck's equipment.

Captain Cassidy confirmed Martin's report and he and every other man from Eight-Two Engine made damn sure they got a good look at the whore house and the four stiffs before the cops came and roped off the crime scene.

SIXTEEN

6:35 PM TUESDAY, OCTOBER 25, 1966

"Bunny, Fredrick wants to speak with Carmine as soon as possible.", Lydia began her telephone conversation.

"So what the fuck. Let him speak with Carmine. I'll set it up for tonight."

"You don't understand – Fredrick knows that Doug was working for the Preacher. He's very upset Bunny. That TV reporter, John Dolan told him that the Police suspect Doug and Larry Carson were killed by the Preacher because of problems with the computer work they were doing for him. Fredrick is afraid he'll be implicated somehow. He wants Carmine to help him. Fredrick doesn't know everything about our relationship Bunny ... Did the Preacher kill Doug?"

"Shut the fuck up bitch! Why the fuck you talking like this on the telephone? Tell your boss Carmine will be in touch later tonight. He'll call him at the usual location. Do you understand what I'm telling you?"

"Yes Bunny, I understand. I'm sorry – I'm just worried that's all. This is not working out. When are you coming to Washington?"

"Tomorrow, I'll see you at your apartment after five." Bunny slammed down his phone before Lydia could answer.

"Stupid, fucking bitch. She probably told Summerfield about Hayes working for the Preacher.", Ennis thought.

Now he was going to have to see Carmine and take shit from him. San Fillipo had invested half a million in Summerfield and Bunny knew that the Family would make twenty times that from the minority businesses that had been set up to take advantage of the legislation Summerfield sponsored.

He also knew that his life was worth less than shit if anything screwed up the passage of the minority business Bill this Friday.

Carmine would be at the club later tonight and could make the call to Summerfield. Bunny checked his watch, it was six twenty, still early enough for him to begin tracking down Monica. He could feel the warm glow start in his guts when he thought about the cool young blond that gave such great head.

"No pop in the brain pan for Miss Monica.", Bunny thought.

He would take out some of his frustration on the bitch – kind of enjoy himself, get it out of his system before he faced San Fillipo.

"She might even like some of what I got planned for her.", he thought.

He drove to her place on West Seventy Ninth street. It was almost seven thirty when he reached the apartment building's iron bound front door, entered and stood before a bank of twenty-five door bells.

Bunny didn't ring Monica's door bell, "why warn her", he thought. Instead, he rang every other bell in the apartment house until some asshole buzzed him through the locked front door.

He figured since there hadn't been anything public about Sal and the girls, Monica wouldn't know he was looking for her. He intended to tell her that he wanted to be sure that his "A number one bitch" was feeling good – that's why he came over "personal" to check her out. All she had to do was let him get close – just close enough to get his strong, oversized hands on her.

He took the slow elevator to the fourth floor and now stood before her apartment door. It was painted dull green and made of steel plating with a double lock and a peep hole.

He rang her bell three quick times; this was the code they sometimes used to gain entry at the whorehouse when it wasn't open to the "public".

Monica had her period and wasn't feeling well. She had been stretched out on her living room couch drifting in and out of sleep and watching TV all day.

Ten minutes before Ennis arrived there had been a news break on CBS TV, reporting that four victims had been found murdered, shot gangland style, at what appeared to be a house of prostitution over on West 54th Street. It mentioned the bodies were discovered as a result of a first floor Pizzeria fire and that the victims included three unidentified women and a male.

The news break lasted less than fifteen seconds but it was long enough for Monica to realize that her life was in danger. The warning also gave her enough time to gather what little money and drugs she had in the apartment, dress and make a quick telephone call to a relative in Queens who agreed to put her up for a few days.

Making the phone call to her cousin delayed her two minutes and saved her from walking into Bunny in the hallway or on the street in front of her apartment.

Monica's hand was on the door knob when the bell rang a quick three times. She hadn't rung anyone through the downstairs entrance and since she recognized the whorehouse bell code, she instinctively knew that Bunny Ennis was standing less than a foot away, just on the other side of her front door.

She forced herself to look through the peep hole. There he was, a smile played across his lips, dead eyes staring back at her. Somehow, he knew she was looking at him. Maybe he could hear her gasping for air, or smell the sweat that soaked her clothes. Monica's knees began shaking. She felt like she was going to throw up. Her chest hurt and her eyes no longer focused.

"Monica baby, let me in. Monica, I know you be lookin' at me. Come on now baby girl, let me in there with you.", he pleaded. "Hey Monica, I got something that make you feel good. Looky here.", Bunny held a small package of heroin in front of the peep hole for her to see.

"This all you need mamma. A little smack gonna make you all better. Now come on – don't be wasting time. Let me on in there so I can get you straight.", his deep voice was soothing.

Five silent seconds passed. Monica stood frozen, her back now pressed against the cold steel door, paralyzed with fear. She nearly passed out when Bunny's foot slammed into the door toppling her onto her knees. He kicked it again and again. Monica could see the door bulge where his foot connected. She began screaming.

"Go away! Go away, leave me alone Bunny!"

"Let me the fuck in there bitch. Open the fuckin' door! NOW!" he roared, his powerful voice echoing up and down the marbled hallway."

Monica covered her ears and squeezed her eyes shut tight. She curled up into a small ball at the foot of her door and remained in this position for ten minutes, afraid to move, praying that she would die before the "Bunnyman" broke his way through the fragile barricade that protected her.

Little by little her brain began to register that the pounding had stopped. She finally dared opening her eyes and view the battered aftermath of his assault. Somehow steel was stronger than Bunny Ennis' foot. It had prevented his entry and her certain death.

Monica sat rocking and mumbling to herself, her heart was pounding loudly. She felt sicker at this moment than at any time she had tried to go cold turkey. Her stomach was cramped, her head ached. Her mouth was dry and there were no tears left to cry.

"The phone.", she thought. I'll call for help."

She couldn't move her legs so she sat rocking for another five minutes until she could. She picked up her telephone and started to dial but stopped before her finger even reached the first number.

"Ha – call for help, that's a joke. Who the fuck is going to help me? I have to get out of here. Get to my cousins.", she said aloud putting the telephone to rest.

Monica couldn't stop shaking; her stomach was still doing flip flops when she rushed into the bathroom and dry heaved; later, a cold wash cloth on her face helped. Feeling somewhat better, she decided to take a chance that Bunny had left. She would exit the building through the cellar and then grab a cab and get to her cousin's place in Queens.

Monica peeked out the front window, slowly checking the street for Bunny or his big red car. She didn't have a great view, but he was no where she was able to see. She returned to the battered front door and looked through the peep hole. The hall was empty and quiet. Monica then went to the kitchen and selected a short, sharp steak knife and placed it in her purse. She turned off all the lights, made sure the windows were locked and taking a deep breath, opened the front door.

Slowly, ever so slowly she leaned her head into the corridor. Monica looked in all directions and when she was certain that he wasn't hiding somewhere, moved through the open doorway still keeping her hand on the door knob in the event she needed to leap back into the apartment. She finally closed the door and locked it, trying to make as little noise as possible.

Suddenly the door of the apartment two doors down crashed open! Monica's heart had almost stopped as she turned back to her door and fumbling with her keys, attempted the impossible task of trying to open the two locks engaged just seconds before.

"What the hell is going on here God damn it!", the old woman's voice screeched down the hallway.

Monica turned and with overwhelming relief, faced her irate neighbor now standing outside her apartment door, her skinny sweater clad arms folded across her fragile body.

This grey headed, shriveled old women was just warming up.

"I'm going to call the god damn cops on you and your crazy friends if you don't stop. I'm an old woman. I have a heart condition. I'm going to call my son; he works for the City. You bastards have no consideration, ringing my bell, pounding on doors!"

"I'm sorry Mrs. Cohen. I'm really sorry we disturbed you. It was my idiot boyfriend. It won't happen again, I promise.", Monica said trying to sooth her neighbor's frazzled nerves.

"Well, it better not, that's all I can tell you god damn it!", she screamed, slamming her apartment door.

Monica exhaled a long sigh of relief. Her heart was pounding and she had almost wet her pants.

"Heh – heh, heh.", she began a quiet, almost insane laugh. "Fuck you, you old bitch.", she whispered to her neighbor's closed apartment door. She knew that Mrs. Cohen was most likely standing on the other side still listening.

Although the suddenness of the hallway encounter had almost caused a seizure, it created enough of a distraction for Monica to overcome her fear of stumbling into Bunny.

"He's gone. I'll be alright if I can just get the fuck out of here.", she said aloud without realizing it.

She took the elevator to the basement and made her way past the deserted laundry room, down the dank, dark naked concrete walled corridor and on toward the steel door that led to the side street and escape. Reaching the door, she pushed hard but it wouldn't open. Monica knew that it was never locked from the inside; it almost felt as if it were blocked by something outside on the street.

"Fuck, fuck, fuck, FUCK!", she shouted, her voice echoing off the cellar walls.

Monica pounded the door once with a closed fist and kicked it twice before turning and stumbling into the waiting arms of Bunny Ennis. Before she could re-act, he spun her around and pinned her arms behind her back causing her to drop her pocketbook.

"Hey baby – I almost missed you.", Bunny whispered into her ear. "There I was, waiting for you in the lobby and then I seen the elevator leave your floor and go to the cellar. Good thing I jammed up this door here or I wouldn't have seen my Little Miss Monica anymore.

Monica turned her head and asked in a calm voice. "Bunny! Oh my god – please don't hurt me."

"Now why would I hurt you baby? You be my favorite lady don't you know."

Monica had seen the results of Bunny Ennis' volatile temper and making a heroic effect to appear calm, continued talking in a soothing voice.

"Let me go Baby. I won't tell anybody anything. Please let me go."

"I guess you heard about Sal and the Ladies.", he said shaking his head. "You and me got to have a talk. All this 'Bunny don't hurt me shit" making me feel real bad Monica. Let's go back to your place and have us a pow wow."

"Alright. That sounds like a good idea. I have some Jack Daniels for you. We can talk. Could you let go of me Bunny; I won't do anything. I swear to god."

Bunny released her but placed his arm around her waist and held her tightly. Monica tried to bend and retrieve her purse from the cement floor but Bunny reached it first and held it in his free hand. They entered the elevator still parked at the basement level and rode it to Monica's floor without speaking. She didn't dare look at him but kept her eyes focused straight in front of her. Her mind was racing, trying to devise a plan to escape.

They left the elevator and made their way back to her apartment door. He released his hold and opened her bag, looking for her keys.

"What the fuck you doin' with this blade girl?", Bunny held up her kitchen knife. "All the time you tellin' me not to hurt you, you gettin' ready to cut my ass."

"No Bunny.", Monica started to move away but he grasped her by the throat and pushed her against the wall. Monica began a muted scream.

"Just leave me alone Bunny – leave me the fuck alone!"

He slapped her hard across the face and covered her mouth with his hand. Her eyes bulged and she tried to knee him. He was too quick and moved out of the way, catching her blow on the outside of his leg. He began to smile.

"I like that – I like that when a bitch show spirit. It get me goin'. Now let me open the door and we have our little chat."

Keeping his hand pressed against her mouth and her head jammed against the hallway wall he managed to open the apartment door and shove her inside.

"Now don't be makin' a fuss Miss Monica. I just want to talk wit you. You understand what I'm tellin' you?"

Monica nodded that she understood and Bunny released her. She immediately bolted for the kitchen. Whether she was trying to get to the telephone or another knife didn't matter. Bunny caught her before she went three steps and began smacking her with his right hand while he held her by her long blond hair with his left. She fell to her knees and he ripped off her blouse. Monica wore no bra and her pink nipples were hard.

"Monica why you being so bitchy? You think the Bunnyman kill Sal and his ladies? That be dumb. Why would I do somethin' like that? I just came to see if you knew anything about what happen. Now calm down. Calm down."

She knew he was lying but her best hope for survival was to play along with him. She stopped struggling and looked up at him.

"Oh Bunny, I knew you didn't do it."

"Now that be better. You and me got to work together on this dilemma. You dig what I'm sayin'?"

He let go of her hair and she stood before him, still half naked. Monica put her arms around Bunny's neck and pulled him toward her. She kissed him full on the lips and he forced his tongue into her mouth.

Bunny still guarded against any attack she might make and Monica could feel his tension. They stood kissing while he ran his hands over her naked back and squeezed her ass. She began moaning and dropped to her knees. Quickly opening his pants, she freed his swollen cock and began sucking him off. She could feel him relax. He grasped her hair and forced her head to move in an in and out motion over his prick.

"That's right baby. Do it. Ah baby, you do that so good. Take it all."

She stopped and looked up at him.

"I want you to cum Bunny. Cum in my mouth."

He reached down and lifted her to her feet.

"Let's go to the bedroom and have us a party.", he whispered.

"Alright, I'll fix you a drink first Bunny.", Monica said starting for the kitchen but he stopped her by grabbing her arm.

"I don't want nothing to dull my brain right now. Come on let's go get it on."

He pushed her roughly into the bedroom and striped her naked but did not remove any of his clothes.

"Lay down there.", he ordered.

Monica obeyed and lay on her bed. Bunny pulled the belt from her terry cloth bathrobe hanging on the door hook. She blanched when he took Sal's knife from his pocket and cut the belt into four pieces.

"What are you doing honey?", she asked wide eyed.

"I'm gonna tie you down girl and then we have some fun."

"No Bunny, please don't do that. I don't want to be tied up. I got my period. Let me suck you off.", she pleaded.

Bunny raised his fist and held it over her face.

"Don't fuck with me. Spread your arms and legs out there. Now!"

She did as she was ordered and he tied her securely to the bed. When finished, he removed the package of heroin from his pocket, held it for her to see and left the bedroom. He returned with her dope preparation added to the "fixin's" taken from her pocketbook. He cooked the smack, filled the needle and popped a vein in her arm.

She felt the immediate rush and an overwhelming glow of well-being. Monica floated free now. Bunny was no longer a threat; he was her main man.

Bunny reached down and pulled the tampon from her vagina.

"Please don't fuck me Bunny! Hmmm. Let me taste that big cock of yours. Come on baby – give it up here."

Her eyes were glazed and unfocussed as she starred up at him. Monica's hips began to squirm and she licked her lips seductively. Bunny's eyes devoured her body as he reached into his pocket and removed something three inches long and cylindrical which he then inserted it between her legs.

"I ain't gonna fuck you bitch – but I'm gonna give you a bang!", he said softly, as he lit the short fuse on the M80.

7:42 PM TUESDAY, OCTOBER 25, 1966

"Fuck me, she said! Fuck me – well fuck her!"

Mrs. Cohen's blood pressure was rising as she picked up the telephone and dialed "0".

"Operator.", came the flat response.

"Get me the cops.", she ordered.

The old lady was still mumbling angrily when the officer answered.

"Officer Shewell, 68th Precinct."

"Is this the cops?"

"Yes mam, what's the problem?", he responded already guessing that this old bitch had a beef with the neighbor.

"Problem? I'll tell you the problem. It's that whore in 4C, now she's shooting guns off. I'm an old lady. I got a bad heart. My son works for the City and I'm going to …"

Shewell cut her off. "What's your name and address lady?"

"What?"

"Where do you live? What's your name?", Shewell loudly repeated, thinking it must be a "full moon" since he had had more nut calls than usual this shift.

"My name is Flo Cohen and I live at 518 West Seventy Ninth apartment A4. Now listen, are you cops going to do something about this or what?"

"Ah … sure we are Mrs. Cohen. Now are you complaining that your neighbor has discharged a fire arm in their apartment?"

"God damn right I'm complaining and that's not all they done. She cursed me out and her friends ring my bell all the time. I'm not well and I can't take much …"

Shewell interrupted for the second time.

"When was the fire arm discharged?"

"Two minutes ago! What are you going to do about it?"

"What's your neighbor's name Mrs. Cohen? I'll send a car to investigate."

Flo Cohen gave Officer Shewell the necessary particulars and twenty minutes later two patrolmen were standing in front of her apartment door. She repeated her story and now stood behind them as they knocked on Monica's battered door.

"She's in there. I know she's in there. I saw her go in with her nigger boyfriend and she wasn't with him when he ran out."

The older cop rapped the door with his nightstick this time announcing it was the police. When no one answered, he turned to Mrs. Cohen, "Looks like there's nobody home lady. Why don't you call us later when she comes home? We'll come back and talk to her. How's that sound?"

"It sounds like shit.", she answered and before either cop could react, skinny old Mrs. Cohen pushed by them, pounded on the apartment door and turned the door knob. Since Bunny hadn't bothered to lock up, Flo Cohen almost fell on her face when the door unexpectedly thrust open and banged against the hall wall.

The cops were pissed off but didn't have time to yell at the old lady because all three could hear the low moaning coming from the rear of the apartment. Mrs. Cohen moved back against the hallway wall, pointed toward the rear bedroom and with a smug look on her face calmly announced: "See ... he probably shot the bitch."

The cops found Monica as Bunny had left her, naked and tied to her bed. The only reason she was still alive was because of the effect of the strong heroin shot Bunny had injected before. The narcotic had slowed her heart rate enough so she hadn't yet bled to death, but death was near.

The younger cop, a rookie, gagged at the sight of Monica's mangled body and the blood-soaked bed.

"Get outa here if you're gonna puke!", his partner ordered. "Take that old lady back to her apartment gather her statement after you call it in."

Needing no further encouragement, the rookie promptly hustled Mrs. Cohen out of the bedroom, and back to her apartment leaving his partner the grim task of ministering to the half dead girl.

The old cop cut the ropes binding Monica's hands and feet tied to the bed posts, careful not to disturb the knots since these sometimes gave a clue to the killer's identity.

"Miss ... Miss?", he softly whispered, but not really expecting a response since she was already too far gone.

"She'll be dead before the ambulance from Sinai gets here.", he thought but he tried again. "Who did this?"

Monica's eyes never opened as she mouthed "Bunny".

"What Miss, could you repeat that for me?", he asked and for the first time recognizing the stench of blood mingled with cordite that hung in this room. "Miss." He had his pad out and ready to note anything she said.

Monica's beautiful blue eyes, the eyes that Larry Carson were so taken by, fluttered open but could not focus. She thought she saw her father standing by her bed.

"What's he asking me?", she thought.

"Who did this to you Miss? Who did it?"

"Bunny did it Pop.", she answered. Then her eyes half closed and Monica died.

SEVENTEEN

8:40 PM TUESDAY, OCTOBER 25, 1966

The Eastern Shuttle flight to New York was on schedule and for once the cab ride to Dolan's Manhattan apartment didn't take longer than the flight from Washington.

Dolan was still uneasy from an incident that occurred at National Airport. He had stopped in the men's room and was relieving himself when the man standing at the next urinal said something to him. Dolan turned and saw that the young black man was staring intently at his penis. The young man's gaze finally shifted to Johnny's face and Dolan instantly recognized the retarded look.

"Bull's with short horns have to stand close mister.", the retarded man said again to him and then laughed.

When Dolan didn't respond, he shouted the same phrase which he continued shouting even as Johnny quickly retreated from the crowded men's room.

Now he was back home. Johnny switched on the living room light, took off his jacket and tie as he checked in with the office. Speaking briefly with the night secretary, Dolan confirmed his midnight meeting with Peterson. He also collected his telephone messages. Aside from the usual, Janet Gibbons requested that he either call her office or her home anytime after seven. He tried her home number but gave up on the tenth ring.

It was now almost nine and Dolan expected Charles Sadler's call. Since he wanted to shower, eat and perhaps nap before his session with Gil, he hoped it would come soon. He didn't have long to wait; the telephone rang at eight fifty-five.

"Hello. Charles?"

"Yes Johnny. Hello. Looks like you made it home on time for a change.", Sadler laughingly answered.

"No problem tonight. On schedule one out of ten times is about normal for the Shuttle. But I guess with your frequent commute to DC you've had a better percentage."

"Worse Johnny."

Dolan sensed that Charles Sadler wanted to cut the small talk and get to the purpose of his call. "Charles, what was your problem with Doug Hayes?", he asked.

"I was indiscreet with him.", Charles answered simply.

"Can you tell me about it?"

"I'd like too but this has to remain confidential, my career and reputation are at stake."

"Certainly Charles, I won't compromise you – but I won't lie for you either. A capital crime has been committed and I have to inform the police of any material information I uncover. If you can accept that, I'll do all I can to help you."

"Johnny, I understand your position and let me begin by saying that I didn't kill Hayes, nor do I know who did."

"Alright, I believe you. You said you were indiscreet; in what way?"

"I met Doug at a reception Summerfield was hosting. I enjoyed Doug's wit; you know he didn't particularly care for "Pope" Fredrick Douglas either. We met a few times in the City before sharing intimacies. He told me he wasn't happily married to Lydia and that she was having an affair with Summerfield which really didn't surprise me at all."

"Did Hayes blackmail you Charles?"

"No, he didn't but his brother tried to."

"His brother. I didn't know Doug Hayes had a brother."

"You didn't know that! Damn ... yes, Doug Hayes had a younger brother – Allie. Nice kid but high strung. He took some compromising photos of Doug and I; why the hell I allowed that to happen I'll never understand. Anyway, he took some pictures and later told me that I'd have to pay to get them. He said he needed money for narcotics. I asked Doug to help and he did. He returned the photos together with his negatives.

I thought everything was straightened out but George, you met George this morning, checked the prints after Doug was killed and found that they had not been made from negatives. In other words, there was at least one other set of photos. I assumed that Allie had them but I don't know that for fact. When Doug was killed, I panicked. I went to Summerfield yesterday and asked him to have Lydia search Doug's apartment on the chance that they were still there. He told me he would ask her to accommodate me but I had to tell him about the photos. Since she hasn't been back to the City, I needed to find Allie and thought perhaps you had spoken to him. But since you didn't know that he was Doug's brother I guess you haven't.", Sadler concluded.

"Allie is dead Charles, and his real name is Albert Summerfield; he's Fredrick's son, not Doug Hayes' younger brother."

"Oh god Johnny, no .... oh my god! I didn't expect that. Summerfield probably had the photos all along, the bastard. I didn't mention it yet but he's strong arming me to back his equal opportunity bill."

Dolan could sense Sadler's despair. He decided to tell him all he knew.

"I've discovered that Hayes and his murdered partner Carson were most likely supplying a computer service to an organization involved with Policy.", Dolan began.

"Do you mean – like in "Mob Policy.", the numbers racket?"

"Yes, and it could mean there's mob involvement in killing Doug Hayes, Charles."

"I'm a dead man Johnny, a dead man. Summerfield already owns me and should the press find out about my relationship with Hayes and if he was killed by the Mob, I'll be utterly destroyed. Is there anything you can do to help Johnny?", Sadler pleaded.

"Maybe, but let's look at this logically. First, if there are any photos still floating around and Summerfield has them, he's obviously going to try to protect you. You can't do him any good if you're out of Congress."

"That's true.", Sadler agreed.

"But if Hayes was killed by the Mob and they know about your affair there's really nothing they can do to you without the photos. Since you haven't heard anything from them yet don't panic. I know Allie Summerfield is dead so he can't hurt you now. He pretended to be Hayes's brother which means he didn't want you to know he was Summerfield's son. My guess is that he didn't have an ulterior motive in blackmailing you. Allie was heavily into drugs and was probably just trying to hustle a few bucks.

Finally, my investigation started because I thought Hayes and his partner Carson were killed because they were homosexuals. You've confirmed that Doug Hayes was gay but I don't think that was why he was killed. Everything I've learned thus far points to a Mob hit. What do you know about Summerfield's Mob connections?"

"There's been talk for years that he's controlled by the San Fillipo Family.", Sadler answered.

"There's an up-and-coming family for you. Do you know if they're into Policy?", Dolan asked.

"Johnny, they're into everything but Policy. When I was a New York City Councilman I sat on an investigatory panel for illegal gambling activities and the only area the Mob hadn't penetrated was Policy.

That's strictly a negro, excuse me, black domain. All New York City Policy is controlled out of Harlem by a black mob headed up by someone called the "Preacher". I don't remember too much more but I could get you a copy of our committee's findings if you're interested."

"Yes, I'd like to see it Charles. But it seems to me that your real threat is if Summerfield has the photos and trades them to San Fillipo."

"I swear – I'd resign from Congress before letting that scum ruin me and run me out.", Sadler said with passion.

"I know you would.", Dolan answered. "Look Charles I'm meeting with my Editor later tonight. I won't mention your name but I'll fill him in on what Summerfield might have on someone in Congress. Gil's an OK guy who's seen it all and between the three of us we might be able to come up with something to get you off the hook and stick it to Summerfield."

Sadler sighed, "Alright Johnny, I know I can trust you. I'll see that you get a copy of the crime committee investigation report and I'll keep you posted on developments down here."

"I'd appreciate that. Oh, by the way – what chance does Summerfield's Bill have with the vote on Friday?"

Congressman Sadler considered the question. "I'd bet that it passes with a wide majority. I'd vote for it even if it weren't Summerfield's. It's good legislation Johnny."

They said their goodnights and Dolan prepared for work. He brushed his teeth, shaved and took an extra-long hot shower letting the pulsating water do its job relaxing his tight muscles. Whenever Dolan took a twenty-minute shower he'd remember the West Point morning ritual of three S's- shit, shower, shave – all three had to be completed in less than five minutes. West Point seemed like a million years ago.

Johnny kept a radio in his bathroom and had it permanently tuned to WNEW, his favorite station because it featured Sinatra and the Big Band sound.

It was on as he dried himself, he danced, leaving wet footprints on the bath mat, keeping time with an old Glenn Miller standard. John Dolan was strangely content. He was beginning to enjoy life again. He knew it was because of the Carson Hayes project which seemed to move with its own momentum and the deeper he got into it, the more important finding its solution had become to him. Tracking this story had given him purpose; he wanted to know why they were killed and he felt he would ultimately find out.

Before dressing, he tried Janet Gibbons again and this time she answered.

"Hello."
Her face flashed before him; she has a "happy" voice he thought.
"Hello Janet."
"Hi Johnny, I'm glad you called. How are you?"
"Tired – but happy as they say in the movies."
"Tough day?", she asked.
"Long day.", he answered.
"You need some T.L.C. Mr. Dolan."
"Along with a good meal, followed by ten hours of uninterrupted sleep. Oh, and maybe a few hefty belts of Jack Daniels sprinkled in there somewhere."
"Well, sorry but the only thing I can supply is the Jack D. along with some very interesting information about Doug Hayes."
"Really now? Can you tell me about it?"
"Not over the telephone.", she answered. "But I can show you. I have in my possession Hospital employment records "borrowed" for the evening. I can't make copies and I need to get them back tomorrow. I'm sorry to drag you out Johnny but you'll have to come over to my place if you want to see them."
"Hey great, that's no problem. I really appreciate your help. Just give me an hour or so to dress for work and get over to your place. Where is "your place' by the way?"
"I live on Park between 51st and 52nd Streets.", she replied and then gave him the rest of her address.
"Low rent district I see.", Johnny kidded about the Park Avenue location, one of the best in the City.
"I'm just a poor working girl from Scarsdale Mr. Dolan, down to her last million."
"Too bad, I'm sorry to hear that. I'll see you in a bit Janet."
"Have you eaten?", she asked.
"Not since lunch."
"I'll fix you something. Steak and eggs OK?"
"Great, but don't go to any trouble."
"Johnny it's no trouble at all. I'll expect you in about an hour."
Dolan dressed and taking his report for Gil, left for Janet Gib-

bons' apartment, arriving exactly fifty-five minutes after their telephone conversation.

She lived in a "grand" old apartment building complete with modern innocuous security. Janet had already called down and told the duty desk she was expecting Mr. Dolan so on his arrival he was cordially greeted by name by the uniformed white-haired man stationed in the lobby who had "retired cop" written all over him. Johnny identified himself and was shown to the mahogany and polished brass elevator. As the door's rolled closed, he glimpsed the security man calling up to Janet announcing his arrival.

Johnny pressed the door bell and waited less than five seconds for her to open the door and usher him in. Her apartment was richly appointed. Its entrance foyer was done in an off white with two oversized gilded mirrors hung on opposite walls each reflecting the huge oriental vase filled with a variety of fresh cut autumn flowers resting on antique provincial three-legged tables positioned directly below. Janet was wearing a magnificent flowered silk long outfit that moved with the rhythm of her body.

"Come in – please come in. Let me take your overcoat. Here come on into the living room.", Janet said all "smiles" at his arrival.

She took his arm and led him to the living room which was at least thirty feet square and had a twelve-foot ceiling framed in gold leaf. There were expensive oriental rugs placed over a highly polished parquet floor and the room was dominated by a bank of four French doors with shiny brass fittings opening onto a deck terrace overlooking Central Park.

"Living room? Janet, this room is as big as the Plaza lobby. If you don't mind me asking, what do you really do for a living – rob banks?"

"You know what I do for a living. I just happen to have generous parents who let their only and favorite daughter use their Park Avenue co-op. The deal is I pay the utilities and supply my own food and booze."

"You have a good deal. My parents would have drunk my booze as part of any deal I had with them.", Johnny responded.

He sat on one of the two eight-foot couches and enjoyed the magnificent view of the uptown New York City skyline. Janet had Frank Sinatra on her stereo which was a perfect background to the perfect night.

She returned in a minute with his drink, handed it to him and placed two thick Guardian Center personnel files-one for Larry Carson and the other Doug Hayes' on the glass topped coffee table. Both files were stamped confidential in inch high red letters.

"You'll want to look at Doug's employment record first Johnny. By the way – how do you like your steak and eggs?"

"Medium on the steak, scrambled well on the eggs thanks."

He picked up the Hayes file and discovered it contained a completed job application, resume, benefits data, security information and performance reviews. The whole file was about an inch thick and every page was stamped confidential.

The first item that jumped out was Doug's full name ... Fredrick Douglass Hayes. His employment application must have caused him concern because he had scratched out whatever he had begun to write for FATHER'S NAME and had boldly written Fredrick Douglass Summerfield. His mother's name was entered as Loretta Hayes.

"Janet! I take it that you saw what Doug wrote for father's name?", he shouted toward the kitchen.

"I saw ... that's why you had to see it for yourself. See how he scratched out whatever he started to write. What do you think, was he really the Congressman's kid?", she finished standing at the doorway. Janet was wearing a simple white apron over her lounging gown.

"Yes, I think he probably was. It's ironic but I only heard an hour or so ago that Summerfield's legitimate son, Albert claimed he was Doug's brother, so I guess he really was. Let's see if there are any other revelations tucked away in these files. Johnny then reviewed each of Hayes' personnel records. He had graduated from St. John's University with a degree in education and had had a part time summer job during his school years with a well-known legal firm connected to the Democratic Party.

Hayes had studied for a time in England and there were other indications that there was money and power in his background.

"Janet, I think we've found another Summerfield son.", Johnny announced with finality, closing the last of the Hayes personnel records and placing the file face up on the coffee table.

His Jack Daniels glass had begun to sweat leaving a small round puddle on the coffee table. It kind of stuck to the table before he raised it to his mouth. He felt the warm, relaxing glow begin with his first sip of the cold bourbon.

Dolan stood and walked to the French doors. Gazing across the terrace at the night sky now muted with the reflected light from a million City lights, he felt an electric thrill pass through his body.

"I'm doing what I love", he thought. After a bit, he returned to the couch and picked up Larry Carson's records.

It was curious that both he and Carson were born in the same Brooklyn hospital, although Carson was ten years his junior. The only negative notation in his file was a less than satisfactory reference Carson had received from one of his former employers – "took project guidance too personal" it said, otherwise, he was well credentialed. Dolan finished reading the Carson file a minute or two before Janet returned.

"All through?"

He nodded.

It's too chilly for the terrace tonight, come into the dining room for your meal.", she said.

Johnny stood and followed her into the smaller but equally ornate dining room. She had set a place for him and the aroma of the steak and eggs reminded him how hungry he was. There was toast, coffee and fresh orange juice as well.

"Janet you are a wonder – this is great. I really appreciate all the trouble you've gone too."

She beamed and sat watching as he ate with gusto. When he had almost finished, she asked: "Well, were the files any help?"

"Yes, I think they were. Especially Doug's. I'll have to prove that he really is Summerfield's other kid. You know, I met Congressman Summerfield today."

Dolan poured rich cream into his coffee wishing it were tea.

"You did; what's he like. I've read about him and seen him on TV."

"Oh, he's a politician and a leader in every sense. But I didn't like him. Guess I'm getting too judgmental for the news business but after you cut through all the standard Washington bullshit, excuse me – there's still a need to find out if there's any humanity in the politician. I didn't feel that Summerfield really gives a rat's ass about anyone except himself. You know if Hayes was his kid then both of his sons died violently – I don't think he cares. Hayes' ex works for Summerfield. Stunning woman, bright, articulate but another vulture. She and Summerfield probably have something going and from what I heard, it started while she was still married to Doug. How do you figure? A guy's old man screwing his son's wife.", Dolan shook his head.

"What happened to the hard headed, thin lipped reporter who's seen it all Mr. Dolan?"

"I'm not sure that I ever was one Janet. I'm still surprised by dishonesty and total selfishness. Too much Catholic education I guess."

"Does all that education mean that you're totally honest and selfless Johnny?", she asked.

"No, I'm not but I'm not representing a quarter million people in the United States Congress either.", he answered.

"Well, - OK, what's next?", Janet asked, obviously enjoying herself.

"A long meeting with my boss to figure where we want to go with this thing. I've got a pretty good idea why Carson and Hayes were killed but I don't have anything to tie it directly back to Summerfield although there may be a common denominator that links it all together. Summerfield may have ties into a crime cartel here in the City and I believe that Larry and Doug were killed by the Mob."

"You mean he had his own kid killed?", she asked with disbelief.

"Maybe indirectly.", he answered. "But I need more time and some help with solving this thing."

"Will you get it?"

"I don't know but I'll find out before the nights over Janet."

"Can I do anything to help?", she asked.

"You already have."

Dolan left shortly after. He told Janet again how much he appreciated her help and promised to call. He could tell that she liked him and had a sense that if he told her he was gay he'd never see her again, but maybe he was wrong. He did have many women friends and he genuinely liked women. Johnny had never made love to a woman and often wondered what it would be like.

EIGHTEEN

11:10 PM TUESDAY, OCTOBER 25, 1966

As usual, their conversation was brief. Neither man wanted to have anything more than a working relationship with the other. When they spoke, or on the rare occasion met, they were very formal, business like and always brief.

San Fillipo began the late-night telephone conversation.

"My friend says you needed to talk."

"Yes. I wanted to know about our friend Doug's tie in with the Uptown group?", Congressman Summerfield asked.

"I don't know anything at this time but if you want, I'll look into it for you."

Silence.

Summerfield finally replied: "In other words ... eh, your group had no connection with our friend's accident?"

"I don't think we need to discuss that – but if it makes you feel any better – no, my group was not involved."

"Alright, thank you. Goodnight."

"Hold it a minute, how does our project look for Friday?" San Fillipo asked sounding like a boss to an employee who has a deadline to meet.

His tone was not lost on Summerfield who smiled at the question. First the President of the United States and now the Don of the San Fillipo Family, both concerned about Friday's vote.

He suppressed a chuckle and answered: "Secure."

"Goodnight my friend.", San Fillipo answered also emulating Lyndon Johnson by hanging up before Summerfield could respond.

Summerfield was still smiling as he climbed into bed and "spooned" his naked body next to Lydia's back while cupping her breast with his right hand. She squirmed her ass even closer and reaching behind her, placed her hand around his already stiff cock and lifting her leg, slipped it between her thighs.

NINETEEN

12:05 AM WEDNESDAY, OCTOBER 26, 1966

Twenty minutes after leaving Janet Gibbon's, Johnny was seated before Gil's desk briefing him on his afternoon interview with Congressman Summerfield and Lydia Hayes.

"He admitted that he was Allie's father Gil and asked that we not make a public thing of the kid's suicide."

"I have no problem with that. But what about Doug Hayes – did you come up with anything there? Did Summerfield know about Hayes' involvement with the number's racket?"

"No, I don't think he did – but Lydia Hayes knew all about it and I think she may have had a rough time with her boss after I left. She mentioned that Doug told her he was working for the king of policy in New York. A guy in Harlem called the Preacher and … "

Gil abruptly interrupted.

"The Preacher – Johnny that confirms it. We hit the jackpot!", he shouted. "Remember when I told you last night about a friend Uptown at the Amsterdam News. I called and asked him if he knew anything about the Carson and Hayes numbers pick list ad. Well, he knew a hell of a lot. It seems that his paper was contacted by an attorney who fronts for the Preacher. They wanted to know who placed the ad. The News told him. My friend figures our guys were contracted by the Preacher and accepted an offer to be his "consultants" as Mrs. Carson put it.

Now here's the kicker, it appears we now have an old fashion gang war erupting between the Preacher's organization and the San Fillipo Family.", Gil was smiling when he finished telling his little piece of information.

"That's the second time I heard the San Fillipo's mentioned today Gil. A politician friend of mine figures that San Fillipo is the likely challenger to the Preacher's policy monopoly.", Johnny added. "What makes you think they're at war Gil?"

"Well, it's obvious you haven't been listening to TV or the radio news the last five hours Johnny?"

"No, I haven't had time. Why?"

Peterson stood. "I want you to see something. Come on."

Gill moved quickly for a big man and Dolan almost had to run to keep up as they made their way to one of the news bureau screening rooms. Gil called an editor who set up a viewmaster with about fifty feet of film.

"This came in this afternoon when you were on your way back from DC.", Peterson said turning on the equipment and queuing up the film.

There was a voice over describing a murder/fire scene and the four victims who had been found dead in what was probably a house of prostitution. The story indicated that the "house" was reputed to be run by the San Fillipo crime family and that its manager, Sal Caputo was one of the victims. There was film of body bags being loaded into the Coroner's wagon followed by a three second mug shot of Sal Caputo.

"Hold that spot Gil. That's the guy in the crowd at the Carson Hayes body site!", Dolan announced.

"What? Are you sure?", Gil asked, stopping the film at Caputo's photo.

Johnny held the crowd scene photo next to the viewmaster and they compared it with Caputo's mug shot. There was no doubt that this was the same man.

"Johnny my lad, I believe we have the inside track on the gang war angle. As far as I know, neither the cops or anyone else has connected the Carson and Hayes murders to this whorehouse hit and we have it in the bag with the Caputo link. And, we still have the additional angle with Summerfield. What do you think?"

Dolan sighed and thought a minute before speaking.

"My politician friend seems to think that San Fillipo already owns Summerfield so let's kick this around a little."

Peterson pushed his chair back, closed his eyes and locked his hands behind his head as he listened.

Dolan stood and began pacing. "First, we have a black man picking up Carson and Hayes at the Keg on Friday night and most likely bringing them to the same whorehouse where Sal Caputo and his ladies were found this afternoon. The whorehouse angle tends to substantiate our theory that our guys were naked when they were killed – probably had engaged in sex before they were tortured and popped."

The face of Pauline Carson flashed before Johnny. He hoped she would never learn about her husband's stop at San Fillipo's whorehouse.

Dolan continued. "We know that Hayes was killed first since he was colder when they found them. So, they most likely killed Doug Hayes to make Carson tell them where his Single Action program was kept. He tells them and the black guy goes to Guardian Center and walks off with it. Since they got what they wanted, they ace Carson.

We know that Sal Caputo and probably this black guy both work for San Fillipo and I'd bet the black guy is Sal's boss and probably the hitter too. San Fillipo needs a black front man to take charge in Harlem and this dude is a real "take charge guy" – cool under pressure isn't he Gil?"

"Like an MBC News Department executive.", Peterson answered dryly still keeping his eyes closed.

"So, San Fillipo now has the Preacher's Single Action program and the Preacher decides to even things up. He retaliates and blows away San Fillipo's property – Sal Caputo and the girls but maybe not San Fillipo's black hitter. Sounds like a fair trade but I wonder if he got Single Action back when he visited the whorehouse? If he didn't, the shooting war may not be over."

"Now we come to Lydia Hayes and Congressman Summerfield." Peterson interjected.

"Yes, let's not forget the beautiful Mrs. Hayes and dynamic Congressman Summerfield. The Preacher may not know that Doug Hayes' ex works for Summerfield but he certainly knows that Summerfield is San Fillipo's property and San Fillipo is trying to take over his piece of the Policy racket.

Since Summerfield seemed surprised this afternoon when Lydia told me about Doug's involvement with the Preacher, I don't think it was Summerfield who told San Fillipo about Single Action. Gil what could San Fillipo do with Single Action?"

"He could break the Preacher's bank. If Single Action stays good at picking winners, San Fillipo would be able to lay some sizeable bets down on the Preacher's patch and eventually the Preacher would go bust in paying off. Just figure it out if the daily payoff is 600 to 1, and the Single Action hit rate is 50%, it wouldn't take long to break the bank.", Peterson concluded.

"You're right, but just suppose killing Carson and Hayes turns out to be a mistake. Suppose San Fillipo can't get Single Action to work, then what Gil?", Dolan asked.

"Then it's business as usual. The Preacher holds on to Policy and it's still up to San Fillipo to take it away from him. In other words, nobody wins for the time being."

"Ok, then the Preacher has to be sure that San Fillipo doesn't have the edge with Single Action.", Johnny concluded.

"What do you think the Preacher will do next?", Gil asked.

"Nothing if he has the Single Action program and knows how to use it. But if he doesn't, then – he'll have to hit San Fillipo again or trade with him. I think we ought to tell the cops what we have and go public, what do you think Gil?"

TWENTY

6:00 AM WEDNESDAY, OCTOBER 26, 1966

"Yes Daddy, I'll get the car and you can ... ", suddenly Daddy's face was very close to hers and he was speaking but she couldn't understand him. He wanted her to come with him and then they were sitting on the couch and she was on his lap and he was holding her ... and touching her. "No Daddy don't touch me there ... ", she tried to squirm away but she liked what he was doing with his hand between her legs. The warm sensation that started from her vagina and rippled down her legs and up her belly and chest was so nice she didn't want him to stop. She put his arms tightly around his neck and held him tightly. She could smell the witch hazel he always used as after shave. When it came, the orgasm was so strong it lifted her hips from Daddy's lap.

"Larry Carson told me to find the black man.", Daddy whispered to her – but he was using Johnny Dolan's voice. "What?", she heard herself ask. "Do you want to come to the beach with me.", Johnny's voice asked from far away. Daddy was now walking toward her with his arms outstretched waiting for her to come to him.

Janet Gibbon's dream abruptly ended with the wake-up sound of flat buzzing from her alarm clock.

Still languid from her multiple orgasm, she moved her wet fingers from between her legs and ran her hands slowly up her body and placing them above her head ended with a full, wide-awake stretch.

"God!", she thought as she entered the bathroom, "I meet a guy twice and then I'm dreaming that he's finger fucking while masquerading as my father no less. Jesus, what would John Dolan think if I told him about this one? Hmm ... maybe I will."

When Janet arrived at her office later that morning, she remembered something important and first thing, made a call to the Hospital Security Department.

"Hi, this is Janet Gibbon ... is Jack available?"

She had forgotten that there was a separate NIH security file kept for every employee of the hospital and research center and it usually contained much more detailed information then the personnel file she shared with Johnny. Since the Government supported most of the research done at the Center, they made sure that anyone who had access to secret projects went through a deep background check and wasn't a secret employee of some drug company. Janet was able to set up an appointment that afternoon with Jack Spellman, the Security Department head, to review the Hayes file. He told her that the NYPD investigator hadn't asked to see it but should they uncover any important information in the Hayes file he would need to advise them.

TWENTY ONE

9:45 AM WEDNESDAY, OCTOBER 26, 1966

Gil Peterson and John Dolan sat in the MBC News Bureau conference room with Captain Gentner, Detective Al Miller and Detective Sergeant George Horrigan who was the investigating officer assigned to the Carson Hayes homicide. Peterson had contacted a ranking Police Department official during the early morning hours, who in turn organized the meeting with the three detectives. It was obvious to the newsmen that the cops didn't want to be there.

"Coffee guys?", Gil inquired trying to crack the ice.

He ordered coffee and pastries and turned the meeting over to Dolan.

"I want to thank you for coming on such short notice. What we have to show you is important. I think we may have uncovered some information concerning the Carson Hayes murders that you might find useful.", he began.

"What do you have Dolan?", Detective Miller asked suppressing a yawn.

Dolan ignored Miller and made his presentation to the other two policemen. He reviewed his investigation only leaving out the details of Allie Summerfield's death and concluded with the tie in of Carson and Hayes' killings to the whorehouse executions using the Sal Caputo photos.

"So, you see gentlemen, Larry Carson and Doug Hayes may have been the first two victims of a gang war over the control of Policy in the City."

The three officers sat quietly for a minute or two before Captain Gentner broke the silence.

"Are we off the record now Gil?" He directed his question to Peterson.

Gil shot Johnny "what do you think" look, picked up on Dolan's subtle signal and answered Gentner with "We're off the record Captain."

Gentner smiled, raised his hands – palms up and shook his head from side to side. "To tell the truth guys, we had a lead on the gang war angle from the git-go. Carson and Hayes' were dumped in front of an afterhours joint run by the Preacher. At first, we figured the hits had something to do with Policy but once we id'ed Carson and Hayes we just couldn't tie two civilians into the picture. Figured it was some kinda screw up by the jokers who dumped them there."

As Gentner spoke, Johnny remembered the excited young cop talking to his sergeant in Mike Denton's video. Most likely that was a "beat" cop who made the Preacher's Club for the detectives.

Gentner continued. "A street bum gave us a half-assed description of Sal Caputo too. Seems Caputo woke the bum who was camped out behind some garbage cans, when he unloaded the stiffs. We got a positive ID when the bum saw a Caputo's morgue photo. We didn't uncover the Carson Hayes computer angle so thanks for the information – that gives us a motive. As far as Congressman Summerfield goes – that's a hot potato. There's nothing at this time to link him to any of this or Doug Hayes' ex-wife either and I don't think that the Department will even consider allowing the investigation to proceed along those lines. Gentlemen, thanks for the coffee and the information. As usual the Department appreciates your cooperation."

Gentner nodded to his associates and all three stood.

"Captain what you added is off the record of course but I'm going public with the rest of it today.", Gil announced while shaking hands with Gentner.

"That's your business Mr. Peterson.", he answered, shaking Dolan's hand and moving toward the door.

"Nice seeing you again Dolan.", Al Miller said while pointedly ignoring Johnny's outstretched hand.

Johnny shrugged off the insult and directed a parting question at Sergeant Horrigan who had remained silent during the meeting. "Sergeant Horrigan ... any leads on the mechanic?"

Horrigan shook his head in the affirmative, "Yes, I think we might be getting a little closer to the shooter who aced Carson and Hayes.

"Peterson jumped on his answer: "We're still off the record Sergeant. What have you got?"

Gentner interjected: "This information is preliminary guys and is still under investigation and may have nothing to do with anything at this point.", he nodded an OK to Horrigan to proceed. "Go ahead George, tell them.

Horrigan leaned against the door frame and rubbed his eyes.

"We think the hitter is a guy named Bunny Ennis, a real sweetheart. He's probably the only black man in the Mafia – a kind of "Jackie Robinson" of organized crime. The FBI gave us access to wire taps and other surveillance material they've been compiling on San Fillipo. Ennis is a regular visitor to Carmine San Fillipo's hangout in Little Italy and since he tends to stand out in that crowd, he's attracted a lot of interest with the Bureau. There was a killing of a San Fillipo prostitute last night that may have a tie in to the whorehouse massacre. She was a regular at the whorehouse and it could be she set up the hit for the Preacher and Bunny Ennis just evened the score for San Fillipo.

Horrigan paused for a second.

"I saw her body last night. It was a fucking brutal take out. He blew her guts away with dynamite or some heavy-duty fireworks. We have a witness, a neighbor of the girl, who ID'd Ennis from a mug shot. We're out looking for him now."

"Thanks George.", Gentner said. "That's it gentlemen. We'll keep you posted."

After the policemen left, the newsmen stayed on and finished their coffee.

"I think they told us more than we told them.", Gil said with a smile.

"They sure did. They confirmed the gang war angle and tied the Preacher into this thing. Are we really going public today Gil?", Dolan asked.

"Yep, I filled in our Division VP and he thinks we have a shot at the 7 o'clock News. It's your story Johnny but here's how I want you to approach the piece. We play up the gang war that's raging in the City. We cover the murders and we cap it with a loose tie in to Washington using Lydia Hayes. Let's stay away from the Single Action computer program details for now. I want to use that angle for follow up. It's still an MBC exclusive. I also want you to see if you can prove that Doug Hayes was Summerfield's other son."

"You got it boss. What else?"

"Are you up to putting the basics together for tonight or do you want to sack out for a few hours on my couch?"

"I'm OK.", Johnny answered. He was lying since he was exhausted. "Besides it's too damn cold in your office. I couldn't sleep anyway."

This was a major career opportunity for Dolan. The 7 O'clock News meant that his story would go National. Dolan knew from the beginning that Peterson had kept his MBC News brass filled in on their progress. The next step was to put together a coherent story that would be tightly edited and cleared with legal before airing. The connection to Summerfield through Lydia Hayes gave the piece national appeal and would likely cause a stir. Johnny was certain that this is exactly what MBC brass wanted. This was not the first time a "tiny crack" grew into a Grand Canyon and the least that would result from tonight's piece would be follow up interviews with Lydia Hayes and a major investigative effort to somehow link Summerfield with the events. This was how the news business worked. The Press would descend like vultures when the story broke – especially now with the public's interest in Summerfield's Bill since it was so close to a House vote. Dolan knew that the next twenty-four hours were going to be very interesting.

TWENTY TWO

3:48 PM WEDNESDAY, OCTOBER 26, 1966

Bunny Ennis enjoyed his flight from La Guardia to DC National. He had arrived at the airport early, bought his ticket and had a shoe shine and a quick drink before boarding. The flight to DC was smooth and since it was early afternoon, not jammed with passengers. The stewardess thanked him for the twenty he slipped her as she placed his Jack Daniels on his service tray.

He took a cab to Lydia's apartment but detoured and made the driver wait while he completed some grocery shopping at a neighborhood super market. Bunny felt like cooking tonight – not to please Lydia but just because he felt like it.

Lydia's apartment was almost sterile. She had a cleaning service and rarely used it for anything but sleeping. All her mail went to her New York address and she dined out most nights. Bunny knew this so he made sure to buy all that he needed for the meal he planned – a "special" Creole jambalaya using a recipe that he had perfected over the years. He even bought a chicory-based coffee blend to add a special "New Orleans" touch to the meal. Bunny let himself in, hung his jacket and tie in the hall closet and put on a brand-new apron to cover his custom made Sulka shirt. He turned on Lydia's stereo, found a DC soul station, pumped up the volume and began preparing his jambalaya. In a little while the whole apartment was filled with the pleasant odor of spices, chicken, ham, sausage and shrimp mixed with onions and green bell peppers. Bunny continuously tasted the mixture adding a dash of this or a pinch of that until he was satisfied.

He was relaxing in the small kitchen with his first Jack Daniels when Lydia came in.

"Something smells good. My baby been cookin' for his sugar?", she said throwing her arms around him and hungrily kissing his mouth.

"I can't wait to taste what you got for me.", she cried.

Bunny was not a man who gave or took praise but for some reason, felt genuine pleasure in Lydia's reaction. He described the meal he had prepared and the two of them performed like and old married couple while he completed the final touches on his jambalaya as she set the kitchen table.

The meal was exceptional and they made love between their first and second cup of coffee. Both were as relaxed as well-fed cats.

"Bunny, why can't it always be like this with us?"

They were lying naked in each other's arms. The bedroom window was open and a cool evening breeze played across their relaxed bodies. The low sounds of soulful sax came from the stereo next to the bed.

"Because we don't have time for this kind a business baby. We too busy being who we are.", he answered, softly stroking her face.

"Who are you Bunny?", she asked with an innocence that came from somewhere a long way back in her past.

Ennis gave up a hearty baritone laugh.

"I'm the man … I make it happen … I say "let it happen" and it happen. Even when I do the white man's work I do it for me, not for him. I'm the "Bunnyman" baby – that's who I am. Now who the fuck are you?"

He had almost whispered the question.

"Nothing. I'm nothing.", she quietly answered and he understood.

At 7:18, Lydia left her bedroom and a dozing Bunny Ennis; she turned on the TV and tuned to MBC news. The tail end of an airline's commercial gave way to the hang-dog face of David Byrnes.

"And now a story from New York. It seems that the City is embroiled in a shooting gang war that has already claimed as many as seven victims and the end is nowhere in sight. We now turn to our

New York City correspondent, John Dolan who will fill us in on what seems to be the cause of criminal unrest."

Byrnes's image faded to be replaced by Dolan's who was standing with a microphone in front of a building on West 54th Street and 9th Avenue.

"It was just two short weeks ago that the bodies of the first two victims were found here. This is a bloody war that is shaping up between two powerful crime interests now fighting over control of the numbers racket – sometimes called Policy – here in New York City. These first two casualties were really civilians who had been unfortunate to be on the periphery of a Harlem based gang headed by an elusive boss known as the Preacher. Larry Carson and Doug Hayes were legitimate employees of the Preacher's organization and were brutishly murdered because of it and their bodies were dumped here, gangland style, in front of this building – owned by the Preacher."

Dolan paused and the camera panned the Preacher's building.

"Policy, ladies and gentlemen is a business that deals daily in nickels, dimes and quarters but whose profits are annually counted in the millions. Up until now Policy has been the sole domain of Black gangland enterprise. But perhaps for not too much longer, because you see the Mafia wants it for itself and will go to almost any length to rest it away from the Preacher's control."

Mike Denton's film of the Carson Hayes scene filled the screen for ten seconds.

"Within days of the murder of the Preacher's men, Carson and Hayes, double vengeance was visited on the Preacher's most probable protagonist – a house of prostitution allegedly operated by members of the Mafia's San Fillipo family, a leading organized crime cartel operating from the streets of Little Italy here in New York.

Sal Caputo, seen here in the crowd at the Carson Hayes murder was found killed gangland style along with three of the women who worked at the San Fillipo "house". Ironically, it was a fire in a business downstairs that led to the discovery of the grisly aftermath of the quadruple homicide."

The scene of the four body bags flashed on the screen and was immediately followed by an attractive photo of Lydia Hayes and Congressman Summerfield. The image held for about five seconds with Dolan's voice over introducing them.

"This reporter spoke with Lydia Hayes and her boss, Congressman Summerfield just two days ago concerning the violent death and possible involvement of her former husband, Doug Hayes one of the first victims, with the Preacher's Policy organization. Although neither she nor the congressman are involved or associated with any of the criminal elements in this drama, they did shed some light on Doug Hayes' possible relationship with the negro run Policy enterprise in Harlem. Mr. Hayes may have been using his computer programming skills to aid in the selection of winning numbers.

There are other curious angles to this story that even now are being investigated by the New York City Police Department the Federal Bureau of Investigation and MBC Television News. For example, unraveling the mystery that surrounds a young prostitute known to have worked in San Fillipo's house – the same house of prostitution where Sal Caputo, its manager and his three young workers were massacred. This fourth victim was found by police in her West Side apartment yesterday evening terribly brutalized and fatally injured. This twenty-year-old prostitute's name is being withheld pending notification to next of kin. It is thought that this latest victim may have switched allegiance to the Preacher and have been instrumental in the death of her four associates at the San Fillipo's house. She may have been murdered in retaliation."

The image of Dolan's face filled the screen. "But only one thing is known for certain – that the brutal gang warfare recently begun here in New York City is not over."

Dolan's image faded, replaced by a pensive David Byrnes who gazed into the camera a few seconds before speaking in his trade mark, halting voice. "Thank you for your report Johnny ... and now ... this commercial message."

Dolan's piece had taken 2:54 minutes of air time and Lydia Hayes knew her life would never be the same because of it.

She now understood that she was responsible for Doug and Larry's murder and intuitively knew that the man lying in her bed was their killer. She also sensed that Fredrick Douglass Summerfield's career as well as her own was destined for ruin.

All this Lydia knew in less than the three minutes it took John Dolan to tell his story.

She was not at all surprised when her telephone rang. It was Fredrick calling and she knew what he was going to say. "Hello Fredrick."

"Has anyone from the Press contacted you?", he said in a strangely calm voice.

"No Fredrick but I expect they will."

"Alright good. Now don't talk with anyone and meet me at the office in half an hour Do you understand?", he said emphatically.

"Yes.", she responded.

The phone went dead. Lydia hung up, letting the receiver drop to its cradle with an air of finality.

"Who the fuck was that?", Bunny shouted at Lydia's naked back as she crossed the bedroom on her way to the bathroom.

She was more frightened than she had ever been. She was trapped between two very powerful men – each about to begin a struggle for their existence but only she recognized that each would be fighting for a lost cause. Ennis worked for the white man and therefore, would be sacrificed without regard; Summerfield believed in his own power and destiny and was blinded by arrogance.

Lydia knew that either could destroy her and she felt powerless to stop them. Her first test would come in the next ten minutes. Would Bunny let her leave? She had been the one who told him about the success of Larry Carson's Single Action computer program and she told him of Doug's bragging about them working for the Preacher. She knew about Bunny's involvement with the San Fillipo Family and their hold on Summerfield. Eventually Ennis, Summerfield or San Fillipo would realize that she was the potential "weak link" that could break and pull them all down.

She had to stay calm and keep her wits.

"That was Fredrick baby.", she shouted from the bathroom. "There's some problem with the Bill and wants to talk about it now … at the office."

She finished dressing in the semi-dark bedroom and came to Bunny who was still lying on her bed.

Lydia leaned down and kissed him on his lips. "I'll be back in a couple of hours baby – keep the bed warm."

Bunny smiled without opening his eyes and turned back to sleep. Lydia left her apartment for the last time and took a taxi to National.

There was only one man who could save her life and he was in New York City.

TWENTY THREE

Fredrick Douglass Summerfield was furious.

"How dare she not come when I call her!", he thought, while placing his key into her apartment door lock. It clicked open and he let himself in.

"Lydia! Lydia where are you?", he shouted, first sniffing and then recognizing the lingering odor of Creole cooking.

The stereo played softly in the empty and darkened living room as Summerfield walked toward the stick of light glowing dimly from beneath the closed bedroom door. "She's still getting dressed, damn it!", he thought and had barely entered the semi-darkened room when he was struck across the back of his head, dropping him like a condemned building to the hard wood floor.

"Stay the fuck where you are if you want to live another minute." Bunny Ennis said menacingly to the man who now lay prone at his feet.

"Wha ... " Shaking his head to clear the pain, Summerfield attempted to stand and was viciously kicked in his side sending him sprawling across the floor.

His face was now even with the bottom of Lydia's bed and he could smell dust and taste blood on his lips. A hot tear squeezed from his right eye and slowly rolled down his cheek to fall noiselessly to the bedroom floor.

"I told you not to move shit for brains!"

The harsh command seemed to come from outer-space but it registered and Summerfield lay perfectly still. He supposed that Lydia had been attacked by this madman and was lying dead somewhere in the apartment. He would do as he was told and prayed he would live. Keeping his eyes closed he slowed his breathing; his side hurt more than his head and he sensed that one or more of his ribs had been broken.

Bunny bent and removed the wallet from the intruder's jacket and discovered that the man lying at his feet was none other than Congressman Fredrick Douglass Summerfield.

"So, you the Summerfield mother fucker.", he said. "Where's Lydia at?"

"Lydia?", Summerfield answered timidly, still keeping his eyes closed as if not seeing his attacker would prevent further harm.

"You deaf – yeah, where's Lydia? Look the fuck at me when I'm talking!", Bunny loudly demanded.

Summerfield opened his eyes and even in the dim bedroom light recognized the menace, his face now inches from his. "I … I thought she was here. I expected to see her at the office about an hour ago. When she didn't show up, I called her here but no one answered. Are you … are you Lydia's friend Ennis?"

"I'm Ennis. Now get the fuck up.", Bunny ordered taking two steps backward from the prostrate man.

Summerfield stood slowly, holding his injured side. He dared another quick look at Ennis and then quickly hung his head.

"You want a drink Summerfield?", Ennis asked in a much softer voice.

"Yes. Thank you – scotch." Bunny's offer calmed Summerfield and he followed him into the living room. Ennis was wearing only undershorts. Summerfield had always suspected that Lydia was intimate with Ennis but he hadn't much cared as long as it didn't interfere with their business and personal relationship.

Summerfield had refused to meet with Ennis and insisted that Lydia handle all contacts. Bunny Ennis was an animal, one of San Fillipo's thugs and the beating he had just received confirmed it. Although Summerfield didn't believe he was in any further danger he decided to tread lightly.

Ennis turned on the living room lights and now stood by the liquor cabinet. Summerfield waited by the bedroom. "Were you here when Lydia left for my office?", he asked re-gaining his composure.

Ennis ignored the question and finished fixing his drink. He then sat heavily on the couch, legs spread before him and motioned toward the liquor cabinet.

"Fix your scotch."

Summerfield did as he was told and stood – and leaning forward to ease the pain, slowly sipped the "neat" double Johnny Black. It tasted warm and smooth and quickly numbed the throbbing pain spreading over the left side of his body.

Ennis watched the politician with amusement. Bunny knew this man, this "negro leader", and was not impressed with what he saw. Summerfield looked old in his pain and was paunchy fat. Bunny knew he was frightened of him and would make him squirm. "You said Lydia never got to the office Senator.", Ennis said loudly.

Summerfield lowered his glass and quickly answered. "Yes, never arrived. By the way, I'm not a Senator; I'm a Congressman. I called her in to discuss the Dolan report on the Hunter Byrnes news tonight. Eh, what did you think of it Ennis?"

"I don't know what the fuck you talkin' about Senator.", Ennis answered with obvious contempt.

It was then that Summerfield realized Lydia had bolted. She probably knew she'd be in danger when Ennis learned the newscast report details. Quickly assessing the potential damage Lydia's leaving offered, he realized that it was considerable. San Fillipo had to be warned.

"I'm afraid Lydia may have gone to the police Ennis, or perhaps to that MBC reporter, John Dolan.", Summerfield announced as calmly as he could – not wanting to set Bunny off.

"Look Mr. Big Shot, just tell me what's happening.", he loudly demanded. Ennis was on his feet and in Summerfield's face.

"Calm down, calm down Ennis or should I call you Bunny?" Summerfield pleaded.

"Call me whatever the fuck you want but tell me what's happening. Where did Lydia go and why?"

Ennis shoved Summerfield causing him to wince before returning to his place on the couch.

Summerfield finished his drink and quickly fixed another. The liquor helped. "Bunny, I think we have a serious problem.", he began. "Obviously you didn't see the report on MBC's 7 O'clock News tonight. John Dolan – eh, do you know who he is?"

"I know who the fuck he is. What about him?"

"Good. Well Dolan did a story tonight about a gang war in the City that's supposed to be between Carmine and the Preacher. He also brought Lydia and me into it through her former husband's relationship to the Preacher's organization."

Summerfield then recounted the specifics of the Dolan piece, leaving nothing out. Ennis kept a steady gaze on Summerfield which he found un-nerving. When Summerfield finished, he took a long taste of scotch and grimaced as he slowly lowered himself into the chair facing Ennis.

"So why do you think Lydia split? Maybe she got hit by a truck on her way to see you.", Bunny asked sarcastically.

"It would be best for all of us if she had.", Summerfield answered. "But Lydia knows the Press will hound the hell out of us from here on and she must have been concerned about them finding out something." As Summerfield spoke, he reasoned that Lydia probably believed she would be connected to San Fillipo through Ennis. Once that was made public the whole thing would come tumbling down like a house of cards.

"There ain't nothing for them to find out Summerfield. I think you full of shit. Lydia probably on her way back here right now."

"Oh, she ran alright.", Summerfield replied with conviction. "I think we can prove it rather quickly Bunny; would you be so kind as to hand me the telephone, I'm having a little trouble moving right now."

Summerfield then called the reservations desk at Eastern and learned that Lydia had just departed on the shuttle flight for New York. He sighed as he placed the telephone receiver back onto its cradle and kept his head lowered while updating Ennis.

"She's heading back to the City but her plane hasn't landed yet. Do you think Carmine could send some people to meet her Bunny?"

"Shit! Fucking bitch ... ", Ennis cursed as he dialed an unlisted number in New York. He spoke with Carmine and explained the situation. Carmine then asked to speak with Summerfield who reluctantly took the telephone.

"Yes, Carmine I think she can cause a great deal of trouble for all of us. I don't want to know anything about your business but did Lydia tell you or Bunny here about her former husband and his partner's relationship with the Preacher?"

Carmine answered his question and Summerfield looked disdainfully at Bunny.

"I understand what you're saying Carmine but we have to protect our position for Friday's vote.", Summerfield reminded San Fillipo. "Bunny and I will wait here until you get back to us on Lydia." He then gave Carmine Lydia's telephone number and continued. "Yes, what do you think we should do? Hmm, I see ... "

Listening to the one-sided conversation, Bunny felt heat rising in his guts. "Who the fuck do these two assholes think they be playing with?", he thought. He didn't appreciate being the subject of their conversation and left out on the planning. He stood and without a word pulled the telephone from Summerfield's hand.

"Go and fuckin' get Lydia at La Guardia Carmine!", Ennis shouted into the mouthpiece.

A surprised San Fillipo stammered back. "Eh ... yeah ... we'll get that bitch Ennis. Now I want to ..."

Bunny cut him off. "You're wastin' time. She be landing in twenty-five minutes Carmine."

Ennis slammed the phone down. "You big shots fuckin' love the sound of your voices don't you Summerfield?", he said this inches away from the congressman's face and then returned to his place on the couch.

It took Summerfield a moment to regain his composure. "I think you made a mistake speaking to Carmine like that Bunny." Summerfield sounded as if he were correcting a rude child.

"Fuck him. You two big ass mother-fuckers would have bull shited all night if I didn't stop you. Carmine got to get the bitch before she get surrounded by the cops or hid out somewhere by that TV news guy. You dig what I'm sayin' to you?"

"I understand. Let me ask you – did Lydia tell you about her husband's relationship with the Preacher?"

Ennis grinned. "The bitch tell me a everything Summerfield. She be a regular polly parrot after you fuck her good. Like to spill the beans so to speak." Bunny yawned and began scratching his crotch. "Do she talk about me after you fuck her or do she just roll over and go to sleep?"

Summerfield seemed unable or unwilling to answer. He never considered Lydia's life outside of their relationship. In his egotistical mind – she only existed for him.

Bunny smiled at Summerfield's obvious confusion and shook his head. "No, from the looks of you – you be doin' the rollin' over. Go fuck yourself Senator. It none of your business anyway."

"Look Ennis, cooperate. I'm trying to save our lives. If Lydia talks, she'll implicate us all. She has information – dates, dollars paid, the works. She'll take us all down to save herself. I just want to know what she told you."

"It don't matter what Lydia told me Senator. She already be a dead woman."

"She's not dead unless we catch her Bunny.", Summerfield responded.

TWENTY FOUR

Lydia's flight to New York City arrived ten minutes late. The minor delay gave Billy G. and Johnny Trips enough time to be at her gate as the passengers deplaned. Carmine had no concerns about getting men to La Guardia in time. He already had them there working as baggage handlers.

Billy G. and Johnny Trips had sweetheart union jobs and didn't really work, they just "hung around" the terminal and watched what was coming in to the City since the San Fillipo Family was always interested in cargos of value. Nobody in the Baggage Handler's Union ever complained about these two. Who could they complain too – San Fillipo controlled their Union?

Carmine had described Lydia to Billy G. and there was no mistaking the tall, attractive black women now coming down the walkway.

The two low level hoods were instructed only to watch and make no move to take her out. If she was met, they were to call Carmine immediately. The airport was always busy and had too much security for attempting a snatch. San Fillipo wanted Lydia watched and when the opportunity presented itself, his people would grab her. A public hit was out of the questions since it would bring further attention.

Lydia sensed she was being followed as she made her way toward the main terminal. She expected Summerfield to sound the alarm when she left Washington so she had made a hurried telephone call from National and had been instructed to take the commuter bus from La Guardia into the City where she was told she would be met.

"Hey Gino, tell Carmine the gash just got on the bus to the City and Billy G. is stayin' with her. He'll call in when they get there.",

Johnny Trips hung up the public telephone and true to his nick name clumsily tripped over the briefcase placed on the ground by the caller at the next phone.

Lydia made the idiot in the blue baggage handlers uniform the minute he got on the bus. She had seen him and another dumbo at her gate area and suspected they were San Fillipo goons. She didn't believe this man now seated two rows behind her would attempt anything during the forty-five-minute trip to New York City.

The real danger was from his idiot partner who had most likely alerted San Fillipo where she was headed. "I should have taken a cab.", she thought.

Lydia would have felt safer if she had known that two new "friends" were seated within touching distance. The young couple that seemed to the world as if they were returning from their honeymoon had also made San Fillipo's blue garbed soldier. They would make certain he wasn't going to cause any trouble.

Just after the bus passed through the Queen's Mid-town Tunnel and only minutes away from its destination, the "bride" stood and began making her way toward the toilet at the rear of the bus.

When she came even with Billy G., she stopped and looked down at him, as if she were about to ask a question. He looked up at her shiny smiling face and when she pointed to the ceiling, Billy G.'s gaze naturally followed her finger, exposing his throat. The straight razor the bride held securely in her right hand flashed even in the bus's dimly lit interior and Billy G.'s hot gushing arterial blood erupted and then squirted obscenely in rhythmic pulses over windows, seats and startled passengers. The soon to be dead soldier slumped forward, head now resting on the back of the seat in front of his, and with sickening gurgling sounds coming from his severed throat tried vainly to stand.

The "groom" who had watched his bride at work, now stood and quickly moved to the bus driver, roughly shoving a very large pistol into his ribs. "Please stop at the corner sir.", he politely asked and pointed to the deserted street ahead. "We've decided to get off here. Oh, and please leave immediately after we exit the bus. Thank you."

He punctuated his order by patting the seated man on top of his bald head.

The nervous driver followed instructions and angled the bus over to the curb and quickly opened the door.

"The Preacher wants you to come with us.", the bride whispered to Lydia who nodded, stood and followed quickly between the exiting couple.

As the bus pulled away, its place was immediately taken by a black Caddy limo – headlights off. Its right rear door opened allowing entry to the two women and man who waited, then closed with a solid thump as it drove off heading in an "uptown" direction.

TWENTY FIVE

"Yeah?", Ennis growled into the telephone receiver.

"Ennis you fuck,", it was Carmine San Fillipo, the boss of the San Fillipo Family, a man to be respected, speaking with a passion he rarely allowed himself, "the Preacher snatched your girlfriend! Tell Summerfield and then get your ass back here – and don't go near your fuckin' apartment, the cops are watchin' it. Call me as soon as you get in!"

The telephone clicked dead. Bunny shrugged and looked over at Summerfield who was half drunk and in obvious agony with his broken ribs. Summerfield raised his head and focused his bloodshot eyes on Ennis.

"Was that Carmine? Did he get Lydia? What happened?", he croaked.

"Yeah, that was the "man". He let Lydia get snatched away by the Preacher. You look like shit Summerfield; want another drink?"

Summerfield shook his head no. In spite of his less than sober condition, he fully comprehended what he had just been told. He forced his head to clear and for the first time in the last two hours showed Ennis some of the toughness it took to become a United States Congressman.

Forcing himself to his feet he slowly and painfully made his way to the apartment door and when he stood by the door for a second and turned toward Ennis; it appeared as if he was going to say something in parting. Instead, he just left and allowed the door to close on its own.

Ennis sat staring at the door a few minutes before going into the bedroom to dress. He figured that Carmine would fuck up the snatch. The only surprise was Carmine's information that the cops had staked out his apartment. He wondered who fingered him. "Lydia?", he thought. "not likely." He wasn't concerned. Nobody had anything on him.

TWENTY SIX

Dolan had finished his Hunter Byrnes piece and at 3:30 am and went back to his apartment to sack out for a few hours. The incessant ringing of his bedroom telephone ended his deep dreamless sleep.

He sat up reached for the receiver and was fully awake when he answered. "Hello."

"Hello Johnny it's Brian."

"Brian ... hey buddy. What's up?" Dolan turned on the lamp and checked the time on the mantle clock across the room. He had slept almost three hours and felt good as he stretched out the kinks.

"I saw your piece on Hunter Byrnes and wanted to give you some advance warning. I spoke with a friend at Justice and it seems you may have tweaked some DC noses out of joint when you mentioned Congressman Summerfield's name. The White House's early warnings alarm went off and they've already jumped on the president of MBC News about irresponsible reporting. They're paranoid right now Johnny because of the importance of Friday's vote on Summerfield's Bill."

"Tough turkey Brian; we had every right to identify Summerfield's staffer's connection to Doug Hayes. The piece was cleared by MBC News council too, so let 'em bitch."

"I think they're concerned about the media follow up. You put a lot of pressure on all concerned to uncover why these two guys were murdered and who did it. And there's always the possibility further disclosures might implicate Summerfield or at the least – Lydia Hayes."

Dolan decided to tell Brian all he had uncovered thus far. When he finished recounting what he had learned, he waited for Toth's response.

"Johnny you're sitting on a time bomb. If it turns out that Doug Hayes was in fact Summerfield's son, people are going to be looking for a political motive for these killings along with the Mafia connection. What do your people plan to do next? Are you cooperating with the NYPD and the FBI on this?"

"Yeah. We're cooperating with the cops, but far too much in my opinion – they don't share shit with us and as far as MBC brass are concerned, they agree with my boss who wants to go "full" public tonight with the Single Action program tie in. You know Bri, computers are something most people don't understand and the reality that somebody figured out how to use them for beating gambling odds should create a high level of public interest. What do you think Brian?"

"I agree – it would be an interesting angle; but what about your original angle – that Carson and Hayes were murdered because they were gay?"

"I don't believe that Larry Carson was gay and I'm still not 100% sure about Doug Hayes, he may have been gay, but I really don't know." Johnny wouldn't reveal what Congressman Sadler had confessed about his relationship with Doug Hayes.

"And I doubt if they were killed because someone thought they were gay. I can't prove it but I think it was their tie in to the Preacher with their Single Action program that in all likelihood cause their deaths. Listen Brian, I have to go. Call me if you hear anything else and thanks for the tip on the White House bitch, I appreciate it."

Dolan rubbed his eyes, now fully awake.

"No sense in trying to sleep now." He thought. "A cup of tea would be just the thing."

TWENTY SEVEN

The "newlyweds" had taken Lydia to a new high-rise on West 120th Street, a location less than a mile from Monica's apartment where she had been brutally killed by Bunny Ennis the day before.

Lydia Hayes was instantly at ease in her new surroundings, a luxuriously furnished penthouse with a magnificent view of uptown New York, dominated by the George Washington Bridge. She stood at the huge windows that rose floor to ceiling and watched, fascinated by the steady movement of headlights from hundreds of vehicles slowly making their way between New York and New Jersey.

The Bridge's graceful arches were further accentuated by thousands of red, blue and yellow lights fixed along its cables and glowing brightly on this crisp October night. She felt safe and protected in this uptown Manhattan tower, safe from Summerfield, San Fillipo and even Bunny Ennis.

Lydia didn't hear the slight, middle aged black man enter. He watched her a full minute standing there by the window. When he cleared his throat announcing his presence, she gracefully turned and smiled warmly almost as if she had known he had been secretly watching.

"Good evening Mrs. Hayes.", he said in a well-modulated and educated voice. Lydia quickly crossed the room and took her host's extended hand in hers.

"How are you? Is there anything that you might need?" he asked, gazing into her deep green eyes and thinking she was the most beautiful women he had ever met.

Lydia took in her host's appearance. He was dressed in a dark conservative business suit accentuated with a subdued tie and gold accessories. Smiling and relaxed, he seemed genuinely pleased in meeting her. She guessed he was about 45, slight build but he carried himself with that certain commanding presence she instantly recognized from long exposure to the shakers and movers in Washington.

But she couldn't know that the Preacher was also a complete gentleman. It was a quality instilled by parents who prided themselves in their gentle and very correct behavior. His father had been a Methodist minister and his mother an outspoken voice for black equality in a generation where even white women were treated with prejudice.

"I'm fine now … safe, and have everything I need, thank you sir. You saved my life." Lydia finally answered.

The Preacher was further taken in by the rich full sound of her voice. This woman possessed a rare combination of ripe, sexuality combined with obvious intellect. "Are you comfortable here then?"

"I am quite comfortable.", she answered. "This is such a magnificent apartment and thank you for helping me on such short notice."

She released his hand as he pointed toward the set of facing couches placed before the dancing and inviting fire glowing in the mahogany and marble fireplace. He waited until she was seated before taking his place across from her. He then lifted the silver tea pot from the low-slung table between them.

"Would you care for tea Mrs. Hayes?"

"Yes, that would be very nice. Thank you."

The Preacher prepared their tea and sighed softly after sipping from his cup. "Ah, there's nothing quite like a hot cup of tea on a cold Fall night." He placed his cup on the table and leaned forward, "Why have you come to me Mrs. Hayes?"

"I needed help and there was no one else.", she answered.

He admired her quick, "matter of fact" response.

"Oh, surely you could have sought help from the police or perhaps even Mr. Dolan from MBC."

Lydia placed her cup and saucer on the table, sat back on the plush couch and crossed her shapely legs. She noticed the Preacher's gaze followed each body movement. "Going to the police would end my career and Mr. Dolan is only interested in what "gossip" he can tell his public Sir."

The Preacher smiled and shook his head in agreement.

"Please call me Preacher, Mrs. Hayes. Yes, you're certainly correct in your expectations from the media but I'm curious – what do you mean "going to the police would end your career"?"

Looking directly at the still smiling Preacher, Lydia un-crossed her legs and leaning forward asked, "Let me first ask you a question if I may?"

"Certainly?"

"Did my late husband actually work for you?"

"Yes, but only for a short time."

"Did you have anything to do with his death Preacher?", she asked; her voice still retaining a certain pleasantness.

"No.", he calmly responded.

"Do you know who killed Doug?"

"Yes, I do."

She waited for him to continue, when he didn't, she then asked: "Would you tell me? It would help me to decide what I must do."

"Doug Hayes and his partner were killed by someone whom I understand is very close to you Mrs. Hayes. He's an associate of Carmine San Fillipo – Bunny Ennis."

There were still a few things that could surprise her and Lydia was genuinely surprised at this revelation. It wasn't as if she didn't believe Bunny was in-capable of violence but somehow, she assumed being close to him acted as a talisman in protecting her and the people around her. She now understood how wrong she had been. Also, the Preacher's information confirmed that she had been correct in leaving Washington. If he knew about her relationship with Bunny, others certainly would as well.

Lydia also realized that she caused Larry and Doug's death. She told Bunny about the Single Action program and how successful it had been. Now she remembered other things she had confided – information that could hurt Fredrick and more importantly, hurt her.

The Preacher was quick to notice the change in Lydia's demeanor; "she didn't fully suspect Bunny Ennis killed her former husband.", he thought, "she's off balance."

Lydia regained her composure. "Preacher, I came to you because you are the only one who can protect me and I hope, appreciate my potential. If I were dragged down with Fredrick there would never be another opportunity for me to reach my objective, which is to be the first black woman to serve in the United States Congress. If I went to the police, I would be forced to tell all I know about Congressman Summerfield's involvement with Carmine San Fillipo and explain my relationship with Bunny Ennis."

The Preacher looked at this woman sitting across from him. She had intelligence, beauty and ambition and perhaps a perfect sense of timing as well; he was ready to take on San Fillipo's Washington connections and she could be his most important asset.

"And if I might ask, just what is or rather – was your relationship with Mr. Ennis in regards to Congressman Summerfields activities?", he asked.

Lydia had made her decision, there was no reason to hold back anything. "Initially, he was our contact man with San Fillipo. Fredrick would pass information on to me to relay to Bunny who would coordinate with San Fillipo. Later on, he and I became intimate … there's no use in denying it, and I was the one who told Bunny about Doug working for you. I guess you already surmised that. I honestly didn't believe that Bunny would have used that information or could I ever imagine that he would have murdered Doug."

Lydia picked up her cup and took a small sip. "Doug was Frederick's illegitimate son. Did you know that Preacher?"

"No, I didn't know. Is that why you and he married?", he asked in response.

"It was a part of the reason.", she answered. "Doug and I met in college; I was attending law school at St. John's and he was a political science major there. He was smart, funny and I liked the positive way he delt with life. We were seeing each other for almost a year before he told me about his father."

"I see. Young love with an added bonus for your career objective. Did you graduate law school Mrs. Hayes?"

Lydia began to feel that she was being interviewed for a job, but perhaps the most important in her life. "Yes.", she answered. "and I passed the New York State Bar as well. I also have a graduate degree in political science."

The Preacher's brow wrinkled in approval. "And when was the last time you saw our friend Mr. Ennis?"

"I was with Bunny last night during John Dolan's report. Fortunately, he didn't hear it or I might not be sitting here. Bunny is a very passionate man and I'm afraid of him."

"Ennis is a thug and a maniacal killer. When I saw Mr. Dolan's report this evening Mrs. Hayes, I anticipated difficulty for Congressman Summerfield when your name was mentioned. But candidly, I don't understand what advantage would accrue to me should I offer you my assistance."

Lydia had considered how she would respond to the Preacher's questions from the moment she decided to contact him five hours earlier in Washington.

She lifted the delicate tea cup to her lips, sipped and then placed it on the table before her.

"Preacher, I have a great deal of information that would most likely eliminate further competition from Carmine San Fillipo."

"Carmine San Fillipo doesn't concern me Mrs. Hayes.", he answered with certainty. His answer caught her by surprise and the Preacher recognized the second flash of confusion registering and then fading from Lydia's magnificent emerald eyes.

He continued. "What does interest me is your political ambition. This country has no elected black political leaders who have the negro peoples interests at heart."

Lydia started to speak and he held up his hand, "Yes I know that we have Malcom X, Carmichael, the Reverend King and many others; but with the exception of King, they are merely black cult leaders who'll quickly fade into obscurity. The Reverend King's movement does have a broader base appeal but his charisma is much like our former President's and his movement will not succeed him I'm afraid."

"I disagree.", Lydia quietly responded.

"History will prove one of us right I'm sure. Now let's consider your personal ambition, indeed the first and last woman elected to the Senate was Margaret Chase Smith in 1949; and she was white. I don't believe the Country is ready for a negro, excuse me, black women in the U.S. Congress – it will someday, certainly in your lifetime Mrs. Hayes." He paused and then continued.

"Now Summerfield of course has his following and has convinced many whites that he speaks for the black minority. You and I know better Mrs. Hayes. His motivation is self-interest and should his interests happen to coincide with his constituency, well so much the better. You could help me since I would be most interested in channeling Summerfield's efforts for the betterment of our people. If you commit to accomplish that objective Mrs. Hayes, perhaps I would be able to support your political ambitions when the time is more opportune."

"Fredrick is on the brink of ruin Preacher. I'm not sure his career can be saved.", Lydia answered with conviction.

"Why don't you allow me an opportunity to evaluate the current situation Mrs. Hayes. Now you must be tired, may I suggest we speak again tomorrow."

"I think we may not have the luxury of waiting until tomorrow Preacher. This would be the best time to begin our planning."

"As you wish. I suggest we start with a telephone call to Congressman Summerfield. He's probably realized that you are under my protection and I want him to know that my protection is available to him as well."

There was no answer at Summerfield's home and Lydia hung up after the tenth ring. "He's either not at home or not answering his telephone."

"No matter. He'll be there eventually and we'll reason with him. Let me have the telephone – there's someone I know is in and will be happy to speak with me."

The Preacher checked the telephone number he was calling in his black leather-bound address book. He was right, the number had barely been dialed when it was answered.

"Yes.", the Preacher began. "Please ask Carmine to come to the phone. Carmine San Fillipo. Tell him the Preacher wants to speak with him. Thank you."

The Preacher winked at Lydia who sat in rapt attention.

"Carmine! How are you my friend? Yes, this is really the Preacher. I know this call is a surprise – but life is full of surprises, isn't it?"

Lydia listened to the one-sided conversation and felt deep admiration for the Preacher. He was fighting for his life and now speaking with his enemy as if they were old friends.

"Yes Carmine, Mrs. Hayes has decided to spend some time visiting. That's the reason I called. If you are available this evening, I think we should meet; there are many things we need to discuss."

San Fillipo made a suggestion to which the Preacher quickly responded. "That will be fine, I'm sure. Just you and I at our meeting of course. By the way Carmine – Mrs. Hayes has confided some very interesting details about your business relationship with Congressman Summerfield and she's anxious to discuss this information with the Press and the police as well. I've prevailed upon her not to be so hasty and she promised she will comply with my suggestion. But I don't know if she'll remain compelled if I were not to be around to provide her with guidance and my protection."

They spoke for another minute and the Preacher was obviously pleased with himself when he hung up. Lydia sat waiting for him to share his plan.

"Well Mrs. Hayes.", he began while pouring himself a fresh cup of tea, "I believe that Congressman Summerfield will soon be working on my behalf."

"That's fine Preacher.", she commented, "but can I expect your support in my career objectives?"

"Mrs. Hayes, I plan to be your most devoted supporter and I promise you will have every opportunity to attain your ambition.

But you and I must work together. Let's start with a quick review of what San Fillipo expects to gain if HR 4800 is passed this Friday shall we."

"Are you meeting with him?"

"Yes. In about an hour.", he answered.

"Forgive me, but is that wise?"

"It's the best thing for me to do. Since you and I are working together San Fillipo will not attempt any overt action for fear you will bring him down. I intend to take Summerfield away from him tonight and he'll have to go along with it. I'll also make him back off on his attempt to take over my Policy organization."

Lydia stood and walked to the window. The Preacher went to her and standing behind her placed his hands on her shoulders.

"I know you're concerned about your safety Mrs. Hayes, ... Lydia, but you are well protected here. The only access to this apartment is with my private elevator and you need a special key to use it. I have five men stationed in the lobby and at the elevator door in the hall. There's also two cars that constantly patrol three blocks in every direction around this building and I'll provide you with a pistol should you wish."

"That's just the point Preacher, I'm your pawn. As long as you have me, your organization is protected from San Fillipo and you'll gain control of Fredrick. Where does that leave me? I'll be your prisoner the rest of my life."

"Trust me Lydia ... you are not my prisoner, you're my partner. I too like Dr. King, have a dream which I'll share with you soon. Oh, and if you're concerned about Bunny Ennis, don't be. His elimination will be part of my arrangement with San Fillipo. Now help me, tell me as much as you can about Summerfield's arrangement with San Fillipo."

TWENTY EIGHT

For once, Bunny Ennis did as he was told. After arriving at La Guardia, he picked up his Caddy and drove directly to Carmine's Club in Little Italy. He parked a block away and now stood across the street hidden in the shadows of the doorway of a closed bakery.

Bunny expected trouble. He knew San Fillipo would hold him responsible for everything, including Lydia's disappearing act. It wasn't his problem that Carmine couldn't get Single Action to work, and it wasn't his fault that Lydia was most likely sleeping in the Preacher's bedroom at the moment he was freezing his balls off trying to figure out how he should handle San Fillipo.

Bunny expected that they would try to take him out. How different it was now from last year when he was welcomed with open arms by the San Fillipo Family. He had some "special friends" hijack a truck loaded with a hundred thousand dollars' worth of bonded liquor and had "given" it to Carmine as his initiation fee into the Family.

He remembered their first face to face meeting. "I want to be the "Man" Uptown.", he told Carmine who answered, "I gotta tell you, you're one ballsie nigger Ennis. Stick with me, I'll make you the "Man".

That was history, now he was a major liability to the Family especially since the cops were looking for him. There might still be a chance if he could convince Carmine that he was the only one able to grab the Preacher's Uptown Policy patch. Bunny's immediate problem at the moment was he had no fire power. He had dumped the piece used on Sal and the girls; all he had was Sal's blade which he now clasped tightly in the pocket of his overcoat.

He expected to be patted down when he entered the Club and since Carmine usually had two or three men with him at all times, there wasn't much he could do against three guns with a switch blade anyway. If he could get Carmine alone there might be a chance for him. For the moment Bunny could only "guts" out this meeting with San Fillipo since he knew there was no running or hiding out from the Mafia.

Bunny filled his lungs with a deep breath of icy morning air and pulling his overcoat tightly around him, started from the doorway at the instant the front of the Club suddenly lit up.

Quickly stepping back into the doorway shadows, he watched. The powerful outside lights had been turned on and when the door opened ten seconds later, two men exited, first looking up and down the empty street. Neither was San Fillipo. They then turned and walked quickly in the direction of the garage where the San Fillipo cars were kept. Bunny noticed that the Club's front door was still open a crack and he glimpsed occasional movement behind it; probably someone waiting for the car to pull up out front.

"It might be Carmine.", Bunny thought; this was the chance he needed. He ran across the street and hit the door hard with full force of his shoulder knocking Gino Fonduci, Carmine's nephew, flat on his ass.

When the kid tried to rise, Bunny kicked him hard in faced and snapped Gino's head back against the floor. His "lights" went out forever and now he looked like some cartoon character with "X's" for eyes and Bunny chuckled softly as he turned and locked the Club's front door.

Reaching down, he removed the piece from Gino's shoulder holster and checked the chamber. It was a light weight 9mm Beretta "Cougar" 934 armed with a full seven shot clip.

Bunny hefted its weight, slipped the safety and walked down the semi-dark hall searching for Carmine. Less than thirty seconds had passed since he bolted from his hiding place across the street and except for a low grunt from a surprised Gino as he hit the deck, there was no other noise that would alert Carmine that anything was wrong.

Bunny stopped cold when he heard the flushing toilet followed by the click of a light switch and the squeaky opening of the Club's private bathroom door.

"Taking a pee pee before you go bye-bye Carmine? No time to wash up?"

Carmine San Fillipo stood in the hallway still adjusting the zipper of his pants. He was wearing his overcoat and a shocked expression. "What the fuck! Ennis you scared the shit out of me – how did you get ..."

Carmine then noticed Gino's lifeless body lying in the front room.

"Sorry about Gino; nothing personal Carmine. I thought you and me should have a quiet conversation with no interruptions so I put Gino to sleep.", Bunny said.

Carmine turned and started to run toward the rear of the building but he had slowed down with the extra thirty-five pounds he now carried and wasn't agile enough to stop Bunny Ennis from grabbing him around his neck and shoving the blue barreled Beretta into his nose.

"Hey where the fuck you goin' Carmine? You got to go to the can again?"

Bunny patted Carmine down and as he expected found he was light.

"Or maybe you runnin' for your piece Carmine? Is that it ... you got a piece down in your office and figured to shoot it out with me. Fuck you San Fillipo and all you fuckin' grease ball wop shit heads. You think you playin' with some kid in the street?"

When Carmine didn't respond, Bunny spun him around and smacked him open handed across his face leaving an ugly red imprint of his hand on San Fillipo's fleshy cheek.

Carmine spat at Bunny, the spittle hitting him just below his left eye. Bunny just laughed as he wiped it off with the back of his hand and then wiped his hand on the front of Carmine's $1,000 overcoat.

"You're dead Ennis and you don't even know it.", Carmine snarled softly, fire burning in his eyes.

"It gonna take more than you to waste me Carmine ... Mr. fuckin' Macaroni."

They stood there glowering at each other until the loud knock on the front door signaled the return of the two bodyguards. Carmine sneered but kept his mouth shut.

"Ut oh, we got company Carmine! Now who can it be?" Bunny roughly shoved Carmine down the hall to the front room and standing behind him slipped the lock on the front door. It swung opened and Fat Jimmy entered.

"Hey it's the fat man. Come on in Mr. Jimmy.", Bunny ordered, noticing the other bodyguard remained at the wheel of the car parked by the curb and hadn't observed what was taking place at the doorway.

To his credit, Fat Jimmy maintained a neutral expression and just looked at Carmine who whispered something in Italian.

San Fillipo could see Bunny's finger tightening on the trigger. "Go ahead Jimmy, tell Nicky to come in.", Carmine finally ordered, figuring to play for time.

Jimmy opened the front door and whistled loudly to get Nick's attention. When the third man entered, Bunny had them lay their pieces on the floor and then stood them facing the wall on the opposite side of the room, hands held high over their heads.

"Now what the fuck you gonna do Ennis?", Carmine demanded.

I'm gonna ask you a few questions Carmine and you gonna answer them."

"Fuck you asshole.", Carmine spat, his response eliciting a chuckle from Fat Jimmy.

"Hey that strike you funny fat man? How about this?", Bunny asked Jimmy turning the barrel of the gun in his direction.

"Pop!", went the Beretta – the 9 mm slug hit Fat Jimmy just below and behind his left knee causing him to fall to the floor. Nicky looked over his shoulder at his wounded partner now holding his leg and breathed, "Christ – this guy is a nut job!" but not loud enough for Ennis to hear.

"Let me hear you laugh now you fat piece of shit!" Bunny then faced San Fillipo. "Why the cops lookin' for me Carmine?"

Bunny waited ten seconds for Carmine's answer; when it didn't come, he calmly turned and shot Nicky in his leg. The two bodyguards now formed a whimpering duo on the Club room floor.

Ennis raised the smoking pistol over his head and turned it a full 360 degrees. "You know Carmine, it be a good thing you wops made these walls extra thick. Nobody gonna hear a sound when I shoot each of you assholes. Now, you gonna tell me why the cops lookin' for me or do I put you on the floor too?"

Carmine considered his situation and quickly answered Bunny's question. "Because you fucked up Ennis. You didn't do too good a job on that bitch whose cunt you blew up. She told the cops your name and half the fuckin' City seen you. The people at the Hospital where you lifted Single Action, the bar where you grabbed Carson and Hayes, the whore's apartment … you got no brains. What do you think – you're the fuckin' invisible man?"

"I be plenty visible to fuckin' blow you away San Fillipo. Now that you mention it, what did you figure out with that Single Action computer bull shit?", Bunny demanded – shoving the still hot barrel of the Beretta roughly into Carmine's belly.

Carmine backed away. "Just like everything else you touch … it's no fuckin' good! The fuckin' thing is useless. You only got half of the god damn thing from the hospital. If you hadn't been so quick to waste the two assholes who wrote it, we might have got it to work!"

Bunny shrugged his shoulders at this news. Nicky and Fat Jimmy quieted and both were now sitting with their backs against the wall, hands clasping blood-soaked pants leg.

"What you lookin' at?", Bunny spat at the two wounded men and they quickly averted their gaze.

"OK, so much for Single Action. That be history. Now where the fuck you goin' this time of night Carmine, I thought we had a date?"

"I got tired of waitin' for you. I was goin' the fuck home.", he answered calmly.

Bunny turned toward Fat Jimmy. "Is that right fat man … Carmine goin' home?"

"Yeah, we was takin' him home.", he agreed, his voice barely concealing his hatred.

"Pop", went the Barretta – this time its slug drilling a neat hole between Nicky's brown eyes. The dead man slumped forward and remained bent at the waist, arms at his sides, palms facing upward as if he were praying.

Fat Jimmy's eyes bulged and instinctively, he shifted his considerable bulk away from his dead partner by bouncing sideways on his ass and then dragging his injured leg.

Ennis shook his head and looked mournfully at Jimmy. "I don't believe you fat man so I'm gonna ask you again ... where was you takin' Carmine?"

"Shut the fuck up Jimmy! Don't tell this fuckin' mullion a fuckin' thing!", Carmine ordered.

Bunny then gut punched Carmine doubling him over and causing him to puke up his late-night dinner all over his pants and highly polished imported shoes.

Bunny's message was not lost on Fat Jimmy. He decided that facing Carmine after this bull shit had ended was better than dying in the next five seconds.

He swallowed hard. "We was goin' to see the "Big" nigger from Harlem ... the Preacher. Carmine and him are havin' a meet.", he spit the words out – as if by saying them fast as he could, they really weren't his.

Carmine straightened up and shot Fat Jimmy a look that acknowledged his betrayal and the eventual retribution that would come. Fat Jimmy looked away from Carmine's accusing gaze.

Bunny smiled at the exchange and lifted Carmine's double chin with his free hand. "So you be getting' together with the Preacher. Now what do you two assholes have to talk about? You gonna end the war; or maybe you gonna trade me for the bitch?"

"Don't flatter yourself Ennis you ain't worth shit in a trade and I'm gonna kill you myself.", Carmine responded pulling his face away from Bunny's hand.

Bunny laughed hysterically. "I don't think you be takin' me out tonight Carmine. Hey, maybe if I get a heart attack from laughin' or somethin' ... I think you blowin' smoke up your ass white man.",

Ennis turned back to Fat Jimmy and roughly demanded. "Where you be meetin' the Preacher?"

Fat Jimmy figured it couldn't get any worse for him and answered without further urging. "Horn and Hardart, the big fuckin' Automat on 42nd Street. Just the Preacher and the Boss at the sit down. It's set for three."

Bunny checked his watch. "Well thanks for the information fat man. I greatly appreciate your spillin' your guts to me." Fat Jimmy almost groaned. Ennis then asked the tight-lipped San Fillipo. "Who set up the meet Carmine?"

"He did.", he quickly answered, finally recognizing the hopelessness of his present situation and deciding to buy time with grudging capitulation.

Bunny thought a moment. "OK ... let's you and me go have a talk with the Preacher."

Carmine was quick to respond. "Fuck no Ennis ... he don't expect anybody else but me, so forget about it. I'll go talk to him. You wait here and I'll be back later."

"Jesus Lord!", Ennis mockingly exclaimed. "You really gonna make me piss my pants and laugh myself to death. Yes sir, Mr. San Fillipo ... I be waiting here Boss for you to come back after your meet and tell me all about it."

Carmine tried another approach. "Look, it was you what fucked up. I know it and you know, but maybe I was wrong. There's still a chance we can pull this shit off together. I don't got nobody else to handle the Uptown thing and you don't got nobody except me. We don't have to love eachother. What the fuck! You still in or what Ennis?"

Carmine then made a move to his inside pocket and Bunny immediately raised the pistol level with San Fillipo's eyes.

"Hey, calm down, calm down, I'm just gettin' a butt.", he said as he slowly removed a pack of Camels from his inside pocket and placed it square against the round opening at the end of the Beretta's barrel. Bunny lowered the weapon and the two men exchanged genuine smiles.

Carmine's eyes went hard but he was still smiling as he lit up and inhaled deeply. He checked his watch while noisily blowing blue white smoke slowly through his nose and mouth. "Well, what's it gonna be Ennis? I only got fifteen minutes to get to the sit down and I don't expect the Preacher is gonna hang around waitin' if I'm late."

Bunny smirked as he replied to San Fillipo. "I think you, me and the fat man here is goin' for a cup of coffee and a piece of apple pie at the Automat."

Ennis then made a jerky up and down motion with the Beretta toward the fat man who sat bleeding on the club house floor. "Get on your feet or die Jimmy! We gots to go see the Head Nigger."

TWENTY NINE

Harry Walker, a low-level aide to the Attorney General of the United States, was under great emotional stress. He was a forty-nine-year-old alcoholic and his career in government was just about over when he was given a final opportunity to work for Lyndon Johnson's new Attorney General. This job was a pay back from the Democratic Party for past services rendered. Walker knew that his particular well had run dry; there would be no more pay backs if he screwed up and at this moment, he was very close to a major screw up. His boss called hours earlier and instructed him to track down Congressman Summerfield and then have him call the Attorney General immediately.

Walker knew something big must be up and for the last hour, his left eye had been twitching uncontrollably, his mouth was dry as a can of year-old talcum powder and his asshole felt like it had been riding a roller coaster without a seat belt ... all because Harry couldn't locate Summerfield.

He had started his search with Summerfield's senior aide, Lydia Hayes and when he couldn't reach her, called every staffer in DC and New York City who ordinarily would know where to find the Congressman, but for some unexplained reason no one did.

Walker knew it wouldn't matter to his boss that Summerfield had dropped off the planet this brisk October evening. He already knew that when he finally reported, the Attorney General would realize that Harry Walker was washed up since he couldn't even handle the simple task of locating the single most important black leader in Congress.

As his final resort, Walker contacted the District Police and requested they check local hospitals and also alert their personnel that Summerfield had to be found "pronto".

There was nothing more he could do but wait by his telephone and pray that some miracle would save him. Harry Walker was a dry alcoholic; hadn't had a drink in over two years but still felt the need. He had decided as soon as he tracked Summerfield down, he would immediately go off the wagon. The thought of drinking himself into oblivion kept him from losing it. He figured that he could alibi some time off work and then he would go on a monumental binge ...

The sudden blast from the telephone he held in his lap ended Walker's reverie and he had the receiver up to his ear before the completion of the first ring.

"Hello." He dryly croaked. Walker's panic was obvious in his voice.

"Hello, is this Mr. Walker?", the high tenor on the other end inquired.

"Yes, this is Mr. Walker. Who's calling?" Harry's eyes wouldn't focus and he felt dizzy. He was suffocating.

"Mr. Walker, this is Lt. McCarter, DC Police. We've located Congressman Summerfield ... "

The miracle had happened – his miserable career was saved! "Thank God! Where is he?", Walker shouted into the receiver relieving the tension of the last three hours. He closed his bloodshot eyes and an image of a dead Congressman Summerfield flash before him. "He's alright, isn't he?", he breathlessly asked. His shirt was sweat soaked and he felt as if he were going to throw up.

"Well no ... he's at Wolbur University Hospital. Came in as an emergency. Broken ribs and other problems Mr. Walker."

"What other problems?", Walker screamed, choking back the vomit that suddenly rose in his throat.

"Well, eh ... he was under the influence when he came in. Said he got hit by a car outside his apartment. We're investigating and I have a uniformed officer with the Congressman now. The hospital people said he'll be OK but they're keeping him overnight."

"Is he coherent McCarter?", Walker inquired, trying desperately to re-gain control – the worst was over, Summerfield was alive and he had found him.

"I couldn't tell you sir, didn't speak with him myself."

"Alright, alright. Thanks for your help. I'll advise the Attorney General. By the way does the Press know anything about this?"

"Not from us Mr. Walker, but I can't speak for the hospital or the Congressman's people. They may have released something. You OK? Is there anything else I can do for you?"

"No McCarter. Thanks for your help, and I'll put a good word in for you with your boss. Goodnight." Walker hung up and rushed into the bathroom and dry heaved for five minutes. He then doused his wrists and face in ice cold water and began to feel a little better.

Harry considered his situation. He had finished the job he was instructed to do thank God, but his boss would still be pissed. The Attorney General wanted to speak with Summerfield and from what he just learned; Summerfield was not currently capable of speaking with anyone. The only course available was to tell his boss where Summerfield was, the shape he was in and see what he wanted to do next. He would call the Attorney General with his report, but first there was another call that needed to be made.

Walker picked up the telephone and with a cold, wet and shaking hand, dialed a private number in New York City. The hour was late but he knew he wouldn't get any complaints.

"Hello.", Brian Toth answered at the third ring

"Hi Bri. It's Harry. Did you get to your good friend Johnny Dolan?"

"Yes, I did Harry and I passed on the news about the White House's bitch to MBC. To tell the truth, Johnny wasn't particularly concerned.""Really? Did he tell you anything new? You know – like what MBC plans to reveal in its next episode of who killed the two "queers". Walker tried being flip to conceal his desperate need for information but Brian Toth wasn't fooled. He and Harry had been lovers years ago when Toth was a young hot shot Labor Union attorney and Walker was a high-level aide in the Office of the Mayor of New York.

"Now listen Harry, if I get crazy and tell you what he told me you're going to have to be very careful how you use the information.", Toth insisted.

"Bri, I'm dying here! I have to pass on some potentially bad news to the Attorney General in a few minutes. You wouldn't believe the night I've spent trying to locate that bastard Summerfield and I just found out that he's in Wolbur University Hospital.", Walker blurted. "If there's something I could tell him – like what MBC intends to do with the Summerfield story – it might go a long way to help me pay for past sins if you know what I mean. And besides, you owe me from the old days Brian or have you forgotten?"

"That was a long time ago Harry. I'll help you but only because you're in trouble. What happened to Summerfield?"

"Hit by a car; was probably drunk when it happened. Now what did Dolan have to say?" Walker sat back, lit the first cigarette from the second pack he had opened in the last two hours. He visualized himself in his favorite bar on K Street sipping an extra dry Martini. For the first time in this nightmare of a night he knew he was going to be alright.

Brian needed to keep this information channel open so he reluctantly told Harry that Dolan would be doing a follow up piece that evening.

THIRTY

After his conversation with Brian Toth and a half hour and two cups of strong tea, Johnny Dolan was fully awake. There was no reason for him to try to go back to sleep. He knew it would be impossible anyway. He had just learned that Fredrick Summerfield was in a DC Hospital – why – an attack from a San Fillipo enemy?

Picking up his telephone, he called the MBC News Department Night Desk and asked if there was anything on the wire about Summerfield. A minute later the AP/UP news manager reported that "there was nothing". Dolan then called the DC News Bureau and was given the same report, even after he had them check the local police log ins for him.

The earlier call he had gotten from Brian Toth from his Attorney General source reported Summerfield's hospital condition. Johnny knew Brian's sources were usually right on the money … "maybe the DC locals are trying to keep it under wraps.", he thought.

This would be especially true if Summerfield had been drunk when he was admitted to the hospital. He had gone as far as he was able so he called Gil at the office and explained the situation.

"It's worth checking Johnny. I'll get some people on it right away. No sense you coming in; I'll call you back when something breaks either way. This could be the big one lad! Oh … and that lady from the hospital, Janet something or other, has been trying to reach you. She said it was important. I don't know … she wouldn't tell me anything."

"I'll call her in a minute. Things are picking up Boss. I'll keep you posted."

Dolan knew Peterson was delighted. Tracking down a hot tip was his element. Dolan knew if Summerfield was in a hospital anywhere in the Western Hemisphere, Gil Peterson would know how hot the thermometer was the next time they removed it from his asshole.

"Oh and hey Gil, I hear the White House wasn't too pleased with our piece last night?"

"Shit! You do have good sources Dolan. Yeah, they called the Big Boss and complained. He told them to go fuck themselves."

"That's great. Listen Gil, I can't sleep. I'm coming in."

"I'll get out your favorite tea bag kid. See ya.", Peterson answered.

Forty-five minutes later Dolan was sitting in Peterson's office listening to him talk with his DC bureau counter-part. He had already called Janet and she had absolute proof that Doug Hayes was Summerfield's son … no doubt about it.

THIRTY ONE

At the moment Harry Walker was sucking in the first long pull on his Camel, Carmine San Fillipo was slowly driving north on the FDR Drive and had just passed the 14th Street exit. Fat Jimmy was seated next to him and Bunny Ennis sat in the foremost jump seat in the rear of the limo.

"You're making me fuckin' nervous Ennis. Do you have to be breathin' down my neck while I'm drivin'?" he said to Bunny whose arms rested across the back seat and his mouth almost even with San Fillipo's right ear.

"You're a hell of a driver Carmine. When was the last time you drove a car?", Bunny asked, amused at San Fillipo's obvious discomfort. He sat hunched over intently peering out the windshield with both hands tightly gripping the steering wheel.

"I don't even have a fuckin' license. I couldn't pass the eye test when I was a kid. I told you that you should drive.", Carmine shouted back at Bunny but not daring to take his eyes of the deserted highway.

Ennis just laughed. "There's no fuckin' cars on the road Carmine. Just keep it straight and get off at 42nd Street. If it goes OK with the Preacher, I'll even drive you home – how's that? You feel better now?", Bunny answered while patting Carmine gently on his shoulder. Turning to the other occupant in the front seat he asked, "That's a good deal isn't it Jimmy? I'll even drive you home too or maybe even better, I'll run you over to St. Vincent's Emergency. You still bleeding all over Carmine's beautiful car Fat Man?"

Fat Jimmy also kept his eyes fixed on the road. "I'm alright Ennis.", was Fat Jimmy's flat sounding answer. He had placed his left hand over the bullet hole in the back of his leg and stopped the flow of blood which had caked and stiffly starched his pants leg. There was another reason for keeping his hand on his leg and out of Ennis' sight – it was only inches from and Ivar Johnson .32 secreted below his seat.

Carmine didn't know about the car's "insurance" piece but Fat Jimmy was certain the Boss would have ordered him to use it on the grinning nigger at the first opportunity.

He'd bide his time and pray that a well-placed bullet would redeem him with the Carmine.

Bunny was loose, almost happy. He had nothing to fear from San Fillipo. He was the survivor – not this Wop big shot who now chauffeured him to a meet with the only other black man that had power in this City. And besides, he had an ace that he'd yet to play.

Living by his wits, ruthlessly taking advantage of every opportunity, Bunny Ennis had clawed his way out of the rat and roach infested existence that bore him.

"Now tell me again Carmine, what's your plan for the Preacher sit down?" Bunny switched the Beretta from his left hand to his right and kept both arms resting on the seat back.

"I told you; he's got your girlfriend and she can lock up a lot of people with what she knows. I'm going to trade Summerfield for her."

"What about Policy … you didn't tell me what you plan to work out with the Preacher on that piece of business." Carmine sighed loudly.

"He don't want a war any more than I do. If he owns Summerfield, he can work all kinda action for himself. I'll make him an offer for part of his organization and throw him a taste of my downtown drug operation to sweeten the pot. That should make him agreeable and Jesus … stop the fuck annoyin' me while I'm drivin' – you want to get us killed?"

Carmine made an abrupt exit at 42nd Street and started up the off ramp that would put them on the street and just a few blocks from their final destination.

Fat Jimmy's left hand now grasped the hidden piece and he

sensed that this was the right moment for him to make his play. He knew that his shot would be awkward if he had to use his left hand so he decided to take a chance and switch the .32 to his right.

"Aw shit Ennis, my fuckin' leg is killin' me.", he whined, he dropped his right hand to his injured leg. The transfer was made in a heartbeat and he brought the barrel up and parallel with his chest, shifting slightly to his left and fired two rounds toward Ennis.

Two things saved Bunny Ennis. The muzzle velocity of a .32 isn't strong enough to give it much stopping power under the best of circumstances and when fired through the Caddy's thick leather covered seat with over six inches of spring upholstery stuffing, it becomes even less effective.

Fat Jimmy's first round tore through the bench seat and was slightly deflected by a compressed steel spring it encountered causing the slug to pass harmlessly by Bunny and finally became imbedded within the plush rear seat. The second round never even came that close. Fat Jimmy had thrown his body down between the front seat and the fire wall to get below Bunny's line of return fire. Dropping down had jerked his aim which caused the second shot to go high and ricocheted harmlessly off the ceiling courtesy light and it shattered the right rear window as it exited the car.

The sudden flash of the pistol startled Carmine and its explosive, double report in the closed car interior deafened all three men. As usual, Bunny reacted quickly and returned Fat Jimmy's fire. Both of his shots hit the fat man but neither was fatal. The first passed through a fleshy arm without striking bone and the second grazed Jimmy's neck and ear.

In a momentary panic, San Fillipo pressed the gas pedal to the floor and crashed the limo hard left into the three-foot concrete wall that paralleled the 42nd street exit ramp. The car's entire left side was gouged and ripped as it pushed against the immoveable barrier; sparks traced its path as it ran along the wall for a hundred feet before coming to an abrupt halt; its engine still running.

Carmine figured they had this guy. He released the steering wheel, turned to his right and grabbed Bunny's shooting arm with both hands forcing the Beretta's 3½" barrel to point harmlessly away from Jimmy. As he struggled with Ennis, San Fillipo tried to push out from behind the wheel but his fat gut wedged him in.

"Shoot him Jimmy! Take the son of a bitch for Christ's sake!", he screamed at the deafened fat man. Carmine was an old street fighter and with a roar sunk his teeth into Bunny's wrist.

Fat Jimmy couldn't hear Carmine but could see him wrestling with Ennis. At this distance Fat Jimmy could have taken Ennis out with one shot but months of neglect had insured that the .32 he held in his fat hand would not be the means of ending Bunny Ennis' life. Jimmy couldn't pull the trigger; its mechanism was locked solid by the accumulated grime it had collected under the car seat. Worse yet, Fat Jimmy was on his ass and stuck fast between the wide bench seat and the car floor. There wasn't a thing he could do to help Carmine, but Bunny didn't know this.

All he could think of was the target he made to the fat man less than three feet away. Carmine's teeth drew blood and as the pain shot up his arm, it turned on dancing white lights behind his eyes. Reaching into his coat pocket, Bunny groped, grabbed and released the blade on Sal's switchblade with his free left hand. He threw himself to the left and as far behind Carmine's body as he could get and brought the opened knife across the front seat and began stabbing Carmine in his gut and chest.

It was over in a matter of seconds. Bunny thrust again and again, sometimes striking bone and feeling the knife deflected and sometimes feeling the blade enter soft flesh and then move freely to its hilt.

Carmine gasped in pain and disbelief as blood gushed from his nose and mouth onto Bunny's wrist which he tightly gripped with his teeth. The sudden, unstoppable force of the knife attack sat him up straight and when he tried to scream no sound would come. He felt he was drowning in his own blood. He couldn't breathe and he became less aware of each knife thrust; his dying brain filled with images of other times and places; there was his long dead mother cooking dinner and there he was riding his bike in the park … His eyes fluttered close and Carmine's lock grip teeth on Ennis' wrist released.

Fat Jimmy watched the knife relentlessly plunge in and out of his boss but he was powerless to interfere; he was only a silent witness to Carmine San Fillipo's death.

The moment Carmine released his arm, Bunny turned, calmly sighted the Beretta's dull barrel down toward the trapped fat man and emptied the pistol's three remaining rounds into his compressed bulk.

All was suddenly quiet in the darkened limo. Both its driver and front seat passenger were dead. No one who hadn't witnessed the viciousness of the life and death struggle that had just taken place would believe it was acted out in less than thirty seconds.

The right rear car door slowly opened and the sole survivor emerged onto the 42nd Street exit ramp, miraculously still deserted.

Bunny dropped the empty Beretta into his coat pocket. He started to close Sal's switch blade and noticed that it was broken off about an inch from the end. He closed it anyway and pocketed it too. He opened the right front door, leaned in and retrieved the .32 from Fat Jimmy's hand. There were four rounds in the cylinder and when he tried pulling the trigger, quickly understood why he was still alive – It had been a close thing. "Lucky for me the fucks like to chow down the macaroni instead of cleaning their hardware.", he thought. Bunny placed the .32 in his waistband. He'd clean it up later.

Ennis knew from the beginning there was a better than 50 50 chance he would have to kill San Fillipo so he wasn't particularly concerned about what had just happened. "In fact,", he reasoned, "it's better I should talk with the Preacher man. Carmine would have just fucked things up."

The Bunnyman breathed in cold early morning air as he trotted down the exit ramp. His wrist was killing him and for the first time, noticed the blood-stained sleeve of his cashmere overcoat. There was nothing he could do about it now. He flexed his right hand – it hurt but was OK. It was only a short walk to the Automat and he didn't want to be late for the Preacher. "That was no way to start a new partnership.", he thought.

* * *

Erwin Shaefer knew his luck had changed from the minute he met Lois in the "Jug" three hours earlier. Erwin had been going to this singles saloon on 23rd Street for over a year and the best action he had so far was a feel job of some blonde's ass who had been jammed up next to him at the crowded bar. And she had been too drunk to notice that his hand had been glued to her backside for over an hour and later, she barely acknowledged Erwin even when he bought her a drink.

Now Lois was different. Her face was a "two bagger" but it came with a body that belonged in a Playboy center-fold. Erwin met Lois when he had accidently spilled his beer on her but she thought it was hysterical. He figured out pretty quick that her "elevator" didn't go all the way to the top floor.

"Hey … what the fuck!", he thought. She had been all over him at the bar and he was sure everybody noticed his hard-on every time he left to take a leek or play the juke box. "Fuck 'em he thought. Let 'em eat their hearts out." Erwin had found a sure thing and he knew he was finally going to get laid.

When they left the Jug, he took her to an after-hours joint downtown where they spent most of the time "tongue dancing" at one of the small tables in the back of the almost pitch-black club room.

Now they were on the road, heading to his place on East 86th Street. He told her he had a swinging bachelor pad and hoped that she was too drunk to notice the army of roaches that would cover the floor of his overpriced studio apartment when he turned on the lights.

His powder blue 1962 Buick Skylark owned the FDR at this time of morning. Erwin loved this car and it showed. He kept both inside and outside immaculate. "The only problem," he would tell his friends, "Was the back seat was too small to get laid in." And his friends always shook their heads in sympathy but thought "Erwin could drive a school bus in South Korea filled with free rice and still not get laid."

He looked over at Lois who sat glassy eyed, staring out at the empty roadway whizzing by. His right arm around her shoulders, he pulled her closer until their thighs touched. Erwin's hand reached down and cupped her solid breast and began squeezing and stroking it. He could feel her tit harden and instantly his cock began throbbing.

"You make me so hot baby.", he said hoarsely without taking his eyes from the empty roadway.

Lois' tongue darted in and out of Erwin's ear as her hand moved to his lap and began massaging the inside of his thigh, causing him to squirm in a futile attempt to loosen the constricting pressure his shorts placed on his swollen cock. Lois lowered her head to his lap, deftly zipped open his fly and reaching inside his pants, freed it from the strangling underwear.

Erwin's exposed prick became a human thermometer – first sensing the cooler temperature of the Skylark's interior but quickly heating up when Lois' hot mouth engulfed its entire length.

He tried driving with her bobbing on it for as long as he could. And when he began weaving all over the road, Erwin's otherwise numb brain sent out an urgent signal that he needed to get off the FDR, park and allow it to concentrate as she finished him off.

The Buick barely slowed as it exited at 42nd Street and was traveling at a solid 40 Mph when it plowed into the darkened Caddy partially obstructing the roadway.

Erwin Schaefer would not get laid again for a long, long time.

THIRTY TWO

The Preacher sat alone by the big window with a steaming mug of strong, almost black tea on the marble top table before him. Slowly and very systematically, he looked about the huge but almost empty dining room. There were a few pockets of single patrons in the Automat, refugees from the night, mostly intent on reading their early morning edition of the Daily News or Mirror spread out before them; each reader located as far from their neighbor as possible.

In a few hours this unique, last of its kind cafeteria would be teaming with office workers eager to finish a last cup of coffee and smoke before starting another long, tedious day pushing paper or making their living in some other equally drudge filled way. But for now, the 42nd Street Automat was a quiet, almost contemplative place.

Bunny Ennis pushed through the oversized revolving door and was immediately enveloped by dry heat mixed with odors of eggs, greasy bacon and other breakfast food heaped on steam tables in readiness for the early morning rush.

The Preacher marked Ennis' almost theatrical entrance and immediately recognized the well-built black man in the cashmere overcoat. He raised the tea mug to his lips, sipped slowly and returned it to the table top. Standing, the Preacher quickly removed his beige Orsini overcoat and placed it on an empty chair at the next table, its pure silk lining shimmering in the room's muted art deco lighting. Removing his coat was the "get ready" signal to the shooter equipped with his high-powered rifle who now waited and watched from the rear seat of the Preacher's limo parked directly across the street.

Standing at the cafeteria's entrance, Ennis saw all and recognized the Preacher's innocent activity for what it was. Bunny had expected to find him seated close to the large plate glass window fronting 42nd

Street. He knew the location was a guarantee his backup would have a clear shot at the first hint of trouble and from what he had just seen, Bunny surmised the "shoot" signal would have something to do with a pre-arranged movement of the Preacher's overcoat.

Bunny smiled to himself and walked quickly to the Preacher's table.

"Mr. Ennis, I believe.", came the Preacher's evenly modulated greeting as he looked up at the expressionless man now standing before him.

Bunny was surprised by the almost soothing, silky sounding voice of this man he had come to admire.

The Preacher kept his hands in sight and slowly gestured toward the empty chair across from his. Bunny knew if he sat there, he would present the best target for any hidden sniper watching from outside.

"If you don't mind. I'll be more comfortable here.", Bunny declined while taking a chair from the next table and positioning to the Preacher's immediate right and up close to the "man". Ennis' body was now mostly obstructed by the Preacher's when viewed from the street.

The ploy was not lost on the Preacher who smiled. "I'm flattered at your trust – turning your back on a room filled with strangers."

"I don't trust any mother fucker. You included.", came back Bunny's matter of fact response.

"A wise philosophy. By the way, I was expecting your associate Mr. San Fillipo. Isn't he joining us?"

"Carmine couldn't make it. Had a little car accident. I didn't want you to drink your coffee all alone, so I came instead."

The Preacher's demeanor betrayed nothing and he since had already taken in Bunny's blood-stained coat sleeve and his swelling wrist wound, he asked, "It appears that you've had a little accident as well Mr. Ennis?"

"Yeah, but I'll be cured.", Bunny responded, eyes locked with the Preacher's as he raised his injured arm and shook it from side to side.

"Carmine's accident was fatal.", he announced.

The finality of Bunny's words was dramatically amplified by the two police cars that raced down the empty street outside the Automat, heading east bound in the direction of the FDR; their siren's wailing and red "Christmas tree" lights vividly reflecting off the darkened office buildings.

In spite of himself, The Preacher's attention was drawn to their sudden passage and he stared fleetingly out the window at them. Turning back, he gave Ennis a mirthless smile.

"Aren't you afraid that your Italian friends will be upset by your actions?", he asked.

"Shit. The grease balls ain't gonna be checkin' me out. They be comin' after you Preacher Man. You be at war with them – not me. Ain't you been watchin' the TV brother?"

The Preacher now realized that the man sitting across from him was cunning as well as vicious.

"You underestimate your associates intelligence.", he answered evenly. "Now why are you here?"

Bunny leaned forward and said in a voice just above a whisper. "I came to tell you that I'm your new partner."

The Preacher's reaction to Bunny's announcement was to slowly rotate his half-filled tea cup on the table's marble surface. "Really?", he responded. "Now why on God's earth would I need a partner and if I did – why should I accept you?"

As he spoke the Preacher's gaze again drifted toward the street and rested on the left rear window of his parked limo. He knew he was going to be leaving the Automat in less than a minute and had decided that he'd first watch Bunny Ennis die.

Bunny sensed what was about to happen even as the Preacher's murderous thought was forming. Unafraid, he boldly responded to the Preacher's question. "Because if I ain't your partner Mr. Preacher, you gonna lose everything you got."

The Preacher snorted derisively. "And who's going to take it from me? Surely not you Mr. Ennis?"

"I don't need to take nothin' away from you – 'cause you gonna be happy to give me what I want. You be an "Uncle Tom" Mr. Preacher and uncle toms is dead meat in today's bad ass world. I can save your black ass my brother and that's why I'm gonna be your partner."

The Preacher released his tea cup and flitted his hand as if he were chasing away an annoying insect. "Mr. Ennis I already know you to be a killer and now suspect you're ignorant as well." His cultured voice showed the first hint of annoyance and as he continued, his voice rose with controlled emotion. "No one, not you, not your Mafia associates or the "man in the moon" for that matter are strong enough to take anything that is mine. Can you understand that Mr. Ennis? Did that sink into your dull mind? I'll be leaving now." The Preacher rose and reached for his coat. He looked down at the still seated Ennis and warned through lips thinned to a straight line. "Don't follow me or attempt to contact me again. If you persist in being foolish, I promise you'll regret it."

The Preacher started to lift his overcoat from the back of the empty chair but Bunny's hand shot out and held the Preacher's coat in place.

Eyes narrowed; Ennis' voice took on a different, more authoritative tone. "You walk outa here now Preacher and I guarantee that the Government be hauling your ass into jail by this time tomorrow!"

"The government? Really Ennis, you're demented. What are you threatening with?", he scoffed straining to remove his coat from the chair back.

Bunny's grip locked the overcoat in place and with his free hand he gestured. "Sit back down and listen to what I have to say.", he ordered. "I'm talkin' bout kid nappin'; I'm talkin' bout murder; I'm talkin' about conspiracy to defraud the U.S. Government – that's income tax evasion. Now that's just openers. Give me time brother and I'll add more shit to the list. Enough to bury you in!'

The Preacher knew he had nothing to lose by listening and he sensed there was suddenly something very different about Ennis. He sighed and sat, this time making certain that Ennis was completely exposed to the street.

"Alright you have my attention. I'll give you five minutes. "Please explain yourself Mr. Ennis."

Relaxing his hold on the Preacher's overcoat, Bunny leaned forward and began. "Three years ago, I was recruited by the FBI.", He paused allowing the full effect of words to sink in and was not disappointed. For the first time the Preacher's eyes registered surprise. Ennis quickly continued "I had been in trouble when I was a kid but had managed to straighten myself out. I even completed law school and was practicing Civil Rights law in Chicago when I was approached by the Bureau."

"Are you joking?", the Preacher interrupted. "You expect me to believe that you're an attorney and you're working for the FBI?"

"I'm deadly serious and if I wasn't "working for the FBI" you'd be sitting in a holding pen on 38th Street right now under a murder indictment."

The Preacher asked: "Why are you telling me all of this? And if you're working for the Feds why are you talking about partnership in my operation?"

"That brings us to the interesting part – it's the reason why I'm here. I know your background Preacher and how you came into Policy. You're a truly successful negro entrepreneur – which is to say, a very rare bird in the United States today. We both know that blacks don't control their crime in New York or anywhere else in this Country for that matter and with the exception of your little Policy enclave, it's the white man that runs all the action; except for Uptown."

The Preacher nodded his agreement.

Ennis continued. "Well, the U.S. Government doesn't think that's fair! They want "equal opportunity" crime along with everything else that's happening with minority rights. A few years ago, when Joe Valachi sang his little song for the Feds, he got them to thinkin' – "Hey maybe a little organized crime might be the start of a whole lot of other opportunities for the colored folks." Think about it Preacher, second and third generation Mafia kids are doctors, lawyers, run legitimate businesses, pay taxes and are good citizens. Same is true for the emigrant Irish and the Jews. So maybe crime does ultimately pay after all."

Bunny had his complete attention and continued. "The Feds even set me up with San Fillipo so I'd get on the job training in how to run an organization. I learned everything there was to learn Preacher. I'm ready.

And now we get to you my brother. You were chosen six years ago when Kennedy first got elected as the beta site for the program. Your mother was the original civil rights activist and your father a revered religious leader. Washington felt you had integrity. You never ran dope, girls or loan sharking. In other words, you were the perfect choice to get the ball rolling."

The Preacher considered the strangest compliment he had ever been given. He grinned and noticed that Ennis now spoke without the street BS and actually sounded well educated. "So, let me be clear, you're saying that the government is willing to back me in an expansion of my business?"

"That's what I'm telling you. To the max."

"And just what would that mean?"

"It means that with me as your partner and liaison to the United States Government, your interests would grow. You'd get inside information on government contracts; the IRS would look the other way, so would Labor and the Department of Justice and the same goes with the City Government. All you'd have to do was make sure that you used the brothers in all your ventures; taught them how to run your front businesses, the community and eventually you'd set up operations in Detroit, Atlanta, Philadelphia and any other place where the brothers and sisters need help."

"Mr. Ennis your proposition is intriguing – but what's the downside?"

"The downside as you call it, is you'd have to be ready to fight the Mafia and any other group that might come along. The Government can't help you much when that kind of trouble comes visiting and that's the other reason why I'm part of the package. You don't have the knack for dealing with these people problems like I do."

"Yes, and that brings up a very interesting point – it appears that you have considerable experience in the art of killing Mr. Ennis. How do I know that I won't be implicated in your recent activities and more importantly, how can I ever rest easy knowing that I might ultimately become another notch on your gun?"

"First off, I'll never be connected to any of the take outs of San Fillipo's crowd. My FBI friends sanctioned it and they just won't allow anyone to look too hard for a connection to me. Now as far as you're concerned, as soon as you sign up with the program, the Feds will protect you as well as they're covering my ass. That coverage even includes protecting you from me."

"Really? You seem to have glossed over the fact that Hayes and Carson were working for me – not Carmine San Fillipo when you killed them. Isn't that a bit of a contradiction to what you just said?"

"Look, I did you a favor when I aced those two. Hayes was a liability to your organization. He had already spilled his guts about what he was doing for you to his former wife and if the word got out that you had stacked the deck against all your five and ten cents' actions bettors with a sure thing computer program, your business would have turned to shit. It was too bad about Larry Carson, I kind of liked that dude. But he had to go too. No tellin' what problems he might have caused if he lived after Doug Hayes said bye-bye."

The two men sat silently for a moment

"Well, are you in?", Bunny finally asked.

"I'll need proof Mr. Ennis."

"You'll have it in a few hours Preacher. Now you and I are going to get up and you're going to give the high sign to your man outside with the gun that everything is cool with us. I'm going to walk you to your car and then go and get me some sleep after I call the Feds and tell them about our little visit. Any problem with that?"

"No problem Mr. Ennis. I think I can find you if I should need to."

"And I know I can always find you Mr. Preacher man. Hey say a big hello to my favorite lady, Lydia. Tell her I'm thinkin' 'bout her and lookin' forward to seein' her real soon."

THIRTY THREE

Bunnyman considered his meeting with the Preacher. The whole idea of the Government's plan from its inception was to establish Ennis within the Preacher's organization. He was instructed to first work his way into the San Fillipo family and then sabotage their efforts to gain control of Harlem policy. He accomplished much more than that ... he eliminated Carmine San Fillipo. He knew that the Mafia would only hold the Preacher responsible for Carmine's murder, so he could continue working both sides of the street if he had to. The first order of business next was to update his FBI handler and come up with a plan to validate to the Preacher's satisfaction that he was working for the Government and would be a conduit to ensure his crime organizations future success. He made a quick telephone call from a pay phone and was told where he needed to go to meet with his FBI handler.

Bunny had arrived early and now stood waiting at the Central Park Zoo entrance for his handler. Ennis had been surprised when he first met him ... he was a black man ... Ennis could never imagine that J. Edgar Hoover would hire black FBI agents but he was wrong .... They had, at least one ... Joe Jackson.

"Joe why the fuck are we meeting here? You have an expense account. You should have taken me to a fancy restaurant. I'm freezing my ass off here."

Jackson smiled. "Let's walk and talk. Did you take out San Fillipo? I just got a call that he got aced. The Bureau is in an uproar. Is that where you got that blood on your coat?"

"I did, along with three of his guys. I didn't really plan on it but they forced my hand. So what's the big fuckin' deal?" Bunny shrugged as if he was explaining to a parent about the mess he made in the kitchen.

"Jesus Ennis, how many is that? You're fuckin' nuts. First, the two civilians, the four prostitutes ... now San Fillipo and at least four of his ass hole mob guys. Anybody else I should know about? The Bureau bosses are getting close to pulling the plug."

"Why? Your bosses told me to use any means necessary. What I did was necessary. So shut the fuck up about it. I need your help .... today. I heard the cops are waiting for me at my pad. Make them go away. Make them stop lookin' at me."

Jackson thought a second before answering. "That's gonna be difficult. The request to leave you alone will need to come from very high up. It means at least one top guy will have to be brought into the plan. I'll do what I can. Call me this afternoon and I'll tell you more. But for the time being ... just stay the fuck out of sight. You need money?"

Bunny didn't like Jackson's answer but realized there was nothing more he could do about it.

"Not what I wanted to hear but there's something else you Feds have to do. I just met with the Preacher and filled him in on who I was and who I was working for. I told him I wanted to become a part of his organization. He agreed if he could have some proof that I'm who I say I am. Your guys will need to make it clear that I work for you and I need to be part of his thing. We can bring him up to speed with the details after I get in. Now my brother can your people handle that too?"

"I'll let you know later. Here's some money ... now get lost and call me after 4 this afternoon."

Joe Jackson took a cab back to his office. "Ennis is a loose cannon.", he thought. "When this is under control, he'll have to go ... disappear for good." But that wasn't his immediate problem nor would it ever be. He had to sell his boss on finding someone high up in the Attorney General's office to kill the local heat on Ennis and figure out how they would convince the Preacher that Ennis should come in to his organization. He had a nagging concern about that MBC reporter too ... perhaps something needed to be done to close down his investigation.

Jackson arrived at his office and called his boss in DC to report … his boss listened to his summary of the Ennis conversation and just said "he'd take care of it."

He then gave Jackson more details about the San Fillipo hit; said there were already Organized Crime agents on site and instructed him to get over to the 42nd Street crime scene ASAP.

THIRTY FOUR

Bunny felt uneasy. Jackson seemed like he might be getting ready to dump him. It wasn't anything he said exactly, just the way he had said it. The FBI didn't exactly sanction killing but they didn't tell him he couldn't … he thought back to the time of his indoctrination, they told him he was an "American James Bond" with a license to kill. He knew too much now and they knew it. If the Government was ever tied into this, careers would be lost, people locked up and whatever civil rights plan they had would be set back 100 years. Bunny needed an insurance policy to protect himself and he knew where he could buy one, the reporter … Johnny Dolan.

Using Jackson's cash, Bunny bought himself underwear, socks, dress shirt, tie and a new expensive overcoat. He couldn't be walking around with a blood stained one. He stopped in a nearby drug store and picked up odds and ends to treat his injured wrist. It still hurt like hell. Last stop … a liquor store for a pint bottle of "Jack".

He checked into the Sherry Netherland and got the most expensive room available. He showered, ordered room service and took a needed two-hour nap. Just killing time until he could call Jackson.

At 4:30 he called Joe Jackson from his room.

"Where are you staying Ennis?"

"Somewhere safe for the time being…. Did you get the cops off my ass?"

"We're working on it. Don't go back to your place till I tell you. It won't be long."

"What about the Preacher … you assholes contact him yet?"

"We're working on that too … don't worry, the higher ups will get to him shortly. Now we may have another problem. The MBC reporter guy, John Dolan, is working on the Policy angle in Harlem and he may have zeroed in on Summerfield. I don't know for sure yet. But this will be a major problem for everyone if he breaks a story about Summerfield and the Preacher. You shouldn't have killed those two computer guys."

"It is what it is. What are you doing about Dolan?"

"That's way above my pay grade Ennis. All I know is the FBI bosses are going crazy right about now."

THIRTY FIVE

Dolan reached the 42nd Street FDR exit in about five minutes. Gil had immediately dispatched him and his camera and sound team the minute the wire report came in announcing that Carmine San Fillipo had been found murdered.

Johnny's heart was pounding as he opened the MBC News van door almost before it stopped. He glanced at the kid looking cop directing traffic around the Exit. Although it was still early, rush hour traffic was already building and Dolan knew that this place was going to be a "zoo and a half" before the morning was over. The 42nd Street exit emptied a steady stream of cars from 6:30 AM until 10 AM and 42nd Street was the City's principal crosstown traffic artery. The fact that the highway exit used for the United Nations, the Ford Foundation and other tourist havens such as the famous Horn and Hardart Automat, made the work of the police and the press impossibly difficult.

"I'm glad I don't have to drive anywhere around here this morning.", Dolan thought while imagining the ten thousand or more commuters who were sure to be late for work.

He and his crew slowly made their way up the exit ramp, pass cops, print and TV press, fire and emergency service personnel. The ramp was packed with police cars, two fire engines, and three ambulances, one labeled "Morgue, City of New York", his cameraman rolling all the way.

It had almost broken Gil's heart that he couldn't come along. This was a big big story. San Fillipo had been killed … did the Preacher do it? Hard to say. Mafia hits, especially bosses, had to be sanctioned. Maybe San Fillipo's associates had enough of his very public "war" with the Preacher and had one of their own taken out.

Dolan stood by while his camera guy did his thing. There was a second car, a Skylark, embedded in the rear of San Fillipo's Caddy. It was empty and the front seat was stained with blood. Dolan wondered if its occupants had been part of the hit team. The Police photographer was running from side to side taking pictures of the Caddy's empty interior.

"What's the details Captain?" Dolan stood with four other reporters who had most likely already asked the senior police officer the same question before his arrival at the scene. The captain seemed annoyed at his question.

"Two dead in the Caddy ... two injured in the Buick."

"Was it Carmine San Fillipo?"

"You assholes know I can't give any information pending notification of next of kin ... there'll be a press briefing later this morning. Just take your pretty pictures and leave us alone. We have work to do ... the road is fucked up enough and we are trying to get this fuckin' exit back open."

Dolan and the other reporters gave a hearty laugh at that and began a full barrage of questions anyway. He had already seen the half dozen serious agents dressed in their FBI jackets milling around the Caddy, talking and taking photos. He recognized two of them as part of the FBI's Organized Crime Unit and noticed the negro agent standing among the group. "That's a first.", he thought.

Dolan approached the black agent now somewhat off by himself.

"Hello sir. My name is John Dolan and I'm with MBC News. Would you care to give a comment? Off the record of course."

The agent stopped making notes and looked at Dolan's extended hand.

Joe Jackson already knew who Johnny Dolan was. There had been many nervous calls and meetings back in DC immediately after his explosive report on the Hunter Byrnes news hour. No one knew anything about this turn in developments. It caught them off guard. Now all were concerned that it would put a monkey wrench in the Government's plans.

Jackson saw no harm in talking with Dolan and took the offered hand.

"Hello Mr. Dolan. My name is Special Agent Jackson. How can I help you ... everything off the record of course?"

Dolan smiled. This was a change in normal investigative procedures ... someone willing to actually answer his questions. "Thanks Agent Jackson. I only have a few off the record questions for you. Was it Carmine San Fillipo that was killed?"

"Yes, it was and one of his associates as well. Anything else?"

"Do you have any theories ... like, who killed him? Did the occupants of the Buick Skylark have anything to do with it?"

"At this point ... no theories, and no, the two people in the Buick were civilians and not involved. Appears they had the bad luck of crashing into San Fillipo's limo."

"Was it a mob hit?"

"Eh ... it's hard to say. The other occupant in the front seat was shot to death but San Fillipo was stabbed to death. Not typical of a mob hit wouldn't you say?"

Jackson took a chance. "Could I ask you about your piece on the Hunter Byrnes report yesterday ... off the record of course."

Dolan shrugged. "Why not.", he thought.

"Sure, Agent Jackson ... as long as it's off the record and you promise to keep me in loop on this hit investigation. What do you want to know?"

Jackson smiled. "Of course, I will. Now Mr. Dolan do you plan any follow-up reports?"

"Yes ... we're still verifying some information ... I'll probably be reporting again in a few days."

"Could you give me a general idea of what you'll be reporting? I know you can't reveal too much ... just an overview."

"Well, in general it concerns criminal activity in Harlem as it relates to the Numbers racket and a possible tie in to some politicians in DC. That's about as much as I can say Agent Jackson."

Jackson blanched. He immediately recognized the implications of Dolan's public investigation not only on the Government's plans to infiltrate black communities through local criminal organizations but the potential impact on Congressman Summerfield's pending legislation. He calmed his churning gut.

"Well now that sounds very interesting Mr. Dolan and I look forward to learning what you have to say about that. Are you sharing your information with the local police, or any government agencies at this time?"

"Sorry ... that's all I can share right now. But it was nice meeting you sir. Thanks for speaking with me and good luck with your investigation here. Don't forget your promise."

THIRTY SIX

The plain but official looking black four door Dodge stopped before the rear entrance of Wolbur University Hospital. Its conservatively dressed driver exited and quickly opened the right rear door for his tall, distinguished looking passenger and was greeted by the hospital's chief operating officer, a middle-aged black man. Ralph Cooper had risen to his position after twenty-six years of dedicated service at the medical center but had never met so high-level Government official.

"It's a pleasure meeting you Sir. My name is Ralph Cooper.", Mr. Cooper said, shaking the hand extended by the visitor.

"Thank you, Mr. Cooper."

"If you'll follow me sir, I'll take you directly to Congressman Summerfield's suite."

The two men entered the medical facility and quickly walked to the elevator, door already opened, waiting for them at the end of the empty corridor. Hospital security staff had closed off the corridor to all but essential personnel.

When the elevator door shut closed and Cooper pushed in the top floor number, the Attorney General of the United States politely asked. "And how is your patient this morning Mr. Cooper?"

"He'll be fine Sir.", came Cooper's quick re-assurance. "Two broken ribs and a minor head wound. Oh, and he's shaken off the effects of the alcohol he consumed. The Congressman had a light breakfast about an hour ago and he'll be able to leave anytime he wishes. But the staff thinks he should take a few days bed rest at home."

The Attorney General listened intently to Cooper's report and was pleased and secretly relieved. "Well, that's great news

Mr. Cooper, great news. Tell me, what has the Press been told about his condition?"

"Nothing. To the best of my knowledge Sir, the Press doesn't even know the Congressman is a patient here."

The elevator door opened and the men exited onto an almost empty VIP nursing unit. Cooper pointed to the left and they proceeded just a few feet to stand before the closed patient room door.

"Good, now let's try and keep it that way Mr. Cooper."

"You'll have our full cooperation Sir."

"I'm sure we will. I'd like to have privacy when I meet with Congressman Summerfield and eh ... we'll arrange for the Congressman's transportation later this morning."

"Certainly. Just pick up the telephone when you're ready to leave." Cooper knocked softly and opened the door, ushered in the visitor and left.

Summerfield was sitting in an arm chair drinking coffee and reading the Washington Post. Looking up, he smiled at his visitor. "Please excuse me for not standing; I'm still a little stiff. Can I order you some coffee?"

The Attorney General shook his head and sat on the chair next to the writing desk. He looked the patient over, sighed and said, "Well Fredrick, you're looking a lot more chipper than I expected. How are you feeling?"

"Under the circumstances – fine. I'll be leaving later this morning. What brings you here Mr. Attorney General? The President send you or did you decide to come on your own and report to him later?"

"The President sends his regards and I'm certain that you'll be speaking with him later today Fredrick. Now perhaps you'd be kind enough to tell me how you arrived in your present condition?"

"Well, I didn't know you cared that much about my condition. But since you asked – it seems that I was hit by a car during my evening constitutional. The scoundrel didn't even bother to stop! Can you imagine that? I'm cooperating with the Metro Police and I'm sure they'll track him down."

"I'm sure they will.", came the droll response.

"Just why are you here Mr. Attorney General – to deliver a message perhaps?"

The Attorney General ignored the not so subtle put down.

"I think you know why. The President is concerned about Friday and he wants to be certain that you'll be able to lead the vote on the Floor."

"Oh? You mean there's nothing else on your agenda this morning? You neglected to ask about last evening's Hunter Byrnes news report. I'll save time – neither my aide Lydia Hayes nor I have any connection with the recent unfortunate demise of her former husband. Is that what you came to hear Mr. Attorney General?"

"Of course, I believe that Mr. Congressman but frankly I don't think you or your aide could stand very close scrutiny on other issues that may come to light during the next few days."

"Really? Now what might those issues be?"

The Attorney General crossed his legs and rubbed his nose as he began in a tone he used often when he was a prosecuting attorney in Michigan.

"Your association with the San Fillipo organization for one and that Lydia Hayes' deceased former husband Douglas Hayes was in fact your son and the substantial evidence that he was an employee of a crime cartel when he was murdered. I'm sure you'll agree that there are some significant issues that need to be discussed Mr. Congressman and that's why I'm here."

Summerfield knew his hand couldn't beat a "full house" and his reaction to the Attorney General's accusations immediately shifted into attack mode.

"I'm afraid you don't know what you're talking about – I have no association with San Fillipo – Damn it! My only son, Albert died years ago, and furthermore, I resent your allegations! Now if you'll excuse me Sir, I need to get some rest before I leave here."

"Alright Mr. Congressman, I'm leaving, but take this as a warning … not an idle threat. If the legislation fails to get the vote Friday because of your indiscretions, I promise that the whole power of the US Justice Department will come down hard on you."

THIRTY SEVEN

The Deputy Attorney General of the United States didn't want to be here in this flee bag Harlem hotel conference room. He certainly didn't want to be seated across the table from a notorious negro gangster and be tasked with convincing him that he needed to join the Government in an "off the wall" civil rights plan.

The man sitting on the opposite side of the table was Philip Alexander Beaumount, but preferred that he be called Preacher. In spite of himself, as they spoke, the Deputy Attorney General liked this man. He was obviously intelligent, spoke with authority and had a gentlemanly manner. They sat alone, without note taking facilities and very quickly, the Deputy felt comfortable in speaking candidly.

"Simply put sir, the Governments goal, the Presidents goal, is to help bootstrap as many negros as possible with financial aid, both direct and indirect. Our surveys indicate a serious breakdown in the negro family unit. Lack of real jobs and work opportunities for men is the most significant contributing factor. Yours is a matriarchal society sir ... we wish to impact that with our money and your assistance."

The Preacher smiled, his thoughts flashed back to his own upbringing where his father ruled his household in a "velvet glove, iron fist" manner.

"Please continue Mr. Deputy. I fully understand the "money" aspect but be more specific .... Where do I and my organization fit into the scheme of things?"

"Certainly ... the first order of business would be to grant a bank charter. Then establish a physical banking facility where funds could be legally received and dispersed. Of course, your name would never be shown on official documents but you would in fact control the bank ... perhaps not on a day-to-day operational level but excerpt the overall control. We would assist in recruiting trained banking staff and allowing them to operate as would any other banking facility. The most significant difference would be a lack of scrutiny in the ordinary time to time federal and state banking audits."

"Alright, I believe I understand where this is going. The bank would have funds to make community loans that would never be approved anywhere else. Am I correct?"

"Yes ... loans for negro startup business, day care centers, community construction work and so on. This bank would be a source for funds to create good paying jobs for negro men and women at the same time greatly improving the infra structure of the community ... repairing houses, creating neighborhood shopping outlets, attracting medical offices and so on. You would be entitled to up to 5% of the loan amount as your origination fee of course."

They continued discussing the details of the plan for the next hour. The Preacher already knew he would participate but had some concerns.

He asked, "We haven't discussed my peculiar business, have we? Where does that fit into your plan Sir?"

"It continues just as it is. If you didn't control it, some outside entity would certainly come in and try to fill the vacuum ... we won't let that happen. May I add Preacher ... that as long as your activities are solely focused on numbers taking, not drugs, prostitution and any other criminal enterprise, you will have our complete support and cooperation. Also, we'd expect your cooperation in investigating any criminal activities that should occur. It would be in our mutual best interests to maintain law and order within your community so that negro families would thrive there."

They discussed the Governments proposal for the next hour and in general, the Preacher was in agreement. Accepting it and his role would be a win for the black community, the US Government and most assuredly for himself.

He was ready. "Mr. Deputy ... I need to think some more about our discussion but in general I favor moving forward. However, I have three conditions for you to consider. First, Congressman Summerfield must go. Second, I will pick his replacement and third ... that thug of yours, Ennis would never be my partner .... He needs to disappear."

"I fully understand Preacher, now may I make a telephone call?"

The Deputy Attorney General spent less than five minutes on the telephone. It appeared that he was speaking with his boss the Attorney General of the United States and seemed pleased when the call ended.

"I have answers for some of your requirements Preacher ... "Should Congressman Summerfield no longer serve in the Congress and within reason, there's no problem for you to pick Summerfield's replacement and now in regards to the Ennis matter... that is already in the works. But please understand, when it come to the actual removal of Congressman Summerfield that presents a decision on the highest level. The Attorney General will be speaking directly to President Johnson within the hour. Shall we wait here for his answer?"

The Preacher smiled and asked, "And shall I order refreshments while we wait Mr. Deputy?"

THIRTY EIGHT

Bunny had no real problem reaching the MBC Newsroom. Of course, he needed to answer the same annoying questions from the three different assholes who directed all incoming telephone calls.

He decided that Jackson and his FBI buddies would never solve the "Dolan" problem ... and this reporter asshole could ruin the Governments and his plan ... he had to be shut down.

While he waited for Dolan, he cleaned the little .32 he had taken from Fat Jimmy. His Baretta was empty and he needed a carry piece. Only four rounds ... not enough. He'd have to chance returning to his apartment and pick up some ammo.

"I'm sorry Sir, Mr. Dolan is out on assignment. May I take a message? He'll be calling in soon I'm sure."

"Yeah ... tell him to call Agent Joe Jackson, from the FBI ... here's a private number where I can be reached. It's very important." He had given them his hotel room phone number.

"Thank you, sir ... I'll see that he gets your message."

At first, Bunny thought he could work out some deal with Dolan to protect himself from the FBI, but the more he thought about it the more he realized that this wouldn't work. Dolan was a reporter and couldn't be trusted to keep his mouth shut. Bunny then decided to get rid of Dolan and shut down his story ... or at least stop it for a while.

A half hour later the room telephone rung and Bunny picked up on the second ring. "Hello, Dolan?"

Dolan was not sure he was speaking to the man he had met a few hours before. "Is this Agent Jackson?"

"No ... just listen Dolan ... I have information on the two programmer guys and San Fillipo take out. I need to speak with you... when can we meet?"

Johnny was caught off guard and stalled to get up to speed. "Yes of course I'd like to meet with you but first you have to tell me who you are?"

"A friend of the Preachers. You wanna meet or what the fuck?"

"Alright, I'll meet ... you want to pick a place and time?" Johnny immediately regretted allowing this guy pick the time and place.

"No Dolan, your call. Tonight would be good."

Johnny thought quickly, it had to be public and someplace where he'd be safe.

"The Skull and Cross. It's a bar on Bleeker, down in Greenwich Village ... 10 tonight. That work for you?"

"See you there."

"Wait ... What do you look like?"

"Don't worry Dolan ... I know what you look like; I'll find you." Bunny hung up. There was another call he needed to make.

* * *

Joe Jackson was exhausted and just wanted to call it a day. He had the feeling he was in trouble with his bosses. They made him the contact man for Bunny Ennis and now they all realized that this was a big mistake, Ennis was out of control and this was Jacksons fault. Now they had him back in the air, on the way to the FBI Headquarters in DC, probably to pull him from this assignment, maybe kick him out of the Bureau.

He had spoken with Ennis before he left and told him that the stakeout on his apartment had been pulled and it was safe for him to return home. He warned him not to do anything stupid and he'd call him tomorrow.

"Don't do anything stupid.", he told him ... "Little chance of that ... this guy was homicidal and telling him to be good was like telling a hungry lion not to eat the gazelles.", Jackson thought.

THIRTY NINE

It was dark now and Detective Al Miller sat alone in his car with the cold coffee in its cup holder getting colder. He knew he was out of line. Captain Gentner had pulled the surveillance unit without any explanations and Miller knew he had no right being here, alone outside of Ennis' apartment. But he was on his own time now so, "Fuck Gentner!", he thought. He hadn't worked out a plan should he see this coon asshole Ennis, but he was sure he'd come up with something should he show up.

Bunny made the cop sitting in the "plain wrap" Plymouth in front of his apartment building. The driver's window was down and the dick had his elbow sticking out, a glowing cigarette dangling in his left hand.

"Fuckin' Jackson ... surveillance pulled my ass.", he thought checking the darkened street for more cops.

"Looks like NYPD is doing this stakeout on the cheap ... only one cop."

Bunny had a choice to make. Go on to his apartment and guts it out with the cop. Just leave. Or take out the single cop. He was the Bunnyman so he would take out the cop. "Fuck Jackson ... fuck the FBI.", He thought.

Bunny moved behind the Plymouth, keeping a low profile and away from the car's mirrors as much as possible. He had the .32 out and ready to go and was glad he had it. Good piece for an up-close head shot without a lot of noise. It was almost too easy.

"Hey mother fucker ... ya been waitin' for me?"

FORTY

Johnny tried Joe Jackson's number first. He called his FBI New York office and they told him that Agent Jackson was on his way to Washington and could not be reached, guaranteeing that it was not Jackson who had called him. He left a message and asked that Jackson contact him as soon as he could. He had wanted to discuss the mysterious phone call he'd just received and see if Jackson could shed some light.

He then called Brian Toth.

"Hi Bri."

They exchanged pleasantries for a minute. Brian was excited about the big Halloween party in Greenwich Village later that night and asked if Johnny was coming down to join the fun.

"Actually, that's why I'm calling you Bri. I'll be down in the Village around 10 .... But not to party; I'm working. I'm meeting someone I don't know and there could be problems. Is that offer to have your "leather boyfriends" watch my back still good?"

Brian was concerned. "Johnny what have you gotten yourself into? You shouldn't be getting yourself into dangerous situations. You're a reporter, not a secret agent for god's sake. What the hell is going on?"

"I'm meeting with someone I don't know, who called me out of the blue and told me he had information about the story I'm working on ... you know, the murder of those two programmers and San Fillipo. I told you about that. He may be ok ... from what he said, he obviously knows someone in the FBI and may even be from the FBI ... I just don't know. But I'd feel better if someone had my back when I met this guy. So, can you help me Bri?"

"I'm not sure Johnny ... it's Halloween and everyone we know has some place to go tonight. I'll reach out and see if I can get my friends to meet up with you. But no promises. I'll try. Now where and when?"

"I'm meeting this guy at 10 ... at the Skull and Cross on Bleeker."

"Oh my ... that's a nasty place. Why there Johnny?"

"To be honest that was the first place that jumped into my mind when he asked for a place to meet. Anyway, it's public and rough. Maybe that's enough protection for me ... I don't know."

"I'll call around after we hang up and let you know. Are you going to be at this number for a while?"

"Yes, but just for a bit ... I have to stop by my office. You don't need to call me back ... if you can find some help that would be great, but if not ... don't worry, I'll be ok. So long for now Bri. Maybe I'll see you later. I'll call when I can. Have fun tonight."

Upon hanging up, Brian Toth immediately called his longtime friend, Big Dick Harris, leader of the Leather Boys Motorcycle Club to ask a big favor.

* * *

Dolan stood waiting on the corner of Fifty Second Street for almost ten minutes before deciding all the taxis in this part of the city were either off duty or occupied. He was cold and after checking his watch realized he was going to be late.

"Damn it!", he thought. "I'll have to take the subway."

The refuse strewn platform was almost deserted. Dolan hadn't ridden the subway since high school and although it looked the same, it felt different to him. It had always been dirty, now it seemed hostile. He knew he no longer belonged in a subway station; too many years riding in cabs had jaded him.

Dolan listened to echoes of a sad melody played by the blind saxophone player he had passed on street above. The distant music echoed off the tiled walls and added to the melancholia Johnny felt this Halloween night. He stood with his back against the gritty wall and stepped to the platform edge when he heard the distant clicking of an approaching train now still half a mile down the tracks.

The sound grew into a hollow rumble which became thunder drowning out all other sounds and blocking thought in Dolan's depressed mind. He had watched its approach through the darkened tunnel, rocking drunkenly side to side on wavy lines of track. Two green identification lights framed the top of the lead car and the car's interior pale-yellow lit the upper body of a passenger standing behind the first car door. Silver sparks ground from steel wheels meeting steel track now mixed with electric blue flashes shot from the third rail connection marking the train's path through the black tunnel into the station.

Dolan stepped back from the platform edge as it whooshed by sucking up dirt and discarded newspapers in its wake then blowing them up onto the platform. This was a short, "off-rush hour", three car train and when it slowed to halt it was a hundred feet from where he stood, making him walk quickly but only to wait by the double doors of the last car.

After a few seconds just one of the doors opened letting Dolan exit the dim platform gloom and enter the brightly lit subway car.

Besides himself and a sleeping bum the only other occupant was a black hooded nun. Dolan thought it strange that a nun would be traveling alone this time of night and then he noticed "sister" was wearing sneakers. She wasn't a nun – she wasn't even a she; just another Halloween reveler probably traveling to a costume party somewhere in the Village.

At West Fourth Street a gang of tough, Irish looking teenage kids boarded with wild shouting and much pushing and shoving. There were six of them, four boys and two girls, all looking about sixteen or seventeen. Drunk and loud, they congregated in the center of the subway car. Their faces were painted with weird combinations of colored makeup and each youth carried a knotted stocking, the toes loaded with flour or some sort of white powder. They constantly batted each other with their flour socks and each contact left a round white circle where it impacted.

Dolan ignored them because they seemed dangerous, ready to challenge anyone. But they didn't ignore him and he heard one of the girls make a loud comment, something like "What's that asshole looking at?", at which one of her male companions answered, "Fuck him … we'll kick his fucking ass."

Dolan tensed; he didn't want any trouble. He was too old and too vulnerable for anything physical. John Dolan was not a coward but recognized his limitations in this situation. He decided to get off at the next stop. It would leave him almost where he needed to be and he could walk the short distance.

But whatever he did wouldn't matter. He could see one of the bigger boys moving in his direction out of the corner of his eye. Dolan took a deep breath and decided to ignore anything the boy said.

The kid sat on the narrow bench seat next to him. He stunk of beer and sweat. As the train lurched from side to side the boy took up its rhythm and slowly and lightly began bumping Dolan with his shoulder. His friends had quieted and watched. The girls began an insane giggle and the boys whooped as the kid's shoulder movements became more vigorous.

"Fuckin' Billy's a riot! Ha ha ha … "

The train had begun to enter the station and Dolan stood and moved to the door quickly followed by Billy.

"Gee, I'm really sorry mister … did I hurt you? Hey mister, did I hurt you?", he asked loudly. "What's the matter mister? You fuckin' deaf? I'm talkin' to you?"

Billy stood behind him and Dolan could see his reflection in the glass door. The kid slapped Dolan's right arm and had raised his flour sock as if he were going to strike out with it when Dolan turned to face him.

It was then that Dolan's world became a slow-motion movie. He was outside himself watching as he turned to face the kid. Dolan's first punch broke the kid's jaw, his second – a left uppercut, caught the kid just below the right eye. "Billy the Kid" stumbled back and lost his footing on the rocking subway floor. He went down hard – arms and legs up in the air. Surprisingly, his five friends stayed put. The train lurched to a halt, its doors hissed open and Dolan was off and up the first flight of stairs in less than five seconds. He could hear the gang shouting curses after him but no one followed.

He was out on the street. The cold night air stung his flushed face but felt good. Dolan noticed he wasn't even breathing hard. He smiled and then laughed out loud. People passing gave him a wide berth.

Johnny Dolan thought about what he had just done and was glad he did it. He visualized the shocked expression on the kid's face as he went down. Dolan's right-hand knuckles tingled as he remembered the hard sensation and flat sound of his fist connecting with the kid's jaw. He could have walked off the train and avoided the violence but something had just snapped inside. Maybe it was all that he had been through the last few weeks. He was tired of being and observer of violence. He was tired of feeling the pain of friends who had been beaten and killed just because they were gay. Maybe this was the only way gays could stop what society was so prone to do to them. Maybe they had to hit back but only harder.

"This is bullshit.", Dolan thought. "Those kids didn't know I was gay. They were just punks. Aw fuck … it's done. I'm not proud of what I just did, but it's done." He would put it out of his mind.

Pulling up his overcoat collar to block the cold wind pushing down Broadway, Dolan quick stepped toward his destination. The further into the Village he went, the weirder the street scenes became. First hundreds then thousands congregated along the avenues and side streets of Greenwich Village – many dressed in costume, other just visitors to the annual Halloween event that was part of Mardi-Gras, part gay activism but mostly they were there just for fun.

But Johnny Dolan couldn't have been more alone in this happy mob. The unexpected violence with the teenagers took his thoughts somewhere else … somewhere cold and bleak, back to a mountain pass in North Korea, encased in his Sherman tank. He could smell the cordite from the spent rounds just fired at the approaching column of T-34 Soviet built tanks. He saw them explode … good tanks, untrained tankers. But there were too many to shoot. As usual, reality returned with the blinding white flash as his tank exploded…

"What the fuck am I doing? Why am I still here?", he thought.

His earlier telephone conversation with Janet Gibbon then replayed in his thoughts. She told him there was definite evidence in the Hospital's NIH file that proved that Doug Hayes was Congressman Summerfields son. And then for no apparent reason, she then told him that she was really attracted to him and believed that he felt the same about her. Johnny then told her that he was gay.... that he genuinely liked her. He told her that they could only be friends and she started to cry. The conversation only added to his depression.

FORTY ONE

Bunny opened the car door and shoved the dead cop's body down between the front bench seat and console. He took his wallet, his .38 revolver, badge, watch, car keys and a wedding ring trying to make it look like a street robbery and slow down identification. He made sure he wiped any surface he may have touched, locked the car doors and left for his apartment. No one had seen him. The whole episode only took three minutes.

He reached his apartment and put all the cop's stuff into a paper bag and added the small .32. He'd get rid of it later and "dump it far from here", he thought. He then noticed a few blood stains on his new overcoat and his hands as well.

"Shit ... I'll have to dump the coat too."

He stripped, took a quick shower and dressed casually ... he loaded the Baretta, put half dozen extra rounds in his leather jacket pocket and looked over his apartment. He knew he may never return here again. It was "clean" should they search it. He'd stay at the Sherry Netherland for the next few days and let Jackson figure out where to stash him.

He left the apartment, locked it and took the elevator down to the lobby. His car was parked about 100 yards from the entrance and he took a quick look at the cop's car, still dark and quiet as he made for the red Caddy. Bunny came from Chicago and still didn't know this City's neighborhoods all that well.

He knew the "Village" was south and drove toward Broadway figuring it would take him downtown to his destination. He had placed his "cops" package on the front passenger's side floor and planned to dump it in the Hudson or East River when he could. Traffic was moderate and he cruised along at 35mph. When he reached the Bowery, he found a parking spot at a bus stop, took his blood-stained overcoat and left the car. He had seen a bum sitting in a doorway.

"Here my brother.", he said tossing the $500 coat to the surprised half-drunk man.

"Thanks ... hey my man, you got any loose change to spare?"

Bunny was still laughing when he returned to his car. "Dude got a $500 coat and still wants spare change.", he thought.

He stopped smiling a half mile later when he found himself locked in the traffic jam caused by the Halloween revelers thronging the streets. He drove around and finally found an overpriced 24-hour parking lot and asked directions from the attendant to the Skull and Cross bar on Bleeker. The guy smiled and looked at him strangely but gave him the information sending Bunny on a long walk, pushing through the crowded streets, to its location.

FORTY TWO

The Skull and Cross was a dump. But a well-known and always busy dump. It catered to tough biker type gay men and all other gays just stayed away. It was also known for its almost daily violence. The NYPD never responded to any calls from either the bar or its neighbors. "Let the homos figure it out for themselves", was the answer any 911 caller ultimately received. After a while, people just stopped calling.

Bunny Ennis hated gays. Not for any particular reason he could articulate ... he just hated all gays. He had become "white hot angry" during his long walk to the Skull and Cross bar. The streets were teeming with gays ... half of them drunk, openly kissing eachother, and wearing outrageous costumes or just running semi-naked, only body paint on exposed asses and sometimes colorfully painted cocks and balls. More than once Bunny had to roughly push a few away as they attempted to touch him. It got so bad he wanted to pull his Baretta and shoot the motherfuckers.

Bunny Ennis looked like someone who might frequent the Skull and Cross. He had the right body look and tonight he unknowingly dressed for the part. Leather jacket, tight jeans, open shirt and a permanent scowl that said, "don't fuck with me motherfucker." So, nobody paid much attention when he made his way up to the long bar filled with "biker types". The Skull and Cross was not all that crowded considering it being Halloween where every other bar and restaurant in the Village was jammed packed.

He looked for Dolan. "The fuckers not here yet. Shit." Bunny thought; he didn't like this place ... wanted to get out. He decided that when Dolan arrived, he'd take him somewhere else, away from all these fag bastards.

The bartender finally came over. He didn't have a biker look ... far from it. Tall and skinny, heavily made up, dressed in a pink flowing shirt fully opened to his waist and a tutu below. In a high make-believe falsetto, he asked Bunny what he wanted to drink.

"What are we drinking tonight Tall, Dark and Handsome?"

He ordered his Jack and Pepsi which got a little titter from the barboy as he skipped off to prepare it. Bunny looked the place over while he waited. He avoided eye contact with the patrons as much as he could. He began to understand that it might be a biker fag bar, the Skull and Cross could be a dangerous place and he would have to tread lightly.

It was a big, dirty barn like space ... all wood wall paneling, black painted ceiling, no televisions, no pool tables, dart boards or anyother BS games to amuse drunks. The back space had scattered tables, a small dance floor, juke box in the corner but the focus point was a well lit raised space or stage that featured a very large wooden "X" like cross with half dozen plastic human skulls fixed in place on the wall behind it. Bunny wondered if the skulls might be real and smiled at the thought.

Bar Boy returned with his drink and got a happy surprise at the large size of Bunny's tip. "Oh my ... handsome and rich too. Thank you, sweetie."

In spite of himself, Bunny smiled. He had been watching the front door and the small distraction caused him to miss Johnny Dolan's entrance.

Johnny had visited the Skull and Cross a few times over the years. Its owner was a member of his club and he had helped a few of the regular patrons avoid problems by using his police and government contacts to intercede on their behalf. He knew he'd be recognized and no one would bother him. He only hoped that Brian had reached out to some of the leather boy friends and they were already here and would have his back if things went "South" with this un-known source he expected to meet.

Bunny finally made Dolan ... still standing close to the entrance waiting for him.

Johnny immediately knew that the rough looking, but out of place man approaching him was his mystery contact. "My name is Dolan. You looking for me?" No handshakes were exchanged.

"Can we talk somewhere else Dolan?"

"No. We'll talk here ... let's take a table in the back. Nobody will hear us or bother us. Come on." Dolan didn't wait, just walked toward the back room. He was glad that he had chosen this meeting place. His contact was obviously out of his comfort zone being here.

Bunny didn't like that answer but he was here ... Dolan was here and he had something he had to finish, so he trailed after him to the back.

When they were seated, without asking, Bar Boy pranced over to the table and brought a refill for Bunny and a drink for Dolan. Bar Boy knew Johnny and as all good bartenders ... remembered his drink.

"All right ... I don't know who you are and I don't know what you're going to tell me so just go ahead. The meeting is all yours." Dolan sat back and took a sip from his drink.

Ennis smirked. Matching Dolan's action, downed his Jack and Pepsi in one gulp and slammed his now empty glass hard on the table, spilling the remaining ice cubes over the table top.

"You're gonna get yourself in a lot of trouble if you keep reporting on them dead programmers and that DC asshole Summerfield."

"Is that what you brought me here to tell me? If it is, you could have saved us both a trip. I think we're done here. Happy Halloween buddy."

Dolan started to stand and Bunny reached out, held his shoulder and forced him back into his chair. "I'm not done yet motherfucker. Sit your ass back down. I'll tell you when we're done."

Johnny wasn't afraid. "Maybe I'll find out something ...", he thought, settling back in his chair. "Allright, allright ... I'll listen ... what else do you have to say? But let me ask you a question first ... did you have anything to do with the death of Hayes and Carson? Or know anything about their murders?"

Bunny's original plan was to try to frighten Dolan and if necessary, just hurt him a little if that didn't work. He already sensed that this guy wasn't frightened. Dolan wasn't going to quit. He would continue fucking up the plan and Ennis decided in a heartbeat that he was going to kill him ... but hurt him first.

"Yeah, I guess you could say I know a little about those two assholes ... I killed them. Is that what you wanted to know?"

Bunny had his wire coat hanger dagger hidden and now brought it from his pocket and with a lightening jab, embedded it deeply into Johnny's left eye. The sharp, white hot pain made Johnny scream and he immediately attempted to stand. The adrenalin that now surged through his body saved his life.

Ennis had begun to pull his Berretta to finish Dolan off with a head shot, but in his effort to rise from his chair, Johnny gave the small table a massive reflective adrenalin laced shove, sending it into the still seated Bunny hitting him in the chest and toppling him to the floor. Dolan blindly staggered away ... holding his bleeding eye and still screaming.

Big Dick didn't know Johnny Dolan but had immediately recognized him from his TV reporter appearances when he entered the bar. He kept close watch from his position, about 20 feet from Dolan's table and reacted quickly when he saw Bunny stab Dolan's eye out.

"Lock it up!", he yelled to Bar Boy who knew the drill. He hit the door lock button and it automatically lowered the outside iron shutter, completely covering the front of the Skull and Cross and barring entrance and any view from the busy street. Bar Boy then rushed from behind the bar and ran to the injured Johnny Dolan while all the bikers attacked the still prone Bunny Ennis.

Bar Boy reached Johnny and put his arm around his waist and led him out toward the back door. "You'll be fine. You'll be fine.", he cooed as they slowly made their exit.

Every one of the bikers brutally kicked and punched Bunny Ennis until he lost conscience. He had managed to pull his Barretta while still on the floor but immediately had his hand stomped and broken by Big Dick's size 12 Engineer boots.

"Don't kill the motherfucker. Stop!", shouted Big Dick. "I got a better idea. Lift him up boys. Strip him and tie him to the cross.", he ordered.

Bar Boy got Dolan to the street and decided to find a cop if he could. The streets were mobbed and many of the revelers they passed laughed thinking the tall skinny guy dressed in a tutu leading the screaming man with "fake" blood streaming down his face was just another Halloween costume prank.

"Thank god." Bar Boy led Dolan to the parked police car. "Officers ... officers, this man is seriously hurt. Can you take him to St. Vincent's? It's his eye. There was an accident. I think his eye was put out. Please help him."

Bunny Ennis was coming to and he hurt everywhere. Three of his ribs, his nose, right hand and shoulder had been broken during the biker assault. He was vaguely aware that he was naked and strapped to something. He knew his left eye was shut from the beating and could feel blood flowing from his mouth. He tried to speak but nothing came out.

Big Dick opened his gravity knife and with a quick motion cut off Ennis' penis and dangled it in front of Bunny's good eye for him to see.

Bunny felt the pain but passed out before the image of his severed penis dangling before him ever registered in his brain.

"Now boys ... let's take something for our "skull collection", Big Dick shouted.

FORTY THREE

A smiling Congressman Fredrick Douglas Summerfield accepted the congratulations, back patting and handshakes from his fellow congressman as he exited the floor of the US Congress. This had been his greatest legislative achievement during his twelve years in the House. His bill had just been passed ... first by acclimation and then by the more official "up or down" vote.

"San Fillipo is dead but I imagine one of his associates will come calling and want to pick up where Carmine left off.", he thought while walking back to his office. His thoughts clouded, thinking about Lydia and her new association with the Preacher. He expected to be blackmailed by them sometime soon. What form of blackmail that would take, he didn't know? He was only certain that it would come sooner rather than later. Ennis was another problem ... a serious, frightening problem for which he had no defense.

Back in his office he waited for a call from President Johnson. He didn't have long to wait. Johnson booming voice came on loud and strong on his phone's speaker.

"Well damn good work over there son. Now we have to get this bill through the Senate. I'll be working on that. Listen Mr. Congressman, there's something I want to ask you. I need a big favor son."

"Certainly Mr. President. Anything ... anything at all."

"I want you to be my new Secretary for Housing and Urban Affairs. How does that sound to you?"

Summerfield was shocked. He was first and foremost a congressman and had never thought of doing anything other than serving in Congress. There was more to this offer than that. Johnson had a plan and he didn't want any part of it.

"I'm very flattered you're offering me that position Sir, but I think I can best serve you and our Party here in the Congress. I'm sorry but I think I'll have to pass on that offer."

"Hmm … now bless your heart Mr. Summerfield, I believe you're makin' light of my offer. I know you're more slippery than a boiled onion so that's why I'm givin' you a chance …." Johnson voice took on an ominous tone. "Take this job Congressman, this is your best and only offer." And with that warning, President Johnson hung up.

Summerfield was shocked speechless. "What the hell is going on?", he thought. Before he had an opportunity to re-think the conversation his office door opened and Lydia Hayes entered together with the man everyone called the Preacher.

"Wha … What's going on? Lydia why are you here? Both of you … get out of my office."

"Calm down Frederick … calm down.", Lydia said. "Didn't you just speak with the President? He sent us to further discuss his offer with you. Oh, and by the way. Have you met the Preacher? Preacher … this is Congressman Summerfield."

"I won't shake his hand just yet Lydia… and I can't say I ever looked forward to meeting you Summerfield. I've always held you as a disgrace to our people. But perhaps that might change now. Let me explain why we've come. You've been offered a better paying and more important position from what I was told; I encourage you to take it. Perhaps then you could actually become an asset for our negro folks if you do."

Events were moving much too fast for Summerfield. He was off balance and Lydia at least, could clearly see that. She had worked at his side for many years, but he was listening … a good sign. The Preacher continued.

"Summerfield, I have been offered an opportunity for collaboration with the Government. One which will benefit our people not only now but for our future. In your new position as Secretary for Housing and Urban Affairs you will play an essential role in achieving our success. Let me explain. Do you mind if we seat ourselves?

Oh, and perhaps you might provide some tea and coffee for us if you don't mind."

The Preacher continued. He left no detail out from his meeting with the Attorney General including how his Policy business would be protected. Summerfield was awestruck. To his credit, Summerfield quickly recognized an opportunity ... not so much for the American negro community but mostly for himself. He could tap into the Government cash cow ... buy real estate at low interest or no interest loans, set up foundations where he could easily include payments to himself.

As he spoke, the Preacher watched Summerfield closely and picked up his subtle agreement signals ... the smile, the head nod, the body movements at the right times. "Summerfield is on board. Time to burst his greedy little bubble.", the Preacher thought.

"I can already see that you want to become a part of the program ... but let me caution you ... the first time you attempt to feather your own nest will be the last. Mrs. Hayes knows where all the bones are buried and will whisper their location into the Attorney General's ear. Indeed Mr. Summerfield, she's prepared to walk over to the Justice Department today if you don't take the job the President just offered. Do I make myself clear?"

FORTY FOUR

Johnny Dolan's left eye couldn't be saved. He remained at St. Vincent's Hospital recuperating for a full two weeks after he was admitted and had two surgeries. Surprisingly there was little media coverage. His attack was announced as an unfortunate accident and there was no further mention of Dolan's investigation of the possible connection of Congressman Summerfield to the murders of Carson and Hayes. Of course, Johnny had no awareness of any of this. He met with a hospital psychiatrist was diagnosed with deep depression which was more than understandable. His TV reporting career obviously would be on hold for the immediate future or perhaps over and his life would be adversely affected over the short term as he delt with both his injury and the trauma of the vicious attack.

FORTY FIVE

Late November, 1966

Gil Peterson wasn't looking toward visiting Johnny's apartment this rainy and cold November afternoon. He had been with him almost daily during his time at St. Vincent's. It was apparent that Dolan was suffering ... from his terrible injury of course, but much more from depression and Gil was concerned. Nobody who knew and loved Johnny seemed to have the right words to help him through the darkness that had taken over. Gil deliberately kept far away from discussing any news that might further his friends deepening despair during his visits.

Johnny had called earlier and almost begged him to visit him at home today. Peterson could hear the sorrow, desperation and hopelessness in his voice during their brief conversation. He wanted to know what was going on with his "story" ... who was working it and why hadn't he heard anything reported.

"I brought you a bottle of Jack and we're gonna have a few belts lad. Help rid the cold from our bones."

Gil was shocked by Dolan's appearance ... sunken eye, unshaved and disheveled when he answered the apartment door. They sat in the living room ... lights off and growing darker with the early setting November sun.

"So, how's the eye. You getting a glass one or just gonna keep looking like Captain Kidd with your eye patch."

Dolan gave Peterson a thin smile. "I'm not sure yet. I have to go back in a week and talk with my doc."

"You in any pain?"

"They gave me pain meds ... sleeping meds. I'm ok. Listen Gil, I asked you to come because I wanted to know what's happening with my story. I'd like to come back and finish it."

Peterson downed his Jack Daniels and stood to pour himself another. "You want a refill? You may need it." He poured the liquor into Dolan's shot glass and heavily sat down on the chair facing him.

"Let me begin by giving you an update on the asshole who took your eye."

Johnny sat back, remembering his conversation with the detective who visited him just that one time at St. Vincent's. He had seemed disinterested even when he revealed that the man who took his eye had confessed killing Carson and Hayes.

"Did they catch him Gil? What's his name? Did he work for San Filippo, or the Preacher?"

Peterson shrugged. "Nobody knows ...the cops eventually traced back to where you were attacked to that Skull and Cross joint. They searched the dump, questioned everyone there, searched the place for evidence, didn't find anything and from what I understand ... they never went back."

"Gil ... the guy warned me ... threatened me ... to stop looking into Summerfield and the murders ... he had to be connected to someone. Why did they stop looking?"

Peterson stood and without asking, turned on a floor lamp. "Too dark in here ... stinks a little too." He poured himself another shot and sat back down. He stared at Dolan a few seconds, sighed and then began speaking.

"Your story ... our story is dead. Done. Never to be told." He held up his hand stopping Dolan from speaking.

"Hear me out first. When the big guy told me to "kill it", I screamed holy hell. I met with him, then the head of MBC News and even the CEO for MBC. At first, they wouldn't tell me anything, just that the story needed to be shelved for national interest. Why, I asked? Eventually they let out that Lyndon Fucking Johnson, President of the United States of America, wanted the story killed."

Dolan sat stunned; not believing that the President could actually want his story killed?

"Why? That's crazy Gil. What's going on in DC?"

"There's more Johnny ... and you're not going to like it either. Summerfield will be announced as the new Secretary for Housing and Urban Affairs sometime next week ... and to top it off, there's a rumor circulating that Lydia Hayes will finish out his congressional term. Oh, and that FBI guy you met, Jackson, got shipped out ... now working the missing Polar Bear desk in Alaska. He probably knew too much or fucked up somehow. There's something big happening and I guess we'll never know."

After Gil left, Johnny pretty much finished off the Jack Daniels ... he then emptied the bottle of pain pills, together with the rest of his sleeping pills, filled his glass and washed them down with his last shot of Jack.

He then laid down on his couch, closed his good eye, and in time, he slept.

Johnny Dolan, like his story, was done.

* * *

Johnny stood in his tank's open turret and watched the ant-like column of North Korean T34s moving slowly along the dirt road 1,000 yards below.

"Get ready kid, we'll have to move fast after we shoot ..."

"I'm ready Sir." The smiling kid soldier replied.

"Shoot shoot shoot!"

Author's Note

I hoped you liked the story. The genesis sprung from my real life... really. (Not the killings, all the sex etc.) I began writing Single Action sometime before 1974, had finished about 60% and then lost interest or maybe life got in the way.

At one time, I was a hot shot computer programmer and in the very early '60s worked for a major NYC hospital where I quickly rose to a departmental directorship. As in the story, one of my staff and I got talking about "Numbers" ... specifically picking numbers, and I thought I could write a program to pick them. I understood the laws of probability and created a large data base of previously played numbers. At that time there wasn't a governmental sponsored number's lottery so I used previously played NYC street numbers which included both the "Brooklyn" and "New York" numbers for my data base.

I then prepared a list every month and noticed some successes. My "partner" had an ad published in the Amsterdam News in Harlem exactly as it appears in the book and we offered our monthly computer pick list for $2. It worked well and he and I made a few bucks each month from the mail ins. One month our list got really hot, three or four winners and we made a lot of money after that. Things were going great until one day my partner came in with the bad news. "Some people uptown want us to stop with the computer thing.", he told me. It seems we had too much success and had gotten noticed by the mob Policy Bankers. Remember at that time, folks really didn't know all that much about computers and for the most part believed that they could do anything, including picking numbers.

Suffice to say, we quickly got out of the computer picking numbers business.

I don't think Single Action could be easily written by anyone born after 1990 … it's not PC and it's a dark, dark story. If they ever make it a movie, I'm pretty certain it will be made in "black and white."

My next book will be a collection of short stories and a couple of plays. I've included a sample story below called "Smoke" … watch for the book … also, you might enjoy my first published book "Beyond Hate".

Good reading all.

Jim

September, 2021

ABOUT THE AUTHOR

Jim Williams is a NYC native. After military service he became a computer program and eventually had his own software development company. He retired at 50 and lived his dream of owning an Irish Pub.

Williams has traveled extensively in the US as well and Europe and Asia.

WHERE THERE'S SMOKE: A Short Story

Ann Breen wiped the lens of the binoculars on the tail of her sweat drenched shirt and raising them, focused on the young man sitting in the fifth row under the sweltering late May Indiana sun. Just as his image sharpened, the crowd surrounding him suddenly rose, blocking her view as they roared approval at the eighty high-tech racing machines passing at 185 MPH.

It was the Indianapolis 500.... the Memorial Day classic and watching their happy faces, Ann knew that some of these cheering spectators might never live to see another.

When the crowd sat, he re-appeared and Ann's breath caught as he turned and looked directly at her. She knew he couldn't see her at this distance but somehow he had, because he was beckoning her to come.

It took Ann five minutes of pushing through the packed stadium before she reached him. He motioned to the empty seat and called, "Sit here Ann. I've been waiting for you."

Her heart pounded as she stepped in front of half dozen spectators finally taking her place beside the man for whom she had searched the last four years. "How did you know my name?" Her chest felt tight and it was hard to breathe.

"I just knew.", he answered gazing steadily into her eyes. His tenor voice was pleasing and somehow comforting. He looked about 25, and his pale face was further accentuated by long blond wavy hair which contrasted nicely with the crisp beige colored linen suit he wore. Ann noticed that although it was over 95 degrees in the exposed stands, he didn't appear affected by the humid heat. The crowd noise and the roar of the race car engines suddenly seemed to diminish and became just faint background noise.

"Are you glad that you finally found me?", he asked.

"Yes I am.", she answered regaining her composure. "What's your name?"

He smiled. "Oh…my name? Let me see…why don't you call me Smoke."

"Smoke…I like that. Where there's smoke,"

"…there's fire." He finished and both laughed as if old friends.

"How did you know I'd be here Ann?"

"I didn't know. I took a chance. I almost found you once before… about two years ago at the

Berlin Air Show."

"Yes, I was there." His smile faded.

2

"I saw you on the news.", she continued. "You were in the crowd right before the accident that killed all those people." Ann vividly remembered the slow-motion film of the aircraft collision played for days on every TV news broadcast; twenty-three people perished.

"Terrible.", he whispered.

"What did you say Smoke?"

"I said it was terrible, Ann. All that fire, suffering; it was terrible."

Smoke seemed genuinely upset at the mention of the accident that made world news two years earlier. "Only two years…it was a life time ago.", Ann thought; or perhaps it had been a double lifetime because she had been searching for him for four years…searching for Smoke.

"Ann, I love ya! We did it!", Jeff Heath shouted lifting his partner from her stool in front of the

Movie-ola editing machine. "Ted just called. We got the contract to colorize fifty "Time

Marches On" news reels; and that's only the start. We're going to be rich!"

Ann and Jeff had set up their little film editing venture six months earlier and it had been touch and go but a major project like this would give them the break they had been praying for.

"Oh Jeff…we did it." Ann's arms circled her 60-year-old partner's neck as she kissed his cheek.

She felt a lifting of some of the heaviness which has held her hostage since Paul and Val's death.

Jeff and Ann had been working together the morning the police came and drove them to Victory

Memorial and Jeff was there when the priest and doctor ended her world by telling her that both her husband and seven year old daughter had died from massive injuries received as Paul drove Val to school.

That was a year ago and now two days later Ann began colorizing the first and one of the most famous disasters ever filmed; the 1937 explosion of the dirigible Hindenburg that killed 33 passengers and crew as it attempted a landing at the Naval Air Station at Lakehurst, New Jersey.

Ann spent a full day "reading" the original black and white film, mapping each camera angle sequence, counting the number of frames and noting their content. Next, she determined the master colors used for sky, earth and fixed objects seen in the film such as buildings. Ann then researched authentic colors of Naval ground crew uniforms and other personal artifacts visible in the four-and-a-half-minute film. The result of her meticulous effort was a creation of a master sequence book which would be used as a guide for loading the computer program profiles that actually created the colorized result.

Ann loved her work and was never bored by the repetitious tasks required to colorize a film. She was an artist by training and had drifted into film editing and later to this offshoot field. She had taken some basic computer programming courses and over time with Jeff's instruction learned the colorization technique. She found it fascinating ...organizing each black and white film, attempting to maintain the original artistic integrity while adding the dimension of color as a story enhancement. There were many film purists who despised this new technical capability and Ann often found herself in heated arguments defending her work when she revealed what she did for a living.

Ann completed the "rough" Hindenburg cut in three days and she and Jeff now sat before her Movie-ola reviewing the results and noting additional requirements.

In general, they were satisfied but had discovered one noticeable problem. It was a three second blip of moving white light which appeared among the ground crew caught below the fire engulfed Hindenburg as it collapsed to earth.

"I'll get that patch fixed this morning. What's next Jeff?", she asked.

"I have about twenty minutes of World War II stuff that needs work; you up for it?"

Ann went back to the original black and white Hindenburg film and advanced to the point where the white blip first appeared. The original showed a knot of terrified sailors running for their lives. As Ann advanced the sequence frame by frame, it appeared that one of the sailors had broken away from the group and seemed to be moving toward the falling Hindenburg. "That can't be right unless the guy had a death wish or something. It must be the camera angle.", she thought.

She went over and over the three second spot and was finally convinced that the guy was running toward certain death. The distance was too far to make out much about him. He was dressed as the others and wasn't a naval officer. Someone had edited the original film because the next sequence had the burning Hindenburg on the ground. Ann searched in vain for the sailor. After a time, she gave up looking for him and wrote some special programming code to correct the white flash in the colorized version but decided to hold off washing it out until she had a chance to discuss it with Jeff. A half hour later it was forgotten as she sat with Jeff and began reviewing the next assignment.

They worked long and hard hours over the next few weeks and Ann gave no further thought to the strange phenomenon found on the Hindenburg piece. She was happy; her days and nights were full and she hardly ever left the office for more than a few hours of mostly dreamless sleep and then back again.

One morning Jeff asked her to review a 1940 piece he had already colorized. It showed masses of Belgian civilians on the road fleeing Germany's Blitzkrieg. Ann was tired and almost didn't notice that the "Hindenburg blip" had returned.

The piece had been shot by an anonymous photographer and was a soundless action sequence which showed an actual strafing of the refugees by the Luftwaffe. The five-inch Movie-ola screen filled with images of dozens of terrified people.... young, old, men, women and children all madly dashing to vacate the tree lined road now under attack. The camera had rocked with the silent crashing of aerial bombs and for an instant it had pointed skyward catching the blurred image of a low flying plane. When it refocused, Ann then saw what might have initially been

Somehow Ann and Jeff's close personal and business relationship changed. He became overly cautious in reviewing her work. He most likely thought she had already played some kind of editing trick and was concerned that she might be still mentally and emotionally unsettled with the loss of her family. They began to drift apart and she eventually ended their partnership. It was then that she began her search for the man in the films.

Smoke touched her hand. Ann felt an overwhelming calmness flood her body. Almost like slowly waking from a deep night's sleep and experiencing the bodies short but perfect sense of total relaxation.

"Are you the Angel of Death Smoke?"

He smiled and laughed, "No, no Ann ... I guess, well ... you could call me the Angel of Comfort."

She was confused. All the days, months, years she had searched, she believed he was a supernatural manifestation of death. She believed she was allowed to see him for some reason.

Later she reasoned that she needed to find him and be with him so she might die and join Paul and Val.

Smoke seemed to read her thoughts. "They're fine. I was there with them at their moment of passing. They felt no pain. I helped them understand."

A warm feeling of contentment engulfed her. "They were fine." She thought.

"Thank you so, so much Smoke. I can't explain how happy I feel knowing they're at peace. You have brought joy back to me."

"Ann, you don't need to be here now.", Smoke said seriously.

She instantly thought about Paul and Val. She thought about her sadness ... about her need to be be with them again.

"There's still time ... ", Smoke released her hand and turned away to face the race track. The bunched-up race cars were getting closer. Inches separating them. Ann then made her decision.

CPSIA information can be obtained
at www.ICGtesting.com
Printed in the USA
LVHW031144220322
714080LV00008B/617